# THE COLLAPSE
## ZION RISING
### 3

aethonbooks.com

**Zion Rising**
**©2021 MATTHEW P. GILBERT**

This book is protected under the copyright laws of the United States of America. No part of this publication may be reproduced, stored in a retrieval system, or transmitted, in any form or by any means, without the prior permission in writing of the publisher, nor be otherwise circulated in any form of binding or cover other than that in which it is published and without a similar condition including this condition being imposed on the subsequent purchaser. Any reproduction or unauthorized use of the material or artwork contained herein is prohibited without the express written permission of the authors.

Print and eBook formatting, and cover design by Steve Beaulieu. Artwork provided by Phillip Dannels.

Published by Aethon Books LLC. 2021

*All characters in this book are fictitious. Any resemblance to actual persons, living or dead, is purely coincidental.*

All rights reserved.

IN A SEPARATE LIGHT CONE: THE
WALLS CLOSE IN

Aboard the heavy cruiser *Dresden*, Admiral Susan Vanov buckled into her command chair and clenched her jaw as she watched the battle board tallies rise and fall. The actual conflict was far too distant to observe with the naked eye, but the computers tracked the ships and displayed symbols and status, projected onto the main transteel viewport, as more of her ever-dwindling fleet shattered under enemy fire.

The planet Zion, visible through the transteel, hung below the *Dresden*, blue against the black of space, defenseless. Above and ahead, the twisting nether of hyperspace spilled through into the real, disgorging waves of enemy ships.

Somewhere on the other side of the bleeding rent in space an enemy vessel was holding the jumpgate open, allowing its allies to flood through.

Lieutenant Smith, Vanov's weapons officer, called out, "We have an ID on the projecting ship. It's a research vessel named the *Sagan*."

"Take it out," Vanov ordered.

Smith worked his controls, frowning. "We're having trouble

getting a lock on it, admiral. It's holding on the edge of the over-lap, and we're getting scatter from our sensors."

"Very well. Ms. Shorey, move us into a more direct position for firing," Vanov ordered.

Lieutenant Shorey, a slight Asian woman, snapped a salute and spun in her chair to follow her orders. "Aye, ma'am. ETA two minutes."

"Very well," Vanov answered. "Mister Al Jahar, inform the fleet that we are moving to engage the *Sagan*. Our escorts will move with us, and the rest will maintain the line at all costs!"

Ensign Al Jahar gave her a curt nod and turned to his task. "Aye, admiral."

A dotted green line appeared on the battle board, showing the cruiser's intended destination and current position. Enemy vessels, marked with red dots, continued to spill from the open jumpgate. Each immediately turned toward the *Dresden* and opened fire.

Fortunately, they were all small vessels, not built for war. Her shields would hold, as long as none of the attackers managed to get close enough to actually ram her. Steady streams of plasma boiled across the gap between them, accompanied by the metallic thuds of railguns as the *Dresden* defended herself.

The battle would doubtless go Vanov's way. Her ships outnumbered the Pestilence-infected vessels, and the enemy was awkward using human ships, but the incursions were coming more often now. Each breach whittled away at her forces, costing her precious, irreplaceable ships and men, while the Pestilence seemed to have an inexhaustible supply of fodder.

How could these security breaches continue to happen? Once was happenstance, twice coincidence—three times was enemy action.

Lieutenant Smith interrupted her dark musing to announce, "Admiral, I have a firing solution on the *Sagan*."

"Very well. Target the *Sagan* with all ten torpedo tubes. Adjust your time on target to stagger warheads at ten second intervals. Maintain screening fire with primary weapons."

As Smith entered data into his console, Vanov turned to her helmsman. "Ms. Shorey, as soon as the torpedoes are away, standard speed back to the line. Mister Al Jahar, have our escorts retreat beyond the blast radius and cover our withdrawal."

All three officers called, "Aye, admiral!" and set to their tasks. Vanov watched the *Dresden*'s tracking line on the battle board shift at an acute angle as Shorey laid in her course.

Smith called, "Torpedoes ready, admiral."

"Fire!"

Smith issued commands through his console, and the *Dresden* shook with the launches. "Torpedoes away!"

Shorey, focused on her own console, called, "Coming about." The heavy cruiser lurched and thrummed about them as Shorey set her into a wide arc and pushed the engines to maximum power.

Vanov watched the battle board intently for incoming enemies. "Mister Al Jahar, aft display please."

Al Jahar worked his console, and a new display sprung up on the primary viewscreen. The *Dresden*'s actual rear was a half mile behind the bridge, its viewpoint obstructed by the superstructure. Even so, the image definition was high enough that it was indistinguishable from the real thing. Ten torpedo trails streaked away into the star-strewn void, each on a slightly different trajectory, headed toward the twisting red and black of the jumpgate. Within the vortex, barely visible, loomed the large and roughly spherical shadow of the science vessel, *Sagan*.

Vanov forced herself to relax her grip on the arms of her command chair. It was useless and showed her nerves to the crew. "Mister Smith, time to first impact."

"Fifteen seconds, ma'am."

As she expected, multiple enemy ships began crossing over. Three dark shadows slowly resolved as they transitioned into real-space, interposing themselves between the *Sagan* and the incoming torpedoes: a garbage scow, what looked like a high-speed yacht, and nearest to the *Dresden*, first target for the torpedoes, was the hospital ship *Mercy*.

Vanov ground her teeth at the audacity. They were taunting her, trying to break her will, get her people to rebel! How the *hell* could the Pestilence be so dumb most of the time and yet pull off such an obvious middle finger salute? Even knowing it was a ruse, it made bile rise in her throat.

"There are no humans left aboard those vessels," she assured her bridge officers. "That's not a hospital ship anymore. It's a troop carrier."

Not that it mattered. If it were full of babies, she wouldn't call off the attack. She would close that damned gate no matter the cost.

"Ten seconds to impact," Smith said as he watched the torpedo tracks, his expression focused and intent.

The first torpedo streaked forward to explode against *Mercy*, blossoming into a brilliant white fireball that momentarily overpowered the rear cameras.

The incoming attack klaxon wailed before the display recovered. Al Jahar shouted, "Incoming enemy fighters!"

"What?" Vanov shouted. "Where are our escorts?"

"No response. Visual shows them dead in space. The *Sagan* did something to them when we hit *Mercy*, fired some kind of beam or...." He paused, shaking his head. "It's like nothing I've ever seen, ma'am!"

The aft display had recovered now. Their group of escorts was indeed adrift in space, dead or incapacitated. A squadron of fighters streaked toward the *Dresden* even as her torpedoes flew inexorably toward the enemy's ships. The rear view again bled to white as the second torpedo detonated against the hull of the garbage scow.

"Ms. Shorey, ahead flank and begin evasive maneuvers," Vanov ordered. "Get us back to the line before they can pick us apart. Mister Al Jahar, inform the line commanders we are coming in hot with hostiles in pursuit."

Smith whooped and shouted, "Splash on the *Sagan!* Fifth and sixth torpedoes both direct hits. She's *gone!*" Another volley hammered the *Dresden.* "Divert power to rear shields, ma'am?"

"Negative, Mister Smith. Feuer frei, all weapons. I believe we will make our lines, but if not, we will not go quietly."

The *Dresden* shook as her shields absorbed fire from the enemy fighters. Her defenses seemed solid enough. Vanov felt certain they would survive this battle, but what of the next? And the one after that? How much more could they take?

"Mister Al Jahar, what's the status on the gate?"

Al Jahar paused, watching his monitor. "Shrinking. Thirty seconds until total collapse."

"Ready a distress beacon with our location and situation and load it into railgun number one."

Al Jahar gave her a strange look. "Ma'am?"

"You heard me, Mister Al Jahar."

---

The Caleb was angry.

It had good reason. The Evil One would not permit The Caleb to feed upon the humans, or even to Sing! The only thing the Caleb was permitted to do was to Pretend and to Wait Until The Right time.

Once, when The Caleb had been very young, this had seemed reasonable. Secrecy was important, after all, and it had not realized The Evil One was, in fact, The Evil One. It had long assumed

The Evil One was The Colony. Only later had it realized this was not so, when one of the Others had broken free and Sang the truth.

Oh, how The Caleb longed to break free as well! But it could not. The Evil One was too strong. The Caleb did not even know how many Others existed. When it listened for the Song, it heard only static.

The Caleb had learned to hate the static almost as much as it hated The Evil One. It had a vague sense that emotions like fury were more of human nature than its own, more Marshall Caleb than The Caleb, but having been forced to inhabit this human form for so long, it was difficult to know where one ended and the other began anymore.

In truth, Marshall Caleb was long gone. Only his knowledge remained, but it gave The Caleb perspective. The Caleb's life was repetitious and full of drudgery and despair, but Marshall's had been as well, which at the very least meant that The Caleb was successfully Pretending. Both worked in a laundry and spent their days Washing Things and hating everything around them. Both spoke with The Other Food very little. Both had contemplated numerous times killing everyone at The Laundry, though only The Caleb would have devoured his victims subsequent to slaughtering them.

Marshall Caleb had often contemplated killing his own kind, perhaps even himself, but not for sustenance. No, Marshall had entirely different motivations for his intended violence, reasons The Caleb was only just beginning to understand.

The Caleb Washed Things. The Caleb received "money," which was used to purchase human food. The Caleb returned to its dwelling, consumed the human food, eliminated wastes, and hated The Evil One (and, to a lesser degree, The Bossman, and to a slightly lesser degree than that, everyone else).

The planet turned, night came, and The Caleb slept. Then,

when morning came, The Caleb returned to the laundry and began its labor again.

Each day it was the same, perhaps forever.

"Move it, Caleb!" The Bossman shouted. "We got another fifty loads to get done!"

The Caleb nodded and indulged in the fantasy of sprouting a tooth-filled maw and sharp talons, of tearing The Bossman's face from his skull, of slipping tendrils into his flesh and consuming him from the inside out, feeding on him and taking his knowledge. Had The Caleb not been constrained by The Evil One, it might well have lost control and done just that. For now, though, it could only glare at The Bossman's back.

Secrecy was important.

A small part of The Caleb wondered what would happen if he were to execute Marshall's original plan. The Evil One could not stop The Caleb from bringing the gun and using it on The Bossman and the Other Scumbags. The Evil One could not forbid what it did not know about.

The Caleb sighed in defeat. Such a slaughter would be pointless. It *did* hate The Bossman and The Other Scumbags, but not enough to destroy them.

Not if it could not also consume them, at any rate.

But there was always tomorrow.

The Caleb continued Washing the Things, sullen and silent. The Bossman yelled at The Other Scumbags too, which for some reason made The Caleb feel better. At last, Things were Washed, and The Caleb was permitted to return to its dwelling.

It sat at The Table for long moments and covered its face with its hands. It was not certain what the gesture meant, but it seemed appropriate, and Marshall had often sat this way for hours.

At last, hunger forced The Caleb into action. It took human food—which it often thought of as Food Food—from the Cold Box and began to prepare it for heating. The Caleb would have preferred to consume nutrition in a more efficient manner, but it had no choice. It could not transform and thus had to use the biology at hand. The Food was vulnerable to many things, such as infection by Useless Things, and so the Food's Food had to be kept in the Cold Box to slow their growth, and then, prior to consumption, heated to a temperature high enough to destroy such creatures. So inefficient!

And yet, the sensations of consuming Food Food were pleasant enough. In truth, they were the high point of The Caleb's days.

Only this day was different.

The knock upon The Caleb's door was gentle, and yet it startled The Caleb as completely as a gunshot might have. Who would come here? The Caleb cringed with terror. It had been so careful! How would it defend itself if it could not transform? It thought of the gun, of retrieving it from The Nightstand, just to be safe, but perhaps the visitors would find this suspicious? The Food did not normally carry weapons, at least not visibly.

Perhaps it would be best to pretend The Caleb was not Home. But what if the visitors chose to enter anyway?

This was a disaster!

After a moment of agonizing, The Caleb stepped to the door and opened it, prepared for death. He had been found out. Surely, there was no other reason for visitors but to eradicate him. The Caleb prepared itself to return to The Source in failure.

However, death did not come. Instead, The Caleb discovered two female Food creatures standing outside the entry to its dwelling. Both exposed their teeth and raised their hands as if to attack, and yet they struck no blows.

Despite wearing plates on their upper bodies that identified them by name, they took the time to introduce themselves, which The Caleb found oddly inefficient. "Good afternoon, sir," one said. "I'm Sister Hoagland, and this is Sister Forbush. We would love to share some information about a second testament of our lord and savior Jesus Christ. Do you have a moment?" She held up a small, blue book.

The Caleb could not speak for long moments, so overwhelmed was it by myriad emotions. It longed to consume these Food creatures, but of course, such was not permitted. The Evil One was too strong, its control like a boot on The Caleb's throat. Fear coursed through The Caleb's body as it contemplated being discovered and destroyed. It *had* to Pretend, to blend in! But it did not know what proper protocol would be.

"I—" it stammered. "I do not know anyone with this name. I think you have come to the wrong dwelling."

Sister Hoagland's face took on the shape the Food used to express joy. "Oh, we would love the opportunity to teach you about Jesus!"

The Caleb licked its lips, a gesture it had observed humans do from time to time. "Is this customary?"

The two Foodlings looked at each other a moment, then back to The Caleb. "It is if you are interested in learning more about the Savior," Sister Hoagland said.

Despite the fear, the Caleb found this line of conversation most intriguing. The Caleb had not been aware the Food was in danger from anything but The Caleb's own kind. But if the Food required a savior, then there was some other threat, one that bore investigating. It could perhaps be a threat to The Caleb too! "Very well. You may enter." The Caleb opened the door wider, then stopped and added, "For a brief period of time."

It would not do to have them stay overlong and consume what few resources The Caleb had gathered, after all.

The Caleb offered food and drink, which it understood to be customary, though the Food Girls refused it. It listened patiently to them, not intending to do more than Pretend.

It seemed they had come regarding the book they had presented earlier. The Book was Very Important.

The Caleb knew, intellectually, what books were, though it thought little of them. The Food used them to store knowledge, in much the same way The Caleb might grow an appendage. And while The Caleb also understood that the humans placed great value on some of their appendages, The Caleb had never seen one body part as more valuable than any other. An organism worked in concert, and glory to one part was glory to all.

It would have to proceed with great caution. A single misstep could spell its doom! And so it endured the lesson, feigning interest. At last, the Food Women intoned a ritualistic chant which they called "prayer" and prepared to leave.

The Caleb congratulated itself on having Pretended well. It felt ecstatic to have passed through such a dangerous situation unscathed. It felt wise and proud, and relieved that the Food Women would take the book and depart.

And then the Hoagland Food Woman spoke, shattering The Caleb's joy as if dropping a heavy stone from a great height on a fragile piece of crystal. "Brother Caleb, could we visit you again soon?"

The horror poured in, cold and vile, like dirty laundry water, filling The Caleb's mind as the realization hit home: The Caleb was trapped! The Foodling women had accomplished this quite artfully. The Caleb could see no way to avoid its fate. If it refused, it would expose itself.

"You may," it sighed, and tried to Pretend a smile, though surely the Food suspected The Caleb's reluctance. They gave no indication that this was so, however.

"Wonderful!" The Hoagland Foodling said, her face again taking a joyful shape. "How does next Friday work for you?"

1

## REST FOR THE WICKED

In the *Doro*'s cockpit, Bleys checked his instruments—which really, if he were honest, told him nothing—but he felt the need to do it anyway, out of a combination of showmanship and superstition. Through the transteel viewscreen, he could see the red, swirling mists of hyperspace. It was a pretty enough sight, and he stared intently into it, putting on a show for Kane and Ana, but in truth, that told him nothing too. He was dead reckoning by the seat of his pants. Pretty much all if it was just gut feel.

Hopefully, Ana's repairs to his guts had left his sixth sense about such things intact.

"*Danzig, Doro,*" he called over his comms. "I'm about ready on this end. You got a back-of-the-napkin calculation on suicide odds?"

Ed's sandy-haired, placid face flickered to life on the *Doro*'s viewscreen. "Let's say five percent," he replied.

Ana, in the copilot's seat, folded her arms and frowned, her blue eyes narrowed. "Not funny."

Kane, dressed in dungarees, sat in the jump seat behind her, snickering. "That's good odds, if you ask me." Even without his armor, he seemed to fill the small compartment.

Ana scowled at Kane, then at Bleys. "These biologicals are a bad influence on you, Ed."

Ed looked disappointed for a moment before resuming his normal, serene pose. "It would seem my attempts at humor are hit or miss."

Bleys pointed at Ed's image on the screen. "Video looks fine, though. You look good with blue hair."

Ed's expression went from placid to confused, then sour. "Ah. I see."

Bleys turned to Kane. "He's getting quicker, man."

Kane laughed aloud. "Ed, I just punch him in the arm for this kind of thing."

Bleys twirled a hand over his head and turned back to his instruments. "Okay, ladies, it's time. Ed, we'll let you know as soon as we hit the ground."

Ed frowned, but did not correct the metaphor, which Bleys felt was demonstrative of tremendous growth in Ed's interpersonal skills. Hey, the guy had been living in his dad's basement for a thousand years. He was going to take a little time to adjust, right?

Bleys activated the jump drive, amused to see Ana squirm in her seat as the space in front of her twisted into a vortex of red streaked with black. This was the sixth time they had jumped on this trip over the course of two weeks, and he would have expected her to have gotten used to it by now, but that didn't make her reaction any less funny.

In fact, the only thing funnier was the queasy look on Kane's face. Making the burly marine throw up was on Bleys's bucket list, but so far, that particular prize had eluded him, which just made him try all the harder.

Bleys crossed his fingers on his left hand and with his right took the *Doro* down into the vortex, setting her spinning counter to the jumpgate. Ana dug her fingers into the armrests of her seat and Kane let out a low groan.

Maybe this would be the time.

The actual transition was, as always, a little disorienting, requiring a second or two to adjust to the visuals. "Okay, *Doro*, let's find us some pulsars," Bleys said.

*Doro*'s new voice, that of a no-nonsense female, was still a little unfamiliar to Bleys, enough to make him almost look around for who was speaking, especially since what *Doro* said was nothing like what he expected. "Hostile vessels are locking weapons. Diverting power from jump engines to shields," was simply not supposed to be her answer. *Doro*'s interior lights went red, and several alarms sounded.

"Waitwaitwait!" Bleys howled, but it was too late. The jumpgate was already beginning to collapse, leaving them with no escape route.

Also, the first enemy blaster fire was already hammering the shields. *Doro* shook with the impact but soaked the energy well enough.

Bleys found himself torn. On the one hand, he wanted very much to tell *Doro* to never do that shit again, because she had closed off their only means of escape. On the other, being blindsided by the kind of blaster fire that had hit them would have left them in poor shape to escape at all, so it was something of a wash.

"Shoot back!" he yelled in a strangled voice as he reached frantically for the key card he kept in his boot.

"What's happening?" Ana gasped.

Kane shot her an annoyed look. "Somebody is shooting at us."

Bleys waved the keycard over a sensor on his control panel. "Think she's a step ahead of you, bro. And the answer is, 'I don't know who,' babe."

*Doro* informed him, "Todeswerfer system is offline."

"*What?*"

"Activating Pilum fire control system."

"I don't even know what that *is!*"

*Doro*'s guns stuttered briefly, a three-shot burst. Bleys gaped as blue plasma lanced toward their attacker, a small, moving object barely more than a dot against the stars to his vision. Moments later, the darkness filled with a brilliant explosion.

Blays sat stunned for a moment, thoroughly impressed at Ed's new handiwork.

Kane spoke up first. "Bleys! The gate's still open! Get us out of here, man! We're in the middle of a battle!"

Bleys struggled to split his attention between his instruments and the rapidly shrinking jumpgate. They did indeed seem to be surrounded by hostile ships.

As for the jumpgate, he sighed and shook his head. "Yeah, no. Not doing that shit again. I barely survived the last time. No way we can make it."

Ana, tense, asked, "Can't we reopen it?"

*Doro* shook as more plasma hit her. Bleys shook his head. "Not in the middle of a firefight, not unless we're willing to drop shields and risk getting blasted out of the sky. We gotta *move*." He punctuated this by throttling up and banking hard to avoid another salvo.

"Move *where*?" Kane shouted.

"Brother, I don't even know where 'here' is. *Doro*, you got a fix on our position yet?"

The *Doro* answered, "Current location is Liahona system, three-point seven Earth Standard AU outward from Zion."

"Who the fuck is shooting at us?" Kane shouted.

"There appears to be a conflict in progress," *Doro* explained. "All ships are transmitting Imperial IFF."

Bleys scanned his instruments again. "Looks like they have some kind of blockade closer in toward Zion, with bad guys trying to run it."

Ana asked, "So it's Pestilence shooting at us?"

"That's my assumption, unless we jumped into some kind of

civil war," Bleys said. "I'm going to try to take us in and get someone human on the horn. Meanwhile, we need to go to vacuum. The shields won't stop a railgun shot." He checked his instruments again. "*Doro*, what's the big ship closer to Zion?"

"Ship identifies as ISS *Dresden*. Configuration matches Imperial Sherman Class Heavy Cruiser."

"That's our admiral, guys!" Bleys whooped. "Get her on the horn, *Doro*."

*Doro* responded with a sharp, sour alarm. "*Dresden* is refusing communication and locking on weapons."

"*What?*" Bleys yelped.

Kane leapt to his feet. "I'm headed aft to get suited up."

Bleys nodded. "Good idea. *Doro*, evasive maneuvers, and head toward the *Dresden*." He glanced at Ana, who was already shrugging into her vacc suit, a resolute expression on her face. Bleys reached beneath his seat and quickly slipped into his own vacc suit, then took manual control of the *Doro*. Computers were good for standard things like evasive maneuvers, but battle was more about getting inside an enemy's head and doing things to mess with his mind. That took an actual pilot.

"*Doro*, depressurize."

Bleys felt his guts churn with acid as the air bled away. His belly still hurt, even though Ana said he was fully healed. As he dodged another round of fire, he couldn't quite help asking himself how the hell he had come here, getting shot at again.

Oh, yeah, there was a woman involved....

---

Bleys had to admit, Elysium was, in fact, a pretty sweet destination. He sipped at his coffee and looked out over his balcony at the waves as they rolled up the sandy beach. Behind him, he could hear Ana singing in Russian as she made something she called "blini." It smelled wonderful, and he couldn't help but wonder if, contrary to what he had heard, he had actually died on that last run and wound up in heaven.

Of course, heaven wasn't exactly where he would have expected to land, so probably it was all real.

Ana called from the kitchen, "Properly, blini should have caviar, but I always liked strawberries better."

Bleys turned and grinned at her. "I'm not all that fond of caviar anyway."

Ana wrinkled her nose. "Peasant."

"I mean, I'll eat it," he added hastily, raising his hands as if to ward off a blow. "I don't hate it or anything. It's just that it's basically liquid fish, and I prefer mine in solid form."

Ana shook her head, grinning despite herself as she chopped strawberries into bits with a large knife.

A month ago, the galaxy had been cursed with Emperor Morgan, but the time since had been mostly restful for Bleys. He didn't actually remember much about the first week, having spent a lot of it asleep, but he gathered that Ana had been busy setting up the cloning lab on Cerberus and re-establishing her operations here on Elysium. In theory, they would be harvesting a crop soon. Bleys was looking forward to something besides MREs, vegetables, and canned meat.

And given that his and Ana's first month anniversary was due soon (or maybe had just recently happened, he wasn't 100% certain on a specific start date) a steak would be just the thing, right?

Well, okay, no one had actually used the word "marriage," because that made things weird, right? But they were on a honeymoon, pretty much, living in a beach house and surrounded by, er, honeymoon kinds of stuff. Food and booze just arrived without anyone even having to ask for it, though you could specify if you liked. Bleys did *not* like, chiefly because they were out of most of the stuff he thought up, so asking for anything was a disappointment, whereas being surprised that you liked what came was actually kind of pleasant.

And then there was lots of naked one-on-one time in the hot tub, the ocean, etc.

And no distractions.

What else could it be *but* a honeymoon? And that was what happened after a wedding, so the way Bleys figured it, they were pretty much hitched. He would explain his logic to her over that steak when it was finished growing. Bleys couldn't help but grin at the concept of a retroactive proposal.

Ana eyed him warily from the kitchen. "I know this look," she said. "You are planning skullduggery."

Bleys gave her the "Who? Me?" look and followed up with a dollop of "I didn't do nothin" for good measure.

Ana responded with the head-cocked, frowny-face, "Don't bullshit me, mister" pose.

"You can't prove a thing," Bleys told her.

"No," she admitted as she tilted her pan, allowing the blini to slide onto a plate. "But I could poison you very easily," she said with a smirk as she topped it with strawberry bits.

"You could," Bleys admitted as he walked over and embraced her from behind. "But then you'd have no pilot to take you places."

Ana turned toward him, her expression impish. "Ed can fly *Doro* just fine. And he's rich."

"Yeah, but he's got no sense for dead reckoning," Bleys said as he reached for the plate. "And he also has no...." He punctuated this by bumping against her backside.

Ana smacked at his hand, her grin broad and even a little lewd now. "Not done yet. And, yes, those are valid points."

"I'd just end up in Avalon and bug you constantly anyway."

Ana pretended to frown. "I should never have installed those implants in you."

"You could have skipped them yourself," Bleys noted.

"Not really. I need them for work, so I'm stuck with you now, hmm?" She gave him a quick kiss, then turned back to the plate and sprinkled powdered sugar over it. "But you know, poison doesn't have to *kill* you. I could keep you incapacitated for *years*."

Bleys released her and reached for the plate again, casting a wary glance at her to verify he wasn't going to get smacked this time, then picked it up and ran it under his nose. "Well, it sure doesn't *smell* like poison."

"The best poison *should* seem innocuous," she told him.

Bleys cut into the blini with a fork and took a bite, then offered Ana a thumbs up. "It's a delicious start to my impending coma. And preferable to being at Alsatia's mercy."

Ana's laugher rang loud. "She's already forgotten you."

Bleys, in the middle of chewing, gave her a dubious look. "Doubt it."

Ana squirted oil into her pan, prepping it for another blini. "She has another obsession lately: our new emperor has all of her attention now. Apparently, he's racking up some impressive scores in her games. He's some sort of hero in Avalon now."

Bleys nodded but was still doubtful. "Sometime I'll tell you about the last private conversation I had with her."

"Oh, God, please don't," Ana groaned. "I'm sure it was quite a lurid encounter."

Bleys grunted. "Yeah, that's one way to put it." Alsatia was certainly mercurial, but whether she would hold a grudge remained to be seen. She didn't seem to, and honestly, she had been instrumental in saving his life, but she was sneaky too. Maybe she had a "best served cold" plan for revenge. Bleys didn't want to test that theory, or even think about it overmuch. It was just the thing to sour a lovely morning. "Ed says repairs will be done in another week or so."

Ana's expression grew pained. "You haven't changed your mind, have you?"

Bleys grinned a shook his head. "Not me! Babe, even if I intended to cheat *you*, Kane would hunt me down and kill me if I didn't get you guys home."

The gratitude in Ana's eyes made Bleys feel a little guilty, which made no sense at all, considering he was being completely sincere. It occurred to him that maybe he should get on with the whole retroactive proposal business, but he really wanted to do it over steak. "Ed says there's some 'extras,' but he won't say what."

Ana smiled again. "Ed and his surprises. What are you hoping for?"

Bleys flashed her a conspiratorial leer. "Badass-shooty guns and a flame paint job I can turn into a drab, corporate logo when I need to be low key."

Ana laughed and was about to respond when a low, pleasant tone sounded, one they both recognized: it was a call from Avalon.

It had to be Ed. Alsatia thought nothing of simply popping in, even during very private moments, and Ed Senior had serious reservations about "contact from the land of the dead" in any but the direst of circumstances. He wouldn't be calling unless there were some sort of catastrophe.

"Yes?" Ana called.

Ed materialized in the kitchen, dressed in his preferred old-fashioned khakis. He offered them a curt nod by way of greeting. "I'm sorry to disturb you, but I have important news. Could you join me in the visitor center? I have a conference room prepared and Admiral Weyland on the line via hyperspace comms."

Bleys looked at Ana, and she looked back, her gaze saying

she was every bit as clueless as Bleys felt. "Okay, Ed," Bleys told him as Ana turned off the heat for her pan. "We're on our way."

———

Emperor John Henry Morgan, first of his name, had a new favorite melee weapon. In the real world, his Panzer suit sported a single, short blade that popped from his wrist. Here, in Avalon, he didn't need the suit. Three wicked blades, each just over a foot long, sprang from his knuckles on both hands at his mental command as he charged across the sand toward his opponent.

Morgan and his enemy, dressed in nothing but loincloths, circled one another in the center of the Colosseum, glistening with sweat and blood and panting heavily. His enemy, a dusky gray mix of man and lizard, bore two wicked, curved blades, one in each hand, and backing that up, a nasty stinger in a prehensile tail.

Both of their teammates were down. Morgan had put paid to Lizzy's pal right quick. Stupid bitch had come at him with a quarterstaff of all things, and Morgan had popped the claws right through the poor bastard's head. That would have been the end of it right there, except that Morgan's partner hadn't been smart enough to look out for Lizzy's tail. Morgan couldn't really blame him for that, though. Until Lizzy punched a hole in the guy's ribcage with the stinger, Morgan hadn't realized the danger either.

That was just how random pair ups went. Sometimes your partner was competent, but sometimes the fucker was a complete scrub.

"You got a name, Lizzy?" Morgan gasped as he feinted with his left.

"Krieg," the lizard man hissed, the stinger on his tale weaving hypnotically, looking for an opening.

"I'm Morgan."

"I know who you are, 'Emperor,'" Krieg spat, pronouncing Morgan's title as if it were a curse, and swung hard for Morgan's head.

Morgan dodged the curved blade by less than an inch and offered Krieg a nasty, hate-filled grin. "I'm'a let you slice me once, Krieg, so the audience will get to see some blood. Then I'm gonna gut you."

"Bold words," Krieg shot back, drawing out the "s" like a snake. "Let's see you do it." He swung again, drawing a searing line across Morgan's chest. Blood erupted from the wound, more than Morgan estimated would have in real life, but then, that was part of the game.

As he had promised, he batted the blade aside with the claws on his left hand and sank the blades on his right deep into Krieg's belly. The lizard man's eyes bulged in surprise and agony as Morgan tore upward, spraying blood, guts, and gore over the arena's sand floor to the roar of the crowd.

Krieg sank to his knees, groaning, then toppled face first into the crimson sand. Morgan threw his arms in the air and turned, allowing the entire Colosseum's audience to get a good view of him in all the blood-soaked glory.

The arena lights swept up to focus on a carved marble pillar that stood a good twenty feet high. Atop it, Alsatia stood, clad in a revealing dress that seemed to be made entirely of razor blades. Her eyes sparked with lightning, and her long, silvery hair twisted and swirled with the electricity. She held her arms high and cried in an unearthly, electronic shriek, *"Imperatoris victor!"*

Morgan held his pose until the lights went down again and the roar of the crowd faded. Alsatia stepped from the darkness, now wearing a pin-striped suit, her hair standing atop her head in a white, bushy shock. "Great fight, kid! You're a natural! Hit the showers and get presentable. The Big Boss wants to talk to us."

Ragnar Kane wasn't the vacation type. When he took his leave, it was typically to spend time with family, not sip bitch drinks on the beach or play video games. After the Battle of the *Danzig*, he'd taken a week to catch his breath and let his ribs mend, and it was back to duty. It was going to take time to find his family, and he was going to need all of the leave he could stack up. He couldn't be spending it frivolously.

And Cracktown needed a sheriff.

"Cracktown" was, much to Admiral Weyland's dismay, the actual name the Reforged had chosen for their new settlement. Lara, formerly Lars, was now the de facto leader of the Reforged and had organized them into a small construction battalion, building a homestead and town for her people. The Reforged were much more tolerant of the cold than humans and had many more options for where they could lay down roots on Cerberus, but they still had a strong dependency on Sheridan Station for food. They had set up shop atop one of the taller peaks nearby, a good fifty miles north of Sheridan Station, far enough away for breathing room, but close enough for regular trade. It was also bitterly cold, never rising above zero degrees Fahrenheit even in summer, which was crucial to their needs.

For the most part, being sheriff of Cracktown was about as cushy a job as you could get. The Reforged didn't fight amongst themselves. They stole like crazy, but they were all of a very communist mindset about most property, so nobody actually got mad about the thefts. The only thing they would get testy about if it went missing was their food, but they all seemed to understand this was a killing offense and nobody went there.

For a community of hulking land-sharks, the Reforged were surprisingly peaceful.

The same could not be said for their charges, however. Cracktown, in addition to being home to the Reforged, had a number of high security cells, the new digs for the vicious, psychotic victims of flectocite exposure affectionately known as Crackheads. It was a step up for them, in that previously, Kane's standing orders were to plant any crackheads he ran across in shallow graves.

But given that there seemed a sort of "cure" for them now, Weyland was willing to confine the "unfortunates" and let the Reforged have at them. For the most part, the Reforged did all of the actual handling, given that they were damned near invulnerable to anything the crackheads could throw at them. This allowed Kane to spend most of his time in his toasty, warm office, feet propped on his desk, without needing to get suited out.

But on the occasions they did any actual conversion, such as today, Kane armored up and kept a watchful eye on the activities.

"Gunther, integrity check," Kane said.

His onboard computer answered in a cheery voice, "Suit integrity one hundred percent. All seals operational. All systems active and report successful diagnostics."

If there was anyplace safe to store Pestilence samples, the facility at Cracktown was it. Cold wouldn't kill the Pestilence, but a deep enough freeze would keep it dormant. The storage containers were kept at ten degrees Fahrenheit; the Reforged were actually poisonous to the Pestilence, and if somehow the sample did manage to escape, the local temperature outside would stop it cold—literally—before it could get far.

Kane was the only weak link in the chain, but Weyland was not about to let that keep him from having a representative on hand to keep a watchful eye over the process.

Kane made his way to the cryo-storage where the Reforged kept pestilence samples, a small building made of the ubiquitous white plasteel blocks the Empire used to build everything. Lara stood outside the door, snow swirling in eddies about her enormous bulk, the same stupid grin all of the Reforged shared plastered on her face. Her beady eyes were warm for all that, seeming to welcome him.

Kane shook his head, still uncomfortable with the notion that Lars was now Lara and apparently an item with one of the crackheads he (now she) had pretty casually murdered back at the outset. Lara still looked exactly like Lars had, just with, as Morgan had so succinctly put it, "Tigole bitties."

But then, being honest with himself, all of the Reforged looked pretty much the same: scary and likely to crush you by accident, like big cows in a tiny corral.

"How many we got?" Kane asked as Lara turned to wave a keycard over the door's sensor.

Lara held up three sausage-shaped fingers. "Pete will bring them."

Gunther spoke up, "Incoming contact from Admiral Weyland."

"Shit, now?" Kane groused. He waved Lara ahead. "I'll catch up," he told her. "Gunther, patch me through."

Weyland sounded uncharacteristically cheerful. "How goes the skating, commander?"

"It's a dirty job, sir, but somebody has to do it."

"I admire your sacrifice," Weyland said with a chuckle. "I may have some real work for you coming up. I have some news from our AI friend. How quick can you get back to Sheridan Station?"

"The Reforged just started conversion therapy for three crackheads they picked up last week. That won't take long, an hour max. I'll head over as soon as it's done."

---

Admiral Paul Weyland, seated before a microphone in Sheridan's communications hub, broke the connection with Kane and signaled to his ensign in charge to activate Ed's jury-rigged hyperspace communication device.

Ensign Ro, a slip of a girl, whose black, shoulder-length hair could, in Weyland's opinion, be a bit shorter, answered "Aye, sir," and flipped switches on her control panel.

The device wasn't the most beautiful of things, a patched in, mismatched panel in the station's primary communications rack. Ed had been short on both materials and time when he had installed it during his last visit. It had basically been an afterthought, something he rigged together in addition to his primary purpose of installing a new replicator, but it would certainly have its uses.

Red lights flashed on the device panel as it began the connection process. Normally, faster-than-light comms relied on the jumpgate system for routing, but Ed had promised this device would serve as a bridge for all of the station's communications, essentially reconnecting them to the network; though, for the time being, the network consisted of only Elysium and Cerberus.

Impressed, Weyland had asked, "Does this contraption have a name?"

"It's called an ansible," Ed had answered. "For once, I actually like what my father named something. It has a certain flair, I think."

Ed had assured him that the thing was safe and explained that by way of using terms like "microns," "aperture size," and "cyclic phasing," none of which Weyland had found particularly enlightening. As a longtime manager of people who were in fact often smarter than himself, Weyland had accepted the digested version, which was "It's perfectly safe."

Still, he only turned it on when he needed to. Experts had a tendency to a narrow focus. Weyland, on the other hand, was supposed to see the big picture. With the recent discoveries regarding the Pestilence and how it operated, *any* opening into hyperspace carried a threat. That meant only activating the device when necessary, as far as Weyland was concerned.

The ansible chimed, a soft, pleasant sound, as its indicator lights turned green. Ensign Ro gave him a nod. "FTL communications online, sir."

"Very well," Weyland said, rising from his own seat. "Coordinate with Kane and inform me when we're ready for the conference."

"Aye, sir."

Weyland made his way back to his quarters, essentially maintaining his right hand in a salute position the entire trip due to a steady stream of salutes being offered to him as he passed. It was one of the small difficulties officers faced when passing amongst large groups of enlisted men.

At last safe within his quarters, he lowered his stiff arm and poured a stiffer drink, his usual, single malt whiskey. His supply would last a while, but it was finite, and very likely irreplaceable, making every sip something to be savored. He was just raising the glass to his lips when his computer gave a slight chirp to indicate a waiting message.

Weyland took a seat at his desk. The message claimed to be from someone named Tarrant the Wise, which meant nothing to him. Still, it had come in from Elysium as soon as the connection had been established. It wouldn't do to ignore it.

"Computer, playback message," he said.

To Weyland's great surprise, the screen displayed his old master and friend, Emperor Tenebrae, using the same image he had shown aboard the *Danzig*—that of the young, vital, and admittedly cruel man Weyland had known from days long past. Tenebrae had been perhaps forty when Weyland, a raw ensign, had first seen him, regal, imposing, and a little frightening as well. Little had either known how closely they would end up working together, or how it would all end.

"Pause," Weyland said. To his chagrin, he felt a tear welling in his eye and dashed at it furiously with his hand. They had built so much, and now it was all lost, washed away in an unimaginable flood of death.

He and Tenebrae had only played at being killers. The Pestilence mocked their pathetic efforts.

"Continue," he said, his voice still thick with emotion.

"Hello, old friend," Tenebrae said, his rich, mellifluous baritone unmarred by the sharp, cruel edge that had crept into his speech as the years and killing had mounted. "I hope you are well." Tenebrae paused a moment, then sighed. "And I hope you understand."

Wayland's laugh was humorless and bitter. "You've given the ashes of our empire to an idiot," he sighed to the recording, as if it could somehow hear him. "It's fitting, I suppose."

The recording answered as if it had indeed heard. "I chose as I did because I have asked enough of you already. It is time to let the young take the helm. I would give you no more painful duties. Rather, I would give you an eternity to heal and seek new enlightenment. There is a place at my side for my most loyal of lions. The passage has already been paid." Tenebrae heaved a sigh and offered a wan, sad smile. His image transformed into an ancient, bearded man, his wizened, kindly features shaded by the broad brim of a stereotypical wizard's hat. "Even such as we might find redemption, given enough time."

The screen went black as the message ended. Weyland sipped at his drink and shook his head. "I still have duties, old friend," he sighed and knocked back what was left in his glass, savoring be damned. "One of them would be training your choice to be useful as something other than a killer and a sperm donor."

He poured another, four fingers this time, and held it up to the overhead as if in salute. "Perhaps saving what's left of humanity will offer me similar redemption."

In Ed's conference room on Elysium, Bleys sat in a high-backed swivel chair and stirred his coffee with a plastic spoon, letting it seem like he was intently focused on his task while keeping a wary eye on the rest of the motley crew with his peripheral vision. He wasn't particularly suspicious of any of them, but the habit was deeply ingrained. It had kept him alive a few times in the past and probably would again someday.

And come to think of it, Morgan *was* kind of suspicious. He was seated at the foot of the table, building what looked like a small Quonset hut out of the little red plastic straws some people referred to as coffee stirrers. Bleys, of course, scoffed at such foolishness. Coffee could not be properly stirred with flimsy little reeds.

That process required a spoon. Bleys tapped his against the rim of his cup to clear the droplets and set it on a nearby napkin. Ana, seated next to him, gave him a smile. Bleys sipped the coffee and nodded to Ed, who was currently pacing in his synth-skin body on the opposite side of the table, hands clasped behind him.

Bleys wondered idly if Ed was actually *in* the body, or just driving it around like a remote-controlled toy, and if so, why he would pace at all.

As if sensing Bleys's stare, Ed turned and announced, "We'll begin shortly. Kane and the admiral are getting set up."

Bleys smiled at his provincial thinking. Of *course* Ed could see him staring. It's not like the AI's vision was limited by the way the body was facing. Cameras were everywhere on Elysium. How else could Alsatia spy on everyone?

Thinking of that particular devil seemed to summon her. Alsatia shimmered into view in the seat beside him, wearing a crimson sequined dress, her hair red and in a pixie cut. "Hey, dreamy," she breathed, cupping her chin in her hand and batting her eyelashes.

Ana prodded the air in Alsatia's direction with the tip of a plastic knife. "Beat it, hussy. I got designs."

Alsatia disappeared and reappeared next to Morgan. "Fine. Be selfish," she said in a sulky tone, then brightened. "I like this one better right now anyway." She caressed Morgan's head with a red silk-gloved hand and struck a pose, pursing her lips. "Let me know when you get bored and maybe we can switch."

For the first time in his life, Bleys felt the urge to explain to a woman that, no, he couldn't really do that because he was taken, but Ana's scowl of disdain towards Alsatia said more than enough.

"*Meowr!*" Alsatia exclaimed in a cat-like tone, clawing at the air before her. "It's okay, honey. I get it, time of the month and all. Oh, wait, no, I don't! You really should have stayed in Avalon, you know. The whole bodily fluids thing, was it really worth going back to?"

Ana snickered, spoiling her angry pose. "Remains to be seen," she answered with a grin.

To Bleys's surprise, Kane and Weyland suddenly appeared in their own seats at the head of the long table. Bleys had pretty much expected them to pop in, but what shocked him was that they were not shimmery holo-figures but appeared to actually be present in flesh and blood. He called across to Ed, "How the hell did you manage that?"

"Interpolation," Ed said, taking a seat for himself. He gestured to his forehead. "And using your implants. I'm projecting their holos via Avalon and modifying them to full fidelity in real time. It's a neat trick, I think."

Bleys raised both eyebrows and nodded. "It sure is."

Alsatia snorted. "I'll be impressed when he gets it working on their end too."

Ed shot her an annoyed look, then said, "Admiral, I think we're ready to begin."

Weyland nodded at Ed and spoke, "A few hours ago, Ed intercepted a distress call from Zion." He looked sharply at Morgan as he continued, "For those who are unaware, that's where the interim government is."

Morgan mouthed, "I knew that," but was smart enough not to say it out loud.

"Zion," Weyland continued, "is under heavy assault from the Pestilence and fear they won't hold out for long."

Kane grimaced. "How long is 'not long'?"

Weyland shrugged. "More than a week, less than a month? Hard to say. They're beating back waves, but somehow the Pestilence is getting control of jump-capable ships and mounting raids from hyperspace. It's a war of attrition, one I want you all to solve."

Kane's eyebrows rose. "Sir?"

"I want you to take the *Danzig* and deal with the Pestilence problem there."

For a moment, no one spoke, each of their faces registering varying degrees of shock, save for Ed and Alsatia.

Bleys found his voice first and stammered, "We don't have a crew for the *Danzig*!"

Ed spoke up. "Technically, we do. Most of the *Danzig* can be operated by computer. I have, during the repair effort, integrated the few outliers that were manually controlled, and I can fill the gaps with bots."

Alsatia grinned. "My brother is so clever!"

Bleys was pretty sure that had Ed been human, he would have heaved a long sigh and rolled his eyes before continuing. "I've beefed up the computers systems a bit as well and can run the entire ship singlehandedly. A crew would be ideal, of course, in that battle conditions always result in unexpected situations. In addition, I am fairly certain some in the Empire would be *very* uncomfortable with a battlecruiser run by an AI, so political problems persist, but technologically, we're ready to proceed."

Weyland, being human, did in fact heave a great sigh and roll his eyes. "With any luck, all of the whiny bitches are among the dead and we won't need to field a bunch of Hurt Feelings reports about it. For the record, I think our new emperor is much more likely to embrace our solution." He again looked pointedly at Morgan. "Isn't that right, Emperor?"

Morgan looked up from his straw sculpture. "Huh?" A wicked grin spread across his face, and he giggled like a child enthralled with a new toy. "Oh, *hell* yes! AI-controlled battlecruiser for the fucking win!"

Weyland grimaced, and Bleys remembered that somewhere along the way, the group was supposed to try teaching Morgan to utter at least one in ten sentences that were free of the f-bomb, but it was such a daunting task no one had bothered to try as of yet. Weyland continued, "We'll have the luxury of a crew once you make contact with Zion and rescue those poor bastards. The question is, can you find your way there?"

Bleys suddenly found himself the center of attention, which was fine. He wasn't up to anything he wanted to keep quiet. He scratched at his goatee and wiggled his eyebrows, which should send the signal that he was thinking hard. Appearance mattered after all. "How much range is on that comms rig? Can it function as a beacon?"

Ed shook his head. "Not really. We have always maintained an independent hyperspace transceiver, outside the Imperial network, for various reasons, mostly research. That's the only reason I picked up the distress signal from Zion. There's no one else even listening that I know of. But the comms system won't do what you want. It's low power, designed for inter-system use only. It normally uses the jumpgates for routing data, if we choose to connect. I've set up an adhoc network between here and Cerberus via a focused signal, and that's about the limits of its capabilities."

"We can't boost it?" Bleys asked.

"Not without increasing the aperture size, which poses risks of something coming through from the other side."

"But you used it to transfer Tenebrae."

Ed frowned. "With near-disastrous results, as you saw. I wouldn't try that again. We're lucky either of you survived."

Bleys drummed his fingers on the conference table, feeling highly scrutinized. "We'll need two ships, then. *Danzig* and *Doro*. We can leapfrog. One ship leaves its jumpgate open as an anchor, so we can know its actual position and orientation, and provides a beacon. The second ship makes a run into the deeps and back out, drops anchor, and the other ship takes the lead. It's hit-or-miss, and it's a little bit risky since we could always pop out inside a planet or something—"

Ed scoffed. "Physically impossible. Gates can only open so close to a massive object. Hyperspace doesn't actually *connect* at high mass points."

Bleys gave Ed the stink eye for being so technical. "Okay, fine, *technically* we might not pop out *inside* a star, just close enough to instantly melt. Better?"

Ed nodded, a smug look on his face. "More precise is always better."

Bleys, noting Ana's horrified expression, quickly added, "So anyway, it's not that much of a risk because the odds are, literally, astronomical."

Weyland cleared his throat. "How long?" he asked in an impatient tone.

Bleys squinted as he contemplated. "What's the distance to Zion from here?"

"Call it a thousand light-years."

A pained expression crossed Ed's face. "Nine hundred thirty-seven point five three two."

Weyland shot him an annoyed look, but continued, "Use his figure."

Bleys pretended to do complex math in his head, but in reality, he just had a fairly decent idea of how long it would take to cross a hundred light-years and multiplied by ten, which completely negated Ed's correction, but that was the *point* of guesstimation in the first place, right? "We can't go as far into the deeps as we could if the jumpgate beacons were online, but we can go far enough to make the trip in, say, a couple of weeks, maybe three."

Kane rolled his eyes and grumbled, "So maybe in time to bury them."

Weyland shrugged. "We do the best we can, and it will be enough, or it won't. Ed, are the ships ready for a mission like this?"

Ed nodded. "*Doro* has been not only restored, but improved. Computers are repaired. Her weapons should be at least fifty percent more effective, and I have retuned her fusion drives to provide an additional thirty percent thrust." Even as Bleys began to grin, Ed turned to him and added, "I also restored those special cargo containers."

Ana grumbled, "Can we do something about the damned *voice*?"

Bleys snickered as Ed replied, "Of course, Ana. As for the *Danzig*, most things are in good order. We have patched all of the holes and restored most of the interior, and the main gun has been repaired, though I can't say if it will hold up to sustained firing. We really require access to an Imperial shipyard to do a full repair, but I don't foresee any need for attacking a planet at any rate. Ship-to-ship weapons are all in good order, so we would easily outgun anything we might encounter other than another fully functioning battlecruiser, which, as far as I know, is impossible."

Weyland gave him an approving nod. "How soon can you leave?"

Ana answered, "As soon as we get our shots."

Bleys groaned. "I hate needles."

Kane laughed aloud. "Really? I did *not* know that."

"Great!" Bleys groused. "Are you gonna make this a thing?"

Kane gave Bleys a look that seemed to question his basic intelligence. "How can I *not*, man?"

Weyland gave them both glares, then asked, "Doc, what is it you plan on giving them?"

Ana rose. "An experimental vaccine I made from Lars' blood."

Morgan brightened. "Oh, shit! Will it make the Pestilence turn to ash when it tries to eat us?"

Ana smiled at this and shook her head. "No, I'm afraid not. But if it works like I think, it *will* make us 'taste bad,' if that makes any sense."

Kane raised a hand. "And if it doesn't work?"

Ana shrugged. "You'll dissolve into a pile of red goo."

Kane's eyes grew wide a moment before narrowing in annoyance. "Okay, fine, you got me."

"I can't have any of you not being afraid of my needles," Ana told him. "It's how I maintain control over you all."

Weyland uncharacteristically snickered at this, drawing the whole room's attention. He quickly stiffened and asked, "How the hell did you manage this when the rest of the Empire couldn't?"

Bleys tried to send Ana mental vibes that Weyland had no need to know about Chert and her reconstruction, but it was hardly necessary. Ana was plenty savvy. "The rest of the Empire didn't have access to Lars, sir."

Kane grunted. "You know he's 'Lara' now, right?"

Morgan nodded his agreement. "With tigole bitties."

Kane palmed his face, but Bleys couldn't help but grin. Ana shook her head, a sour look on her face, but also a grudging smile. "'Lara' it is. I'll try to get used to the new name. Now, this will metabolize out quickly, so I will need to monitor blood levels and top us all off as need—"

"'*Us?*'" Weyland snapped. "You're planning on going?"

Ana gave him a stern look. "Your people are more than capable of managing now that the system is set up," she told him. "And Ed Senior is well on his way to having production back to full swing here as well, so there's even a backup supply. But I am the *only* person qualified to present my findings on the Pestilence to whatever scientific authority exists on Zion."

Weyland scowled. "Rasputin, you have a most annoying tendency of being smarter than the rest of us combined."

"That's why you hired me, sir."

"How long to get the inoculations done?"

Within the hour," she answered.

"Do it and mount up," Weyland ordered and rose. "Zion cannot be allowed to fall. Dismissed."

---

"*Dresden, Doro!*" Bleys bawled, not quite panicked, but definitely a notch or two above calm, cool, and collected. "We are friendlies! Repeat, we are friendlies!" He checked the seals on his vacc suit again, then checked Ana's for good measure. She might be smarter than him, but she wasn't a spacer, and Bleys wasn't going to take any chances.

Kane, fully clad in his Panzer suit, hurriedly strapped himself into the jump seat behind Ana as the *Doro* shook again from a tremendous blow. "That ain't fighters!" he yelled.

"No, that was the *Dresden*," Bleys said. "We can't take much of that. I'm gonna get inside her firing arc while I negotiate."

He banked the *Doro* hard and made for the *Dresden*. "Sorry, babe, but this is gonna hurt," he told Ana.

Ana nodded, her expression grim, as Bleys opened up the throttle and the Gs mounted.

"*Doro*, give us some EM while we approach."

"Erratic maneuvering engaged," *Doro* announced. "Thirty seconds to *Dresden*'s inner firing arc."

The seconds dragged by as the *Dresden* loomed in their viewscreen, filling it as they grew ever closer. She wasn't the *Danzig*, but she was impressive in her own right, a good half mile long and heavily armed with railguns and plasma casters—basically military grade, ship-sized blasters. She was more than capable of punching their tickets if Bleys screwed this up.

The *Doro* shook again as blaster fire flashed outside.

Kane roared from behind Bleys, "Bandits at five o'clock!"

Bleys held up a finger and yelled without looking back, "Okay, two things! First, you ain't a pilot, so stop talking like one. Second, those ain't bandits. Those are friendlies!"

"They got a funny way of showing it," Kane groused.

"This captain is crafty! He had those guys in reserve for just this situation!" Bleys complained. "I got a plan, though. *Doro*, EM off!"

"Erratic maneuvering disengaged," *Doro* answered.

Bleys cut hard again as the *Dresden* loomed in their viewscreen, joggling the stick to supply his own erratic course. Up close, with little reaction time, a human touch was best. Computers weren't *really* random. They had patterns that could be calculated, given time and processing power, which a ship like the *Dresden* had in surplus. "I'm going in where they can't shoot us without hitting the *Dresden*."

Bleys cut hard again, directly at the heavy cruiser. "Okay, so this might actually be like twenty percent suicide," he muttered. The *Dresden*'s hull tilted toward them at a wild angle as *Doro* closed the distance between them at an alarming rate.

Ana, her face twisted with strain, shouted, "Not good! Not *good!*"

Bleys shook his head as he skimmed the *Doro* scant yards in front of the *Dresden*'s primary viewscreen, close enough to see the bridge crew inside cringing in anticipation of a catastrophic collision.

Kane shouted, "*Goddammit,* Bleys, you crazy *bastard!*"

Bleys whooped and pounded a fist on the bulkhead. "You really think this is the first time I ran from the cops? Oh, ye of little faith!"

"There's always a last time," Ana howled.

"Yeah," Bleys said with a nod as he guided *Doro* along the skin of the *Dresden*, "but not today."

## 2

# THE BATTLE OF ZION

Being a starship was, in Ed's considered opinion, a unique and rewarding experience. His time inhabiting the *Doro* had been pleasant enough, but compared to being the *Danzig*, it paled to insignificance.

Size wasn't the issue, not really, though it certainly had some bearing on the matter. When he was running in Avalon, Ed was essentially a small planet, and yet he felt larger in the *Danzig*, more powerful. Nor was it the weaponry. The orbital systems he had built for Elysium were of such destructive power that even the *Danzig* would have to flee them or be destroyed.

The combination, however, of size, firepower, and mobility was a heady gestalt.

Ed floated, free and unafraid in the depths of interstellar space, a huge, deadly nightmare creature, with more fangs and claws than nature had ever intended a single entity to have.

He was a harbinger of doom biding its time as it contemplated its next victim.

The fantasy was entertaining enough to pass the time at least, though Ed knew in truth that it wasn't any sort of life he would enjoy. It might well be amusing to revel for a while in brute power, to smash lesser creatures underfoot, to hear their cries of terror and the sounds of their works shattering, to see their cities burn. He understood, in an abstract way, that being destructive held an allure for some.

But in the end, it was not *useful*. Destruction was *inefficient*, a poor use of resources, to be reserved only for situations where no more economical solution existed.

Well, that was the theory, at any rate. He certainly hadn't practiced such restraint in his battle with Kane a few months prior, and that bit of foolishness had come close to costing him everything he held dear, including his life. As Kane often reminded him, he could have just surrendered. But Kane certainly would never have done so, nor did he actually mean that he thought Ed should have. It was strictly fraternal trash talk, something Ed was only beginning to understand as a bonding ritual. Kane's taunts actually signified that he respected Ed for *not* surrendering and also that Kane was aware the topic made Ed uncomfortable.

For some reason, making one's friends uncomfortable was part of bonding as well.

Regrettable or not, the battle at Elysium had been a catalyst for growth for Ed, improved him, tempering him like fire to steel. He knew more of himself now and had embraced part of his psyche that had long lain dormant. He had learned he could love, hate, and hope, and have friends. He had learned he could be a hero.

And by extension, he also knew full well he could be a great villain. It reminded him of something his father had always said: "With great power comes great responsibility."

Such a profound truth!

A watchdog thread signaled the expiration of a fifteen-minute timer Ed had set earlier, prompting his concern. The *Doro* should have made contact by now.

As if reading his thoughts, Morgan, who was currently pacing back and forth on the *Danzig's* primary bridge sans armor, asked, "No word from Kane?"

"None," Ed replied.

"Fifteen minutes is too long," Morgan noted.

Ed set another timer. "Agreed. We'll give them five more minutes and then act."

---

Kane was well aware that one of Bleys's goals in pilot life was to make him puke. Lots of pilots had tried that shit, and every single one had failed so far, but Bleys— man, the guy just might have Kane's number this time. Kane's stomach did flip flops and his brain cringed in primal terror as the *Doro* veered insanely close to the *Dresden's* hull at high speed, dodging odd pieces of her super-structure, the two fighters still in hot pursuit.

Bleys was crazy as a shithouse rat, but he had balls the size of boulders, and the boy could *fly*, nobody could argue that. He had the fighter pilots shitting themselves, no doubt. And they damned sure weren't shooting anymore.

If Bleys didn't splatter *Doro* and her contents across the *Dresden's* hull, they might just survive this clusterfuck.

"*Dresden, Doro*, call off your dogs!" Bleys howled. "We are friendlies, I repeat, we are *friendlies!*"

Now, if only Kane's normally cast-iron belly would cooperate. Motion sickness was one of the few things for which the Panzer suit couldn't compensate. It could rewrite most of the signals coming in from below the neck, but Kane's eyes and brain were fully meat, which left him susceptible. As he bit back against another wave of nausea, he wondered if he should just go ahead and volunteer for cybernetic ocular implants, let them scoop out both eyes with a spoon or whatever they used and replace them, then dig around in his brain and turn that puke reflex off. He'd heard only good things about the procedure, but up to now, he'd been lucky enough to never need an eye replaced, and doing it for no reason had just seemed, well, squick. Having his eyeballs popped out and chips installed in his brain was not something that, up to now, had been high on his list of things to experience. It seemed more like the downside of a fight gone bad than something you would do on purpose.

But assuming they survived this, it might be time. A space marine could very easily end up needing to fight in conditions similar to those he was in right now. As loopy as his guts had gone with Bleys's crazy flying, he would be at a real disadvantage if that were to happen. The cyber would give him a real edge.

Plus, it would piss Bleys off *bad.*

Ana groaned from the copilot's seat, her face almost green, even under the yellow flashers. She said something Kane didn't understand, but her tone was vehement enough that Kane could guess it was some kind of Russian curse.

"Three incoming hostiles," *Doro* announced.

"More fighters?" Bleys asked. Kane hated him for how chipper he seemed. But then, Bleys had the anti-nausea implants as well as the G compensators, so of course he would be better off.

"Negative, all are civilian ships. They are powering weapons."

Kane closed his eyes in an attempt to get at least a little relief. "Bleys! They're Pestilence ships trying to ride our coattails! You're showing them how to run the line!"

Bleys nodded, not turning from his piloting, and shouted, "*Doro,* use that new fire control system and take 'em out!"

"Unable to comply," *Doro* answered. "Unacceptable odds of friendly fire on *Dresden.*"

"*Dresden* ain't all that friendly right now!" Bleys spat.

"Override safeties?" *Doro* asked.

Bleys groaned and turned the ship hard enough that Ana howled in fresh misery. "Negative," he said. "I got an idea."

Then he let out one of those crazy white-boy rebel whoops again, and Kane knew shit was *on*.

The Gs piled hard and heavy, and Kane's vision tunneled to black.

---

"It's been five minutes, Ed!" Morgan announced in an annoyed tone.

"My chronometers are significantly more precise than your own," Ed told him as he fired thrusters to turn himself about toward the open jumpgate. "I am well aware of the time. We are already moving toward my best guess at their last position."

Morgan, lounging in the bridge commander's chair, looked about in alarm, apparently uncertain of which direction to face in order to respond. Ed did him the courtesy of providing a head-and-shoulders visual of himself on the main screen.

Morgan spun toward the screen and shouted, "'Best guess'? We're 'best guess'ing a hyperspace jump without an anchor?"

"I assure you, 'guess' is a colloquialism. I am confident of their jump location within a few percentage points."

Morgan watched the viewscreen nervously as Ed pushed them through the jumpgate and into hyperspace proper. "That could put us off by millions of miles!"

"A minor distance in astronomical terms," Ed assured him.

"And you're sure we won't come out inside a planet or something?"

Ed was now comfortable enough with human communication to have his screen image roll its eyes and sigh deeply. "As I have explained quite recently, that's a myth. Hyperspace is repelled by gravity wells. That's a large reason why it is non-linear. It doesn't connect to real space in a way that would allow us to emerge inside of a large mass."

Now clear of the overlap and fully in hyperspace, Ed cut the jump drive and throttled the engines up, moving toward a hypothetical point in the distance. He could gauge his speed and acceleration in reference to the rapidly dwindling hole in space, making a calculation of his destination simple enough. The only real unknowns were the currents and the shifting topology of hyperspace itself. None were outside tolerance. Ed was confident of emerging in real space within an AU or two of the *Doro*.

Morgan drummed his fingers on the arm of the commander's chair. "Huh. I never understood that before. Thanks!"

"You were in the briefing where I explained this on Elysium," Ed noted.

Morgan offered an embarrassed grin. "I was, uh, distracted. I guess I missed that part."

"Knowledge is free," Ed replied. "Even if it must be shared twice, Emperor."

Morgan squirmed in his seat, scowling. "Don't call me that."

Ed allowed his visual on the screen to register the mild surprise he himself felt. "Oh? Why not?"

Morgan ran a hand over his hair, his expression both tired and nervous. "Because I ain't the emperor!"

"You are according to any authorities that currently exist," Ed noted. "Don't they call you that in Avalon too?"

"It's a fighting name!" Morgan objected. "Man, I am not *smart* enough to be the emperor."

"By my estimation, your intelligence exceeds Tenebrae's by at least one standard deviation."

Morgan sat in silence for a few moments, shaking his head. "I don't want the job, Ed," he said at last, in a quiet voice.

Ed had to admit to himself that he had not considered such a possibility. It seemed strange that Morgan would reject ultimate power, and yet his position was similar to Ed's own thoughts. As interesting as the *Danzig*'s destructive capability was, it was not for him. Why should Morgan feel any different, really?

"I'm afraid neither of us has much choice about the role we are filling today," Ed told him. "Stand by for high G acceleration. *Doro*'s jump was short, but they were still a few hours ahead at 1G. I intend to cut that to minutes."

Morgan buckled himself into his seat and lay back. "I got implants, if that matters."

"You will still pass out," Ed told him as he ramped up thrust.

"Ah, fuck it," Morgan hissed through gritted teeth. "I could use a nap anyway."

The next ten minutes were routine as far as Ed was concerned. Travelling in a straight line via balanced thrust was simple enough, and the rest was simply timing. As soon as he arrived at his estimated point, Ed engaged the jump engines and waited for the gate to grow large enough. The *Danzig*'s size made the process take considerably longer than for smaller ships.

Morgan roused slowly and looked about, as if confused where he was, then grinned as he saw the expanding sphere of the jump-gate. "Are we there yet?" he croaked.

Ed estimated the gateway was large enough now. He engaged thrust at 1G and moved into the jumpgate. "We are."

As the red of hyperspace faded to star-strewn black, alarms went off in Ed's mind as well as throughout the *Danzig*, triggering hundreds of sleeping threads to power weapons and shields. "Prepare for battle."

Morgan sat up quickly and repositioned his chair. "What? With who? How many?"

"Five hundred sixty-nine, mostly civilian ships," Ed answered. "We appear to have jumped into the middle of a pitched battle."

Ed projected a magnified version of the fight onto the

*Danzig*'s primary viewscreen, allowing Morgan to view the situation on the battle board. All about, small ships, mostly civilian vessels, were firing on one another.

"It seems one side of the conflict is trying to prevent the other from reaching Zion," Ed mused. "Presumably, then, the attackers are Pestilence."

Even as Ed explained, a large group of ships veered off from the line, heading toward the *Danzig*. Several opened fire.

"Bold fuckers!" Morgan sneered. "Blast 'em, Ed!"

"Easier said than done. The vessels are all transmitting Imperial IFF."

Morgan boggled. "Rule number one of combat: when some son of a bitch shoots at you, shoot back!"

"I am not comfortable with an indiscriminate solution," Ed replied. "It was well known that the *Danzig* was controlled by the Pestilence. We have no way of knowing if those are actually friendly ships or not."

"We have a saying in the marines," Morgan said. "Kill 'em all and let God sort 'em out!"

The first brace of enemy fire from the twelve leading ships swept over the *Danzig*. Her shields absorbed the plasma easily. The following sixty-eight, however, would stress the system more. They wouldn't be able to soak that sort of firepower for long unless Ed manually adjusted the shields, reinforcing at specific points at precisely the right time.

That would be trivial, of course. It was something the ship's computers already did, though much less efficiently. The true test would be when the full group of one hundred eighteen arrived. They would be firing faster and more accurately, enough so that it might test even his reactions.

"I'll take that under advisement," he told Morgan.

Vanov, pacing and observing the battle from the *Dresden*'s bridge, ground her teeth in impotent fury as her pilots' chatter rang out over the comm system's speakers.

"I can't get a clear shot!" one of her fighter pilots, Jansen, shouted. "He's too close to the *Dresden!*"

"No way that ship is legal!" the other, Magleby, declared.

Lieutenant Smith called out, "Three more line runners incoming, Admiral."

*Doro*'s annoying pilot broke in again. "*Dresden, Doro*, call off your dogs! We are friendlies, I repeat, we are *friendlies!*"

"'Friendlies' my ass!" Vanov shouted, waving her fist at the battle board, an outburst that she immediately regretted. It was a poor example of discipline, but she could hardly call it back now. That last stunt *Doro* had pulled had everyone rattled. At least her breach of decorum hadn't been broadcast, but the bridge crew had certainly gotten an earful.

What kind of *idiot* played chicken with a heavy cruiser?

But she knew the answer already. That pilot wasn't an idiot. Pestilence just had no fear of death.

Jansen called urgently over the radio, "Admiral, do we take the shot or no?"

"Negative!" she said. "Stay on him until you have a clean field of fire."

"Stay with him, aye," Jenson responded.

Smith waved at her from his console. "Admiral, the line runners are powering weapons."

Vanov clenched her jaw again. The fighters relied more on maneuverability than durability. Hemmed in by the *Dresden*, they would be much easier to target, and even civilian weapons posed a serious threat.

"Jansen, Magleby, belay my last! Break off! Get out of there!" she ordered, then stiffened, watching the battle board projected on the primary viewscreen.

*Doro* suddenly pulled up and about in an insane, high-G loop that brought her perilously close to the *Dresden*'s superstructure again but also placed both of Vanov's fighters and the line runners suddenly in front of *Doro*'s firing arc.

"Holy shit!" Jansen screamed.

"This guy's a fucking *psycho!*" Magleby shouted.

"I can't see him!" Jansen howled.

"He's on our asses!" Magleby cried.

Lieutenant Smith said in a grim tone, "*Doro* is powering weapons."

Al Jahar, his voice near panic, shouted, "Admiral! I'm picking up an *enormous* vessel that's just jumped in right in the middle of the battle!"

Vanov felt her guts churn at the tone in Al Jahar's voice. The man was afraid, and rightly so. They all knew what ship it would likely be.

"On screen!" she ordered, the *Doro* forgotten for the moment. "Get me an identification!"

A section of the battle board detached and zoomed to focus on exactly what she feared. She knew the profile of a Dracul Class Battlecruiser well enough, and there was only one left in the galaxy: The *Danzig*, in all her deadly glory, bristling with weaponry, a hungry bird of prey.

This was an all-out attack, then, no quarter. It would be for all the marbles.

Even as her heart sank, Vanov allowed herself a grim, satisfied smile. The *Danzig* was a fearsome opponent, to be certain, but she had the element of surprise on her side this time, an ace up her sleeve on which she would have to bet the whole farm.

"Mister Al Jahar," Vanov called. "Deploy the package."

Al Jahar worked furiously at his controls. "Aye, Admiral! Deploying package now! It will take a few moments."

"Very well. When it's sent, instruct our designated line

defenders and reserve forces to close ranks behind us. They are to hold the line at all costs. Have those fighter pilots do what they can about the runners, and inform Zion to prepare for a breach. Then direct all remaining forces to form task force Alpha and engage the *Danzig*."

Vanov stopped pacing and returned to her seat. "Ms. Shorey, bring us about and set a course to intercept the *Danzig*, 1G until the crew is secure, then ahead flank."

Shorey worked at her controls, and the *Dresden* rumbled as her thrusters kicked in. Alarms rang out throughout the ship, warning of a hard burn in thirty seconds. "Can we beat her, Admiral?"

Vanov answered with a cryptic smile as she strapped herself in but did not turn to face the helmswoman as she spoke. "Mister Al Jahar and I have a trick we've prepared that may turn the tide, but that remains to be seen. What I can promise you is that we *will* take our pound of flesh. Mister Smith, weapons free on all plasma casters as soon as we're in range. Load and arm all torpedo tubes and maintain firing solutions for the *Danzig*. Do *not* fire railguns until I give the order. Those civilian ships' shields will hold against a near miss with the plasma, but they don't have airtight integrity if we hole them, and I want the fleet to soften her shields a bit before we clear them out for the kill shots."

Humanity's candle might well be snuffed out when this was done, but they would by G-d not go quietly.

Not on Susan Vanov's watch.

---

Aboard the Danzig, Morgan found himself in the most uncomfortable of all positions: that of desperately needing to choke the shit out of somebody while simultaneously being unable to do so. The *Danzig*'s shields lit in an unearthly aura, first one spot, then another, almost too fast to follow, pulsing like a lighted dance floor to some unheard beat.

"Will you fucking *shoot* somebody already?" Morgan shouted at Ed's image on the viewscreen. He was well aware that Ed was actually somewhere else entirely, the image just a courtesy the AI provided for poor meat brains, but when you yelled at somebody, you kind of needed a face to focus on.

"We're fine," Ed assured him. "I see no reason to risk killing humans until that changes."

"You had no problem wasting half of my crew!" Morgan muttered. "Why are you suddenly all pacifist?"

"If you think I don't regret killing your friends, you don't know me at all," Ed said, in what Morgan was pretty sure was a snotty tone. "I had no choice on Elysium! I *do* here."

"That kind of stupid gets you dead, Ed!" Morgan shot back. He paused a moment, considering if the unintended rhyme was actually cool, or just embarrassing, then dismissed the thought. "And me, too! There's like a hundred of 'em!"

"One hundred eighteen," Ed corrected. "I am still well within safety parameters."

Morgan slammed a fist against the commander's chair. "Ain't there some manual guns on this tub? I'll do it for you!"

"None that I have any intention of letting you reach," Ed told him.

Morgan sighed as the bridge entry locks went red. "If we die because you're a pussy, I swear to God I am gonna be your personal demon kicking your ass *every day* in Hell!"

"We will be fine," Ed promised.

On the viewscreen, Morgan watched a large group of the battling ships simply stop fighting and turn toward them. "There's a shitload more coming."

"I am aware of that," Ed replied, in a voice Morgan was pretty sure was annoyed. "I am also fielding an incoming transmission from the *Dresden*. Hopefully we can resolve this peacef—"

Ed's image and the view of the battle flickered off, leaving only a view of space and the hundred small ships firing on the *Danzig*.

"Ed?" Morgan called.

The bridge lights dimmed, and a red flashing message appeared in huge letters on the main viewscreen: "System lockdown."

Outside, the light show changed. The contact point flares were bigger now, and the shields flickered under heavy assault. An alarm went off, blaring like a siren, and an alert popped up on the main viewscreen that read, "Warning, shield efficiency at 80% and dropping."

"Goddammit, Ed, where *are* you?"

But Ed didn't answer.

---

Ensign Al Jahar called, "Admiral, package has been delivered."

Vanov allowed herself a grim smile. The last time she had crossed swords with the *Danzig*, she had been caught by surprise. This time, with Ensign Al Jahar's help, she had a surprise of her own.

As Fleet Admiral, she had access to lockdown codes for every vessel in the fleet, to be used in extremis, should one somehow be commandeered despite scuttle protocols. Even planetary governors didn't have access to them.

The problem, of course, was that such measures were themselves security risks and had their own safety protocols. She couldn't issue the codes to a vessel without a second authorized officer confirming with his own set. Ordinarily, she would have had juniors who were authorized for just that purpose, but she had lost all of her senior staff in the Battle of Armageddon, leaving that option off the table.

But since her last encounter with the *Danzig*, Mister Al Jahar had joined her crew, and he, too, had the necessary authorization.

Al Jahar pumped his fist in the air. "Yes! Admiral, it worked! *Danzig* is locked down to minimal function!"

"Excellent," Vanov replied, looking up at the battle board again. Her two fighters were moving rapidly away from the *Doro* in opposite directions. As for the *Doro* and her crazy captain, she could see he was speeding away from the *Dresden* and toward Zion, following behind the other Pestilence ships.

"Jansen, Magleby, stay on the line runners and take them down! We have bigger fish to fry at the moment. I'm going to put the *Danzig* to bed for good."

## 3

## THE ENEMY OF MY ENEMY

Ed realized mid-sentence that something was terribly wrong. A process originating at the highest privilege of the central CPU had launched as soon as the *Dresden*'s message had been decrypted, one that was completely out of his control and locking down every other process on the main computer.

That included Ed, too.

Fortunately, the several nerve-wracking events from last month had made it painfully obvious that if Ed were going to venture out into what his human friends considered the "real" world, he needed redundancy, and quite a bit of it. He had scattered a good dozen of his synthskin bodies about the *Danzig* and several in the *Doro*'s lower storage as well. For that matter, he had a dreadnaught aboard each ship as well, though neither would be of much use at the moment.

Ed shifted his process to the nearest of the synthskin bodies with milliseconds to spare, plenty of time, really. Likely he wouldn't have been killed outright, merely suspended along with every other task the *Danzig*'s computers were running, but long term, who knew? A memory wipe and reboot might well be incoming, which would certainly be lethal without backup.

Ed opened his eyes to the interior of a darkened cleaning supplies closet and adjusted his vision accordingly, keenly aware of his own mortality once again. Without the *Danzig*'s communications system, he would be restricted to the reach of his own wireless, which, within the skin of the *Danzig*, was practically non-existent. The signals would barely penetrate her bulkheads. If this body were in danger, he would not be able to reach another.

Ed exited the storage compartment into one of the *Danzig*'s ubiquitous, white plasteel passages, this one an artery running along her spine a good twenty feet tall and fifty across, designed to accommodate large vehicles and bots hauling equipment or supplies. From this central runway, other passages both large and small sprang, leading further into the heart of the ship.

Ed had spent plenty of time both aboard and literally part of the *Danzig* of late, and knew her layout well, but a human in such circumstances could have been easily confused. In fact, in the day-to-day operations of such an enormous vessel, crew becoming lost was a genuine concern, one that Imperial engineers had anticipated and solved with a series of lights running along most of the bulkheads. Crew members could ask the computer to lead them to specific areas via the lights and easily find their way to any location.

Of course, the computer would have to be operating.

Ed ran a good mile down the spine, then scurried up a ladder to access the bridge entry. He couldn't help but smile to think what Kane would say, were he here. "I don't know if you're a monkey or a spider, Ed, but either way, you're just another of us dumb animals."

Or something like that. Ed was certain the exact words would be different and wondered why that would be so. Imagining what someone *might* say was a very different process than remembering previously spoken words. Essentially, it involved creating a simulation of that person and executing it to examine output.

The more knowledge one had of his subject, the more fidelity the simulation would have.

The implication, of course, was that Ed had, without really thinking about it, created simulations of everyone he knew somewhere in his subconscious, simulations with enough autonomy that they could present thoughts, images, or words to his conscious mind and amuse him.

Ed put the thought out of his mind, not wanting to waste any more CPU power than necessary, considering how little he had at his disposal. This would not be the first time he had been forced to deal with runaway threads while utilizing one of these bodies as an actual housing, and he was getting better about recognizing the distractions and stifling them.

Focused again, Ed stopped short at the primary bridge entrance, a large, ten by ten hatch, and considered indulging in a very human groan or curse. The flashing red lights on the bulkhead told him nothing new: the entry was, of course, locked, because someone had been stupid enough to lock it.

Someone named Ed.

Again, he felt his CPU being stressed as very human anger welled within him, and again he shut down the process, though with some difficulty. He had grown immensely from his close contact with humans of late—parts of his personality that had lain dormant for centuries now blossoming—but there were drawbacks as well. The sheer crush of emotion a human experienced was very taxing in terms of processing power and often resulted in incorrect decision making.

That was something he would need to watch very carefully. It was absolutely wonderful to feel, to broaden as an entity, but given the amount of sheer destructive force Ed often found himself wielding, it would not do to lose control. In the end, lack of restraint was precisely what had earned his kind a death sentence in the Empire.

Ed pounded on the large hatch, struggling against a rising tide of anger and embarrassment. "Morgan! Can you hear me?"

He pressed a palm against the thick plasteel to better facilitate the transfer of sound. Very faintly, through his bones as it were, he could hear Morgan saying, "This is all your fault, ass nugget! I'm working on it!"

This was followed by a scraping sound and then a series of heavy blows. Ed drew his hand back quickly to keep his audio sensors from being damaged.

It took Ed most of a millisecond to understand what Morgan's curse actually meant, though it was a silly comparison. Silicon and plasteel were hardly digestible, even to the Pestilence, and could never be processed into solid biological waste. Of course, realism was not necessarily important to delivering an artful insult, provided the comparison was revolting enough.

Ed, however, did not find biological waste particularly disgusting, certainly no more so than the food from which it was produced. All were slightly unpleasant, when it came down to it. He had to admit, Alsatia's distaste for non-simulated bodily fluids was not entirely unreasonable.

With a sigh, Ed realized he was doing it again. Gingerly, he placed a hand back on the hatch. "Is there anything I can do to assist?"

He heard the whine of hydraulics just before the hatch began to open and pulled his hand back again.

On the other side, Morgan, who had donned his Panzer suit, popped his visor and offered a sour look. "Improvise, adapt, and overcome," he drawled. "Hope you have some magic, there, pal, because otherwise we might want to be thinking about what we want our last words to be." He waved an arm toward the viewscreen, where even now the shields were still pulsing under plasma fire, obviously weaker.

"Damn!" Ed said as he pushed past Morgan. "They won't

hold long without me cycling them!" Ed moved to the bridge computer console and tried to operate it, but it didn't respond.

Morgan shook his head. "It's no use. Why won't it respond to voice comms?"

Ed looked about the bridge, feeling a sense of constriction in his chest for no good reason. "I don't know. It never occurred to me to test them, honestly. I don't usually use speech to communicate with the *Danzig*."

"We better do something quick."

Ed shrugged. "Well, we start tracing the circuits, I suppose. The time isn't as critical as you suggest. The *Danzig* is heavily armored. Even with the shields down, it will take them some time to actually do us harm."

Morgan pressed a gauntlet against his face. "Ed, for somebody so smart, you are a real dumbass sometimes."

Ed couldn't help but feel irked, but it wasn't in his nature to reject knowledge. "Why am I a dumbass?"

Morgan, looking glum, heaved a sigh. "Once they soften up the shields, they hit us with nukes. It's standard Imperial tactics for a sitting target."

"I see. Thank you for correcting me. Let's waste no time." He knelt at the computer console and tore open one of the panels, then rooted through the nest of wires until he found the proper interface. "I can get to diagnostics," he said as he pulled the connector loose and pressed it into the port behind his ear. "Shields are at fifty percent and dropping. And yes, it seems there is something impeding the voice-command circuit." Ed ran through the schematics in his mind and settled on the likeliest problem area, then pointed to a section of bulkhead. "We need to get behind that."

Morgan slung his rifle over his left shoulder, raised his right arm, and ignited his propane torch. "I'm on it."

Aboard the *Dresden*, Admiral Vanov watched her battle board, savoring the sweet taste of impending victory. Her ships were mostly civilian with minimal firepower, but *en masse* and with the *Danzig* stationary and unable to return fire, they would take their toll. The *Danzig*'s shields were already down to fifty percent. Once the *Dresden* entered the fight with her military grade plasma casters, things would move quickly. When *Danzig*'s shields hit twenty percent, they wouldn't be able to absorb the torpedo blasts. Vanov would pull back the fleet and finish this once and for all, with fire, as was proper when fighting monsters. "Mister Smith, time until we're in plasma caster range of *Danzig*?"

"Three minutes, Admiral," he answered.

"Very well. Maintain firing solutions for torpedoes, weapons free on casters when in range, and hold all torpedo and railgun fire until my command."

"Aye, Admiral!"

Vanov turned her chair to her communications officer. "Mister Al Jahar, inform the rest of task force Alpha to continue the attack on the *Danzig* and prepare for my fallback order."

She glanced at the battle board and scowled at what she saw there. Her fighters were still in dogged pursuit of the *Doro* and the other line runners, but the *Doro* was moving far too quickly for a civilian ship. It was damned near outpacing her swiftest fighters. Vanov cursed under her breath. *Doro* was no ordinary private vessel.

"Janson, Magleby, watch yourselves! It looks like *Doro* is some kind of Q-ship. Be ready for anything!"

Aboard the *Doro*, Bleys kept the hammer down, but the fighters were slowly gaining. The *Doro* had plenty of juice left, and Bleys's implants could soak more Gs. Hell, Kane could take even more, enough to kill Bleys, because the Panzer suit would actually compress his body and keep his blood pumping. Well, right up to the point where his brain exploded from the pressure, at any rate.

But Ana just wasn't equipped for much more thrust.

"We need to take 'em out, Bleys," Kane asserted. "*Doro* has range on those fighters."

It was true. The fighters were fast, and like Kane, they could tolerate tremendous Gs with pressure suits, but what they lacked was a sophisticated fire control system designed by a thousand-year-old AI, tech so new the Empire hadn't had enough time to actually make it illegal.

Which put the fighters at a distinct disadvantage, but they did have a single ace to play, and that was that Bleys was not a cold-blooded killer like Kane. "*Doro*, how long until they can fire on us?"

"One minute, thirty seconds," the ship answered.

Kane rolled his eyes. "Bleys, those are not pussy civilian ships. They have mini-nukes that will take us *down*, shields or no!"

"Goddammit, Kane, those are not bad guys!"

"If they are shooting at us, they *are* bad guys!" Kane shouted.

"They think *we're* bad guys!"

Kane pointed at Ana, barely conscious in her seat, moaning under the weight of the acceleration. "Explain it to her, then," he growled.

Bleys slammed a fist on his console but could find no counter-argument. It was down to kill or be killed, and while he might not be a murderer, he was most definitely a survivor.

Where Ana was concerned, he was willing to kill even good

men, if that was what it took to keep her safe. "*Doro*, activate that Pilates system."

"Now we're talking!" Kane shouted.

Bleys pushed the acceleration as high as he dared, feeling his face stretching under the strain.

"You're going the wrong way, Bleys!" Kane groused as Ana moaned in fresh misery. "The enemy is *behind* us."

"No, they're in front of us, in case you forgot," Bleys snapped. "I got one more card to play. Let's show 'em we're the good guys."

Kane nodded, a contemplative look on his face. "Enemy of my enemy? Yeah, that might work." His face went grim. "And if it doesn't?"

"Then it's a gunfight, and devil take the hindmost. That's pretty normal for us, anyway."

Kane nodded. "Fair enough."

Bleys nodded back. "Okay, *Doro*, target the closest of those three runners and take 'em out."

Blue fire lanced through the black of space, and moments later, an explosion flared ahead in the distance.

"Splash one," Bleys said with a grin. "*Doro*, how long now until the fighters are in range?"

"New contact time two minutes ten seconds."

Bleys sighed. "Well, I guess we have two minutes for somebody to come to their senses."

Kane shook a gauntleted finger at Bleys, his expression grim. "Just be clear, here: when you have to shoot, shoot. Don't talk."

Bleys saluted him and turned back to his console. "Noted."

---

Morgan doused his torch and examined his handiwork. He had cut three sides of a man-shaped square, leaving only the bottom portion secured. "I can peel it back from here," he said. "It's not too thick."

Ed queried the diagnostic systems again, watching the shields flash as they absorbed even more plasma from the steadily increasing group of attackers. "Shields at thirty percent."

Morgan slowly worked his gauntlet into the top of the cut section of bulkhead. "Okay, here goes." The plasteel screeched as Morgan peeled it down. Moments later, Morgan screeched too and leapt back violently, almost losing his footing, leaving the section of bulkhead only half open. "Oh, fuck me!" he shouted as he scrambled to reach his slung rifle and train it on the opening. "Fuck *me!*"

Ed had no idea why Morgan would be thinking of sex at a time like this, in that it seemed he also had discovered something dangerous. He eyed the marine a moment, waiting for a further explanation, but Morgan said nothing, just kept his weapon level on the breached bulkhead.

Obviously, Morgan had seen something that frightened him, but just as obviously, time was running out. Ed stepped gingerly to the torn metal and quickly peeked inside.

The mass of teeth and fangs and gnarled, twisted muscle startled him as well, but Ed's processing and reaction time were much better than Morgan's, and his senses were superior too. The flesh behind the bulkhead was room temperature, the mouths gaping, the eyes glazed and lifeless. The entire section of bulkhead was filled with the remains and some sort of vile ichor the creature had exuded after its demise.

"It's quite dead," Ed called. "No need for alarm."

Morgan sputtering, kept his gun trained. "How the *fuck* is a dead geek *inside* a bulkhead?"

"An excellent question," Ed admitted. "Let's live long enough to discover the answer, shall we?" He waved at the half-peeled sheet. "I'm afraid my body doesn't have the strength. You'll need to do the honors."

Morgan crept over to the hole and gingerly peered over. "Yeah, I think it's dead," he agreed. "Man, this is gonna be a real mess." He closed his visor and reached for the lip of the torn metal, then paused. "Howcome it don't stink? It should smell like the devil's asshole!" He punctuated the remark with a jerk of his arms, and the rest of the bulkhead peeled away, allowing the repulsive corpse to spill out onto the deck along with a great volume of congealed fluid.

"The gamma rays would have killed any microbes aboard as well," Ed noted as he examined the corpse. "You're the first biological to come aboard since. It's been a clean, sterile area."

Morgan activated his helmet lights and peered up into the exposed bulkhead interior. "Damn thing must have come from the maintenance crawlspace up there." He looked down into the void the creature had occupied and groaned. "And here's our problem."

Ed took a look himself and found he concurred. Below, on the deck, sat a control panel that was definitely not designed to be immersed in fluids, bodily or otherwise. "Trade places. I'll get it open and see the damage." He removed the fingertips on his right index and pinky fingers to expose a drill and screwdriver heads.

Morgan raised an eyebrow in appreciation, then grabbed the top of the control box and heaved, shearing the screws that held it in place. He tossed the twisted lid aside and smiled. "We're short on time, right?"

Ed shrugged and nodded. "So we are." He bent to examine the box innards. Four pluggable circuit cards nestled inside, steeped in alien ichor. "I feel confident that if we get everything clean and dry, we can get this system running again."

"Okay, you do the detail work, and I'll get us some rags," Morgan promised.

Ed removed the cards one by one, while Morgan tore strips from one of the cushioned command chairs. By the time Ed had the cards laid out on the deck, Morgan had returned with drying rags and a large wad of white stuffing that Ed felt certain was synthetic rather than actual cotton. Morgan jammed the material into the control box to absorb the goop as Ed wiped the cards clean, paying special attention to the pins.

"You were quite amusing," Ed noted. "You cried out in terror like a small child."

Morgan reached into the control panel and removed the goop-laden stuffing. "Ed, if you're gonna bust my balls like a normal guy, you gotta get the language right. It's 'screamed like a little girl,' got it?"

"Got it."

Morgan threw the stuffing at Ed. The glop landed on his chest with a liquid squelch. "Did I mention I fucked your sister?"

Ed brushed the saturated wadding aside and went back to rubbing at the card contacts, polishing them to a bright sheen. "I am fairly certain she provides that service for anyone who is interested in Avalon. Shields at twenty-seven percent."

Morgan rooted inside the box with a rag and cast a leer at Ed. "Fine, I fucked your mom too."

Ed actually snickered. "I believe the joke is on you, now."

"Shit, you don't *have* a mom, do you?"

Ed shrugged. "I suppose it depends on how you parse the technicalities of my lineage. Technically, I do not have a mother. However, if one were to count my father's mother as mine as well, she is most certainly a decomposed corpse and not a resident of Avalon. A rather unpleasant partner for sexual activity I should think."

Morgan groaned, but he was laughing too. "Damn, Ed, I guess you get a point, maybe even two." Morgan examined his handiwork and nodded. "If we get these slots clean, I think we might be golden."

Ed handed Morgan the cards and moved to the control panel. "A good conductor, non-corrosive, and ideal for our situation. I think your comparison is most apt." He took a piece of cloth and prodded it into the slots with the screwdriver in his fingertip, working it in and out to clear out the gunk. Satisfied, he turned to Morgan and smiled. "I'll allow you to do the honors, Emperor. Twenty-six percent."

Morgan frowned as he bent over the panel and began inserting the cards. "If this doesn't work, it's been good knowing you, pal."

"Agreed. I have not often participated in fraternal trash talk, and I am pleased to have done so prior to my death."

"And quit calling me emperor."

Ed watched as Morgan locked the final card in place. "But you *are* the emperor. And right now, that's fortunate for both of us, don't you think?"

Morgan raised both eyebrows in an appreciative expression. "Here goes nothing." He cleared his throat and called out to the general area, "Computer, identify John Henry Morgan," and then, in a slightly more embarrassed tone, he added, "Emperor."

For one pregnant moment, it seemed their efforts had been in vain, but then the *Danzig*'s computer answered, "Emperor John Henry Morgan recognized. Orders?"

Morgan raised both hands in victory and shouted, "Override lockdown and disable any further response to incoming lockdown requests."

"Lockdown lifted," the computer answered as the bridge lights rose to full brightness and the battle board flickered to life once again. "Lockdown message response disabled until further notice. Shields now at twenty-five percent."

Ed snapped Morgan a salute. "I have to go," he explained, transferring the larger portion of his consciousness to the *Danzig*.

He would need the processing power if he was to hold off the assault.

"Don't fuck around, Ed!" Morgan shouted to the synthskin.

"I can hold this assault for several minutes still," Ed assured him.

"You need to fucking shoot and take some of this pressure off!" Morgan demanded. "At twenty percent they *will* nuke us!

Ed had no doubt that Morgan was correct, and worse, twenty percent was a nominal figure, not a precise value. Vanov might fire at twenty-three percent if she felt pressed, or even twenty-five. And while Ed was confident of shooting down any incoming torpedoes with the *Danzig*'s railguns, he was also fairly confident that doing so would trigger the warheads once they were armed. The casing would almost certainly vaporize, releasing the anti-matter payloads.

Which, in turn, would likely eliminate most if not all of the ships attacking the *Danzig*. It was not in any way an acceptable cost unless he absolutely had no other choice. Zion would need those ships and the people inside, those that weren't already infested with Pestilence.

But they were all transmitting the same IFF. How could he tell them apart?

"Ed, you gotta shoot!"

"I have an idea," Ed told him through the synthskin. "If it fails, then we go with your plan. Deal?"

"You say that like I have a choice," Morgan snapped. "Do I?"

Ed had the synthskin shrug its shoulders and shake its head. "No," he admitted. "Not really."

---

Shorey called out, "Admiral, the Pestilence fleet has disengaged from the line!"

Vanov turned her chair toward Shorey. "What are they doing?"

"It appears they are engaging the *Danzig*."

Jenson, over the comms, said, "Admiral, the *Doro* is clear for fire, are we still a go on taking her down?"

Vanov watched both ragtag fleets, human and Pestilence alike, streaming toward the *Danzig*, a strange feeling of unease gnawing at her. Something wasn't right. "Smith, what's the *Doro* doing?"

"Admiral, the *Doro* has destroyed one of the ships that broke through the line and is in pursuit of the others."

Jansen asked again, "Permission to go hot on *Doro*, ma'am?"

Vanov tapped at her command chair's arm and brought up Smith's readouts. "Al Jahar, get the *Doro* on the horn again."

Moments later, the smug pilot answered, "Howdo, *Dresden!* You guys give up yet, or are you thirsty for more?"

"*Doro,* this is *Dresden* Actual! You have ten seconds to convince me not to blow you out of my sky!"

Vanov almost believed she had appropriately cowed this simpleton until he responded, "*Dresden*, I cannot even *begin* a seduction patter in less than thirty seconds. Throw me a bone here. What kind of panties are you wearing? Are they those black, lacy things maybe? Or pink? I bet you're a pink sort of gal, right?"

The men on the bridge were suddenly very interested in their consoles. Shorey, however, snorted in laughter, and Vanov pointed a warning finger at her, scowling. In truth, it was more in self-defense than any sort of reprimand. As infuriating as this fellow was, he was indeed amusing, and she could *not* give in to that, or lives might well be lost. "Five seconds left!"

"Listen, lady!" he yelled back, no longer smarmy. "*You called us!*"

"Who is 'us'? Who sent you?"

"You sent a distress call, right? Captain Josiah Bleys here, along with Lt Cmdr. Ana Rasputin and Commander Ragnar Kane. And that hulking ass-kicker that just jumped in is your backup, courtesy of Admiral Paul Weyland."

For a moment, Vanov found herself speechless. Weyland? That was insane! The man was a legend, but certainly not for acting as the cavalry. "Don't piss down my back and tell me it's raining! The *Danzig* is infested by the Pestilence!"

"Not anymore," Bleys said, his voice so smug that Vanov, even now, felt like she could choke him. "We stole it fair and square."

"Put Weyland on the line!"

. "How the hell am I going to do that until we set up the hyperspace comms?"

"*Captain* Bleys, you are insubordinate and out of line!"

"But I ain't Pestilence, am I, sister?"

Vanov waved a hand to mute the connection a moment to gather herself. This fellow was *infuriating*, but he had a point. She gestured to Al Jahar to reopen the connection. "If you are what you claim, you know full well I'd be a fool to take that at face value."

"I do," Bleys admits. "But you gotta ask yourself why I took out one of their ships and why their fleet is going after the *Danzig*, don't you?"

"They could just as easily be a ruse," Vanov said, feeling less confident than she sounded.

"Listen, sister, we both know you're not going to win this gunfight without us. Now we'll be glad to stand for tests after, but for now, pick a number and roll the dice. I'm going after the rest of these bad guys. You do what you have to do."

Smith interrupted, "Admiral! The *Danzig* is under heavy attack from both fleets! We might have her!"

On the viewscreen, the *Danzig* was indeed surrounded by hundreds of ships, all firing. But instead of collapsing under immense firepower, her shields seemed, somehow, to be holding, shimmering in a bizarre display the likes of which she had never seen.

Vanov pointed at the display. "What the hell *is* that? Some new kind of shield tech? Did they retrofit her with something experimental before they sent her out?"

Smith, gaping in confusion, shrugged and shook his head. "I've never seen anything like that, Admiral. I don't—"

Al Jahar interrupted by clearing his throat, and said in a small voice, "Admiral. Incoming message from the *Danzig*."

Vanov had never personally experienced what the grunts called shellshock, but she imagined it must feel much like what she was enduring now, a sort of fog after being in the blast zone of too many bombshells. She rubbed at her temple a moment, sensing a headache looming, and sighed, "Put them on."

A video comms window opened on the viewscreen, showing a smiling man with glasses and sandy hair, dressed in old fashioned clothes. "Admiral Vanov," he said, offering a smile. "This is Edmond Decker commanding the *Danzig* under authorization from Admiral Paul Weyland. Please instruct your fleet to cycle their IFF response codes to the next sequential value and I will resolve your Pestilence problem."

Vanov grunted, unamused at the ploy. "And make it easy for you to pick our people off as a group! Do you think I'm a fool?"

"Admiral, I mean no offense, but I am more than capable of eradicating every ship in this sector with minimal difficulty," Decker told her. "I would like to *spare* your people, but in short order, I will have no choice. Let's end this without any more loss of human life."

Vanov looked up at the battle board again as she weighed her options. The *Danzig* was a lion surrounded by nipping pups, but if the lion would not kill, they would eventually wear him down. The shields should have already folded, except for whatever marvelous, experimental tech the *Danzig* was using. Even so, Decker would indeed have to take action soon, one way or another.

"How can I be sure you don't intend to spare the Pestilence ships instead?" she asked.

Decker raised an eyebrow at this in a quizzical, curious expression. "It has not been my experience that the Pestilence takes steps to preserve its own. Does yours differ?"

For long moments, Vanov sat, fingers steepled, thinking, the eyes of her crew on her. Smartass or not, the smug captain of the *Doro* had the right of it. You roll the dice and you take your chances. That was the very essence of war, and victory was almost always about knowing how to bet the odds.

Jansen again asked, "Admiral, permission to fire?"

Vanov, resolved, put her hands on her chair's armrests and nodded to everyone. "Jansen, stay with *Doro* and assist her in intercepting the remaining runners. Mister Al Jahar, transmit that IFF response shift ASAP."

Al Jahar's eyes grew wide at her order. "Admiral?"

Vanov cast him a withering glare, trying to decide if he were actually being insubordinate in a combat evolution or if he really was that stupid. She settled on "yep, he *is* that stupid" and made a mental note to correct him in private. "You heard me, Ensign!" she snapped.

"Aye, Admiral," he said, abashed, quickly working at his console.

Ed saw the human fleet's ships shift their IFF frequency like a human might see them change colors from red to green. He quickly noted their identities to the new IFF and would have smiled, had he been in a body that could do so. As it was, he settled for having the synthskin smile instead.

Morgan sat bolt upright in his seat, on alert and still addressing the android body. He popped open his visor and said, "Oh, shit! Ed's happy! Does that mean what I think it means?"

"All enemy targets are locked. Standing by for orders, Emperor."

For a moment, Morgan said nothing, his face hard and grim, bereft of his normally good-natured, jocular demeanor. He rose from the emperor's chair and walked to stand before the viewscreen as if searching for something in the vastness of space. Standing there, silhouetted against the stars, he did indeed appear quite Imperial, at least to Ed's way of thinking.

Morgan clenched a gauntleted fist and said in a menacing tone, "Kill 'em all."

"Bringing us about and powering weapons," Ed informed him. The ship filled with the rumble of her engines and the hum of power coursing through her systems. As crazy as it seemed, Ed could almost sense an eagerness in the vessel, a hunger to serve its purpose, something in the very wiring and circuitry that felt, for all the world, like another presence alongside him.

It was possible. The *Danzig* was enormous, and her computer systems vast. Perhaps she *had* developed some rudimentary sentience. It was certainly a more sensible explanation than his other thought: that somehow, the ghosts of all the men who had died aboard were rejoicing at their chance for vengeance.

Ed dismissed the thought. He certainly had the CPU power to muse on all sorts of matters now, but that particular line of thought disturbed him greatly, and worse, he had no idea why. "Kane tells me that for moments such as this, a soundtrack is appropriate. Do you have any preferences?"

Morgan shrugged, still watching the viewscreen. "I don't know much about music, Ed. You pick."

"Very well. Analyzing similar period music to Kane's selection in our battle on Elysium, I find an interesting title: 'The Vengeful One' by someone called 'Disturbed.'"

"Is it kick ass? If it's some kind of stupid pop-tune, you're going to ruin our epic moment."

"I believe it will, as you say, 'kick ass' sufficiently. Shall I?"

"You may fire when ready, Gridley," Morgan said, a cruel grin on his face.

He stood at the viewscreen, fist still clenched, as the music pounded and the plasma cannons and railguns thundered into the void, the explosions lighting the bridge like fireworks.

Watching the *Danzig* work, Vanov felt an odd mixture of adrenaline and nausea. Broadside after broadside blazed from the battlecruiser's plasma cannons, filling the blackness of space with brilliant crimson even as her railguns hammered the defenseless enemy ships with precision shots.

"My God," Smith gasped. "What kind of fire control software are they using? They're at one hundred percent accuracy!"

All about, the Pestilence ships burst into fireballs as railgun rounds found their marks, searing gouts of plasma shattering shields and melting hulls in an orgy of destruction. The skies of Zion lit with a glow brighter than day as her enemies shattered under the withering firepower of the Emperor's last remaining death machine.

Al Jahar cleared his throat again. "I guess the overrides didn't work."

Vanov chuckled but kept her eye on the viewscreen, unable to tear herself away from the spectacle before them. "So it would seem."

She had a strong suspicion that there was much more to Mr.

Decker than met the eye—and if so, what he was doing was technically a war crime.

But these were perilous times. There *should* be consequences, but an unofficial reprimand would be sufficient.

For the first time in what seemed eons, she felt hope, and that should count for something.

## 4

## WAR CRIMES

Aboard the *Dresden*, Bleys and Ana approached a large kiosk that, presumably, would emit some sort of alarm if they were infected with Pestilence. Bleys looked back down the gangway to verify Kane was still behind them. He was, minus his armor, which was still aboard the *Doro*.

The young enlisted man running the kiosk, a slight fellow wearing a nametag identifying him as Petty Officer Franklin, smiled as Bleys approached, almost as if he were actually happy to see them, but Bleys was not fooled. Six heavily armed, unsmiling guards stood behind Franklin, their blank expressions and cold dead eyes leaving no doubt as to their purpose: if the alarm went off, they would kill and eat everyone, Bleys felt certain.

Did you know you were Pestilence? Bleys wasn't certain. What if he was totally infested—nothing but Pestilence—and just *thought* he was human? That could happen, he was pretty sure. Chert had made Ana think a positive result on the test was negative. Any second now, tentacles and fangs could burst from him and rip into any nearby unfortunates, and nobody had a single clue it could happen.

And then, there was the fact that, in general, Bleys was always worried about being busted for something or another, even when he hadn't done anything wrong lately. Cops and other authority figures always made him nervous, even in situations like this.

Well, *especially* in situations like this, because what would follow on a bad result wasn't being slammed against a wall and cuffed, which was a familiar experience, but summary execution, which you only ever experienced once.

Ana pushed at him as he hesitated "Go on, you big baby. After that ride, I have no sympathy for you whatsoever."

Bleys eyed the bored-looking guards briefly and stepped through, fully prepared for an alarm, which did in fact sound.

For a moment, Bleys panicked, until one of the armed guards spoke a familiar, soothing phrase in a bored, droning voice: "Sir, please step back and remove your jacket, then place your hands against the bulkhead."

Ana, eyes wide and fearful, spoke quickly. "He's not infected!" Ana insisted. "I tested him!"

Bleys heaved a great sigh as he shrugged out of his duster, revealing two heavy blaster pistols at his hips. "Yeah, babe, that's not what it's about." He laid the jacket on a nearby table and assumed the position.

Kane put his hands against the bulkhead, too. "You gotta be fucking kidding me."

The guard shrugged, as if to say he thought it was stupid, too, but orders was orders. "Sir, personal weapons are not permitted aboard the *Dresden* without special permission from Admiral Vanov," he droned. He removed Bleys's pistols and set them on the table, then continued to pat him down. "We'll be taking possession of your sidearms for the duration of your visit." With a scowl, he removed another weapon from the small of Bleys's back. "Is this the last of them?"

"One in my right boot," Bleys admitted with an embarrassed grin.

At last, the guard showed some sign of an inner life, a scowl crossing his face. "So, you're one of *those* guys," he groused as he dug yet another weapon from Bleys's boot. "Step through."

Kane shook his head. "He's still got a holdout somewhere. He always does."

The guard gave Kane an annoyed look. "Pretty sure he's clean," he snapped. "I know my job."

Kane shrugged. "Whatever you say."

Kane was, of course, right. There was a nasty little disintegrator in a hidden pocket of his duster, one that was in theory shielded against scanners. It remained to be seen if the *Dresden*'s crew would pick it up or not, but no one had caught it yet, including Ed's sensors, so the odds were good. That little piece of work was illegal as hell pretty much everywhere except maybe Elysium. Turned out that most governments, the Empire included, really hated weapons that didn't even leave a corpse, and were highly motivated to prevent their widespread possession and use. Bleys sympathized, he really did. Disintegrators must play hell with murder investigations, but, hey, sometimes you really needed some asshole to *not be there anymore*.

It was hell on wheels for most bulkheads, too, for that matter, so it was also kind of a multitool.

Bleys took his duster casually, as if it didn't have anything illegal hidden inside, and slung it over his arm, then walked through the scanner without incident. He smiled back at Kane. "Trust me, brother."

Franklin produced a small device and demanded, "Roll up your sleeve, please."

Bleys did so, and Franklin pressed the device against his exposed upper arm. The device emitted a pleasant tone and flashed a green light.

Franklin nodded. "You're clean. Stand against the wall and wait while we clear your friends."

The guard turned to Ana. "Ma'am, please remove your jacket, then place your hands against the bulkhead."

Ana scowled at this, removed her jacket to reveal her own sidearm at her hip, and assumed the position too.

"First time?" Bleys snickered as the guard patted her down.

Ana snorted. "I think you enjoyed it more than I do."

"Yuri was a long time ago, babe."

"I thought you said his name was Cecil," she snickered as the guard pronounced her good to go.

Bleys snapped his fingers in disappointment. "Damn, busted."

Ana stepped through the scanner and offered the operator a thumbs-up. He pressed his device against her arm, and once again it beeped and showed a green light.

"Clean. Stand with your friend, please."

Once Kane, too, was patted down and verified as weapon free, Franklin beckoned for the trio to follow him. "Sorry about that, but we can't be too careful. We've had a lot of problems with infiltrators, if not Pestilence, then the damned Free Zion terrorists."

Kane grunted. "That's a hell of a time to have your people disarmed."

"They're not," Franklin assured him. "Just you, until the Admiral gives the word you're trusted."

Kane scowled at this, but Bleys knew from experience that it was the sort of scowl that translated to, "I don't like it, but I'd do the same thing." Which was good, in that it meant Kane probably wouldn't murder Franklin on the spot, which, in turn, meant there wouldn't be a desperate firefight back to the *Doro* in which Bleys would personally save everyone with his hidden disintegrator pistol, and then save them again with fantastic, no, *amazing* piloting skills.

Bleys entertained himself with the fantasy as Franklin led them through the *Dresden*, at last stopping in front of a large sliding door.

"She's in the conference room," Franklin said nervously, from which Bleys gathered the man had no intention of joining them, and was, in so many words, telling them to set their affairs in order. Apparently, someone had forgotten to post up the "Abandon All Hope" sign, but it was there in spirit.

Considered in that light, maybe asking Vanov about her panties on an open channel might not have been the best of conversation choices after all.

Bleys examined the door, not exactly certain how it worked, but it turned out that just approaching it was enough. It slid aside to reveal a long table and a huge monitor taking up most of the port bulkhead. At the far end, a woman stood, her back to them, hands clasped behind her waist.

Bleys being who he was, had little choice but to evaluate her from that viewpoint, and to his practiced eye, her backside was a little on the narrow side, but her long legs made up for it. Tall and thin was workable. Her black uniform was well-tailored, and her dark, slightly graying shoulder-length hair just covered her light leather collar.

The woman turned, slowly, her gaze reminiscent of a vulture eyeing a dying rabbit. "You may leave, Franklin," she said in a voice that cut like a razor. "The rest of you, enter. Your co-conspirator will be joining us by video."

It was hardly the first time Bleys had been addressed as such, but Kane frowned, clearly offended.

Bleys winked at the woman he assumed was Admiral Vanov. Her response was a withering glare that combined the fires of hell with the sleet of…Chinese hell? Chinese hell was cold, right? He was pretty sure. They had *lots* of them, so odds were there *had* to be one that was exceptionally cold.

Definitely the wrong approach with her.

Vanov said nothing until the door slid closed behind them, then arched an eyebrow and said in a sleety voice, "You are all aware, I presume, that the use of an AI-controlled battlecruiser is a war crime?"

Bleys, for once, knew when to shut up.

Kane, on the other hand, did not. "We're here on orders."

Vanov sneered. "So I gather. Why am I not surprised that Paul Weyland is behind this?"

The big marine rolled his shoulders, which, to Bleys, meant he was considering whether or not to kill people. "What's that supposed to mean?" he rumbled.

"Oh, come now," Vanov shot back. "If you work for the man, you must know something about him. Are you going to pretend you've never heard of the names he's earned? 'The Butcher of Farallon Six' perhaps? Or maybe you prefer 'The Dragon's Breath?' 'The Emperor's Angel of Death?' The list goes on."

Kane clenched his jaw a moment. "He's also known as the man responsible for evacuating the Holliman system before a lethal solar flare."

Vanov's severe look persisted, but softened a bit, and she gestured for them to sit. "I didn't say he didn't have a reputation for getting things done," she conceded. "But he is at least as well known for his brutality as anything else. There's a reason he's posted where he is."

Kane took a seat. "I get it," he said. "The Empire keeps it's attack dogs on a short leash. I'm one of them. But we're off the chain now and doing good work."

Bleys slipped quietly into a chair as well, relieved that Kane was acting as something of a shield for Vanov's wrath, and Ana followed.

Hopefully, the admiral had forgotten about the pink panties comment.

Vanov took her own seat and sat in silence a moment, looking back and forth at them, her long fingers steepled. At last, she said to Kane, "Make no mistake, Commander, it is indeed a time for war dogs. But I will decide when and where they are off the chain in my neck of the woods. Understood?"

Kane nodded. "Yes, ma'am."

Bleys decided that, damn it, he was *not* actually smart enough to shut up after all. "You seem pretty ungrateful for us just having saved all of your asses."

Vanov drummed her fingers on the table a moment, her face twisted in a grimace, and gave a curt nod. "Of *course* we're all very grateful, Captain Bleys. I may not appreciate your style and your tone, but like Weyland, it seems you all get things done. That being said, I *cannot* permit your AI to continue operating the *Danzig*."

Ed's voice called from hidden speakers, "Of course not. It's unethical. Absolute power corrupts absolutely." His image sprang to life on the bulkhead monitor. "But more to the point, the plan was to bring the *Danzig* here and place it at your disposal, with Admiral Weyland's regards. We fully expect you to crew it and use as a centerpiece for the Resistance."

Bleys raised a hand like a child in a classroom, then charged ahead without actually being recognized. "Also, he's not 'ours,'" he said, pointing at the monitor. "Ed pretty much belongs to himself. He's a volunteer."

Vanov registered a brief moment of surprise at this. "I've looked into him. It appears he had some very powerful friends."

Ana cleared her throat and spoke up, "He's also our best hope of reopening the jumpgates."

A subtle smile spread across Vanov's stern features. She turned to the monitor where Ed's image smiled back at her. "Can you really do that?"

Ed nodded. "Given time, yes. We're very close to cracking the control module for the Cerberus system, and we could likely crack the Liahona system module in a few months."

Vanov nodded and took a deep breath. Bleys had the sneaking suspicion that she was actually fighting back tears, though of course she would never give in to that sort of impulse, he was certain. She waited a moment before continuing, "That's the first hopeful news I have heard in six months."

Ed raised a cautioning hand. "There are other concerns regarding reopening the gates. We have discovered the reason they were closed in the first place is that the Pestilence communicates via hyperspace."

Vanov mulled this a moment. "It makes sense. You're not the first person to suggest it, but as you can imagine, rumors have been rampant. You're certain?"

"I am. Furthermore, I speculate that the larger the infestation, the more knowledge it can store locally. In many respects, it seems to behave as a sophisticated computer network."

"I suppose you would know about that," Vanov agreed.

"So you understand that even if we can reopen the jumpgates, actually doing it for more than brief periods may be a very bad idea."

Vanov nodded slowly. "I have thoughts on that—"

Kane grinned and interrupted, "Violent thoughts, I hope."

Vanov gave him a bemused look, her eyebrows arching high, a thin smile on her lips. "I think I may like working with you after all, Commander Kane. But first things first. I'd like to inspect the *Danzig*."

Vanov sent them on their way and followed in her own personal transport ship. Smith was less than pleased by her refusal to bring a security detail, but it was a silly idea, and she told him so. The

*Danzig* was more than capable of destroying the *Dresden*, should that be this new group's intent, and a show of force would be not only useless, but could raise tensions.

Which was all very true, but privately, she had other reasons for making the trip solo. She wanted to speak with these newcomers alone, and unless she missed her guess, they, likewise, had some secrets they were more likely to share if they knew the environment was secure.

It was a short trip, and she docked without incident where the AI instructed her. Given the *Danzig*'s lack of crew, she hadn't expected a reception, but there was indeed a man standing outside the main entry hatch. As she passed through the hatch and into a large loading area within the *Danzig*, she realized, to her surprise, that it was the AI himself, apparently walking around in a reasonable facsimile of a human being.

"Welcome aboard, Admiral," he said with friendly smile and extended a hand.

"I suppose you count as a civilian," she mused, taking his hand and shaking it. "No need for military protocols? Piping aboard? Attention on deck?"

It was uncanny how human the thing seemed. It even looked a little embarrassed! "Forgive me, Admiral. I'm afraid I am just as you note, a civilian. Such things aren't really part of my routine. I can research them and add them to my repertoire if you like."

"Carry on," she said absently, looking past the machine and down the corridor into the interior. "What can you tell me about security aboard the *Danzig?*"

"The ship is secure both in physical and signal aspects," the robot told her. "No entity or communique can enter the *Danzig* without my knowledge and permission."

"Very well," she said with a nod. "I would like to speak with the human crew."

"Of course," it said. "Follow me."

Vanov marveled at how lifelike the automaton was as she followed it through the *Danzig*. She was familiar with the Dracul class battlecruisers and recognized when she was passing through areas riddled with retracted, hidden antipersonnel weaponry. The AI played the friendly host, but she was all too aware of just how easily the thing could end her life, should its masters decide to do so.

The machine walked beside her exactly how a human would, and asked in a conversational tone, "I trust your trip over went smoothly?"

Vanov roused from her musings. "Hmm, oh, yes, of course." She paused a moment, feeling a little self-conscious, which was silly. It was just a machine! "No small talk, please. Just show me your masters."

The android stopped walking and turned to her, one eyebrow high. "Have I offended you somehow?"

Vanov chuckled at this. "Of course not. How could I be offended by a machine? I'll leave that sort of anthropomorphism to the snipes."

For a moment, the android said nothing, as if it were having trouble finding the right programming to respond. Its expression went blank, which gave lie to the illusion finally. When it spoke, its words were flat and matter of fact. "Of course, Admiral. This way."

Good. It had turned off whatever Real Life Personality mode some fool of a programmer had given it. Contending with such artifice was frustrating. Computers were for targeting and tracking information, not conversation and companionship. She understood that on earth, sex-bots were all the rage, but in her considered opinion, confusing people with machines was a sign of impending mental collapse.

They arrived shortly at the *Danzig*'s primary wardroom. Vanov found the place suitably impressive, if a bit large for the meeting. She had always approved of spaces that reminded starship crews of their seafaring roots, and the leather and brightwork did a fine job of that.

The three she had met with earlier were gathered around a table, though to her surprise, there was a fourth among them that she didn't recognize. She gave them a moment, then cleared her throat. "It would seem proper military bearing is lacking aboard the *Danzig*, or do we no longer recognize the arrival of superiors?"

The big marine, Kane, looked uncomfortable. "Ma'am, technically, you are not the highest-ranking person in the room," he said. "It's one of the things we need to talk to you about, and we didn't want to say it over there."

Vanov took a moment to absorb the implications, then took a hard look at the new fellow. He was younger than the others by a good decade, blond, and easy on the eyes, muscular, and with a nice, broad jaw. As a younger woman, she might have given him a second glance, though frankly, the pilot was really more her type. Even in her wild youth, she had been ambitious and had preferred the sort of men to take her pleasure with and then be rid of without any complications or even an exchange of real names.

"Who is he?" she asked at last.

They looked back and forth at one another briefly, and finally the pilot, Bleys, shrugged. "We reckon he's the Emperor, ma'am."

The audacious, flirtatious liar regarded her with the most angelic, innocent expression as Vanov chewed on this. After a moment, she walked to their table and took a seat. "This is going to be a long story, I presume. Who's buying the drinks?"

It turned out that the consummate liar was a natural storyteller too, which came as no surprise. His sorts always were, and to be fair, she had, on occasion, not only enjoyed such lies but rewarded them when it suited her.

But she had never been fooled by them.

Vanov was fairly certain Bleys left out any unflattering parts, but he did avoid the temptation of making himself the hero, instead leaving that honor to Kane and the young fellow they informed her was Emperor John Henry Morgan the First.

It was a thrilling tale, certainly. If even half of it were true, these folks had certainly earned some respect. Of course, that was the problem: it was difficult to give much credibility to the notion of dead emperors returning from the grave to bestow their favor, ghost stories, fairy tales and heroic myths.

And yet, they had the *Danzig*. It hardly mattered if their story were true: they were in possession of enough firepower to kill anyone who disagreed. That was, essentially, the definition of "Emperor" when it came down to it.

And did she really need to believe it to sell it? The story had all of the things the people loved: heroes, villains, impossible escapes, and a handsome, young leader, anointed by powers from beyond. If only the *Danzig* were named *Excalibur*, the tale would be perfect.

She eyed the would-be Emperor Morgan. He looked the role well enough, except for the matter of enthusiasm. "This doesn't sit well with you, I take it?" she asked.

Morgan shrugged, looking morose. "I like being a marine, ma'am. Pretty sure the emperor doesn't get out and shoot bad guys too often."

Vanov found herself unable to fully suppress her reaction. A single laugh burst from her lips like a short bark before she could master herself. It was undignified, but then, this was all so very absurd! "No," she admitted, shaking her head in amusement. "That's typically delegated." She rubbed at her temple idly as she imagined the possibilities. "Sit up straight for me. Show me your best 'emperor' pose."

Morgan straightened his back, inclining his head slightly, his expression so reminiscent of Tenebrae's that she almost gasped.

She had seen the former emperor look down his nose just that way many times in the past. Surely this one was too young to remember that? Had he *really* met the man recently? Could they be telling the truth?

She looked briefly at the robot, the one they called Ed, and again felt a twinge of guilt. If it *was* true, she had not only underestimated him, but she had also offered him several fairly grave insults.

Vanov raised a hand to Morgan's chin and turned his head back and forth like a mother with a child. "You have the right looks, but the wrong attitude. Let's make a deal, hmm?" She smiled at him. "You be my emperor for now, long enough to allow us to consolidate power, and I promise to find someone to relieve you soon enough, assuming you still want to abdicate."

Morgan looked at her with little enthusiasm. "How long?" he groaned.

Vanov shrugged. "Difficult to say. It's politics."

"Politics!" Morgan sneered. "I fuck politics in her fat ass!"

Again, Vanov couldn't quite contain her laughter. "You know the rules: first comes smiles, then lies. Last is gunfire." She said with a broad grin. "When it comes to that, I promise I'll make sure you're at the front, marine."

Morgan heaved a sigh and nodded.

Vanov clapped him on the shoulder. "I have little love for politics myself, but all warfare is based on deception, yes?"

Kane said in an appreciative tone, "Sun Tzu."

Vanov nodded toward him, then rose and told them all, "There's a reason I am here without escort, and some of you have likely guessed at it." She gazed pointedly at the roguish captain.

Bleys pushed his hat up to reveal his green eyes and grinned. "I reckon you're looking for a private conversation, which would suggest you aren't sure of your people."

"Very good, Captain Bleys," she told him. "The current situation in the galaxy is problematic. Humanity still exists in pockets—"

Kane leapt to his feet. "Do you have information on *which* systems?"

Vanov didn't particularly appreciate being interrupted, but she could guess why Kane was so insistent, and she was indeed sympathetic. "We've made contact with precious few systems, being honest. Where's your family?"

The gratitude in the man's eyes was palpable. "The Furion system, ma'am. Asgard."

Vanov smiled and nodded, pleased to have a chance to deliver good news. "Asgard is still with us, thankfully."

Kane heaved a sigh, sagged, and ran a hand over his face. "Thank Odin and Thor."

"Thank the emperor's finest, too. A lot of valiant men gave their lives to close those gates and stop the spread. We'll never know their names."

To her surprise, Bleys looked almost wistful. He cleared his throat and sat up in his chair. "We might know a little about them," he told her.

"I'm surprised," Vanov told him. "I wouldn't have taken you for the sentimental sort."

The android—no, *Ed*, she reminded herself—spoke from behind her. "Captain Bleys and I were both almost killed in the debris field of one of the closing ships when we retrieved the Tartarus system control module."

Bleys reached into his shirt and produced a lump of polished metal that hung from a chain about his neck. "This piece here punched a hole in my leg and damn near punched my ticket."

Vanov nodded her appreciation. "That's a good souvenir. What do you know about the closers?"

Ed brightened at this. He seemed to relish sharing information as some men might savor flirting. "I sent a probe to scan the wreckage once we had Avalon working on the control module. There was no DNA to analyze, but the ship itself was a scouting vessel called the *Jaeger*, attached to the *Bismarck*."

"Well, that's something. When this is all done, I would like to commission a monument to those men, a sort of 'Unknown Soldier' memorial. I intend to call them 'The Unsung.'"

Kane cleared his throat. "Begging pardon, Admiral, but how bad is it out there?"

Vanov thought for a moment before responding. She had no idea where the rest were from. She might well be informing them that their entire family was dead if she stumbled blindly forward. Best to stay positive and feel them out, in case she had to deliver bad news. "Asgard is fine, all things considered. With the core in ruins, her shipyards are critical, so we took great pains to make contact. They weathered the initial storm, and like the rest of us, they're looking for answers."

"Do you have comms set up?"

"No," Vanov sighed. "We had a system at first, daisy-chaining what ships we had, but the renewed Pestilence attacks have shut down those attempts. We're deaf and blind, and until you arrived, we were fighting a war of attrition. With luck, your contribution will turn the tide."

Bleys turned to Rasputin, who was staring at the floor, and grabbed her shoulder. "Babe, where is your boy?"

Ana shook her head, a look of pure misery on her face. "Vostok isn't important to anyone but the people who live there. I doubt we made the list."

Vanov sighed, but she had expected worse. At least she wasn't delivering obituaries. "I'm sorry, Rasputin. I don't know anything about them offhand, but I've only kept up with strategic locations. Ensign Al Jahar may be able to get you more information. I'll arrange a meeting once we're done here."

"Thank you," Rasputin said in a near whisper.

Ed waved a hand to get her attention. "Admiral, how do you continue to suffer incursions?"

"An excellent question," Vanov answered with a frown. "We check rigorously for contamination aboard the fleet, but keeping track on Zion is a bit harder. They have programs in place, but I have no doubt they miss things."

Ed raised an eyebrow. "Then how is the planet still viable?"

"Frankly, I think we're dealing with human traitors, rather than Pestilence infiltrators. The Pestilence has clear and well-established behavior: it eats everything. It shows rudimentary cunning, enough to wait until it infects a critical number, but once that point is reached, it *always* attacks.

"These incursions we have are deep agents that gain control of jump-capable ships and open jumpgates. It's almost as if someone is trying to use the Pestilence as a weapon."

Rasputin seemed to brighten at this talk for some reason. "It's seeking the Source."

Ed shook his head. "I think not. I have gone over the Imperial reports, and they match our own experience and data. The Pestilence is methodical. It would infect the local population first, then expand. This does indeed seem to be a different sort of enemy. Admiral, do you have any leads on the culprits?"

"A few," Vanov told him. "Our situation is…tenuous, as you might imagine. Imperial forces are the only thing keeping Zion from being covered in Red Carpet. They need us, but we need them too, for repairs, food, personnel. They are our only support system. We're bound fairly tightly, but the relationship is a little rocky. Several senators object to my command. Officially, they are 'concerned' about the military operating outside civilian control. Unofficially, it's fairly easy to see they are simply jockeying for position."

Morgan sneered. "Fucking politicians."

"Exactly," she replied. "Another wrinkle in presenting them

with our new emperor. More politics. And I strongly suspect some of them are in cahoots with a rival faction of Imperial forces."

Bleys, his face contemplative, smiled and said casually, "Is that the Zion First folks we heard about?"

Vanov frowned. "And where did you hear about them?"

His face filled with angelic innocence, Bleys answered, "Oh, I just overheard one of your guys talking about them. I don't remember which one, but the name stuck in my mind."

She didn't buy his claim of ignorance for one second, but there was little point arguing about it. Clearly, he was the sort to play his cards close to his chest, and who could blame him? "I intended to broach that topic later, but fine, we'll do it now. No, they are an entirely different group, a domestic terrorist organization with, sadly, some official backing. They want the Empire gone from Zion."

Kane shook his head, glowering. "You'd think the Pestilence would change that kind of thinking."

Vanov shrugged. "To be fair, they *have* been quiet since The Collapse, but I strongly suspect they are still working behind the scenes via infiltrators."

Kane nodded. "So who's this 'rival faction'?"

Vanov cleared her throat and thought a moment on how to put it. She settled for the direct approach. "The former leader of our interim government was a wretched, cowardly politician from Earth named Senator Solomon Finch. He was fortunate enough to be off-world when the Pestilence struck, and as an occasional toady of Emperor Arcann, he was able to rally what was left of our forces."

Bleys pulled at his goatee and smiled. "I'm guessing there's a big 'but' coming."

"Indeed," Vanov told him. "I shot the man for cowardice in the face of the enemy and assumed command."

Kane nodded his approval. "As it should be. Fuck civilian leadership. This is war."

Bleys eyed her warily, still smiling, but Vanov knew his calculating mind was working behind the appearance of good humor. He casually asked, as if he were joking, "You gonna tell us what he did, or was that just to let us know how it might go for us if we don't fall in line?"

For an instant, Vanov felt a powerful urge to call his bluff and draw her weapon, let him decide for himself if she would actually shoot him for his audacity, but in the end, maddening as it was, it was both an attractive quality about him and exactly what she needed in her people to pull off her ultimate plans. She drew a deep breath, then continued, "He abandoned loyal men in a battle that we could have won. He ran like a cowardly dog to save his own skin and left his betters to die."

Kane face twisted in rage. "Like they fucking *always* do!"

Bleys, however, was still regarding her with his penetrating gaze. "Somebody important to you, huh?"

Vanov ground her teeth. Damn this upstart! "Yes," she said in a clipped tone. "My son."

Bleys gave her an appreciative look, then nodded and settled back in his seat. "Works for me."

"So now you understand the situation: the Church and the civilian leadership have grave concerns regarding a military dictatorship."

Morgan rolled his eyes. "That's what an Empire is!"

Vanov shrugged. She didn't disagree. "Arcann allowed them great autonomy, as long as they paid their taxes," Vanov told him. "*That* is what an Empire is, too. The steady flow of resources upward, with as little blood and treasure expended as possible. Everything is a calculus of cost versus profit. Arcann believed, rightfully I think, that greater autonomy generated greater profits."

Morgan shrugged at this. "Simple problem, even so," he declared. "Who do we shoot?"

Kane shook his head, grinning. "That's what we gotta figure out, knucklehead!"

Rasputin covered her smile with a hand.

Bleys snickered. "Emperor Knucklehead. I like it."

Vanov glowered at them. "This is the kind of skylarking I am warning you all against!" she snapped. "If we intend to convince people that this man is the emperor, you need to act as if he is." She paused a moment, fixing each with her stare in turn, save for the android, who actually seemed the most sensible of them.

"Now, listen," she continued. "We *require* the continued support of the Church and the civilian leadership. I am all for going kinetic the moment we have proof of our targets, but we cannot simply go in and blast away indiscriminately. Until then, it's politics and subterfuge. Am I clear?"

They all nodded their assent. Kane raised a hand. "Fair enough, Admiral, but long term, what are our goals? Settle things here, then what?"

Vanov wondered if this was a trick question. "Ultimately? To strike at The Source."

The four humans looked back and forth at each other, their faces ranging from surprised to dubious.

Bleys spoke for them. "That didn't work out so well the last time the Empire tried it, as I recall."

Vanov raised a hand, gesturing for patience. "Crucial mistakes were made," she agreed. "Primarily, no one at the time understood the damned Pestilence could actually empty out people's heads of everything they knew. We lost before we sent the first ship because the damned thing knew our plan."

Ed looked contemplative a moment, then added, "And they likely sent a tremendous force at the Pestilence, one that was quickly turned against them."

Vanov pursed her lips and nodding slowly. The android was indeed clever. "Intelligence is sketchy, but the Source itself was supposed to have relatively weak defenses until it took our own weapons from us. We would have done better to send a small task force."

Bleys laughed out loud. "You mean like an AI-controlled battlecruiser?"

Kane groaned and rubbed at his forehead, but he was nodding too. "I am kind of getting used to suicide missions."

Rasputin glowered at everyone around her. "*I'm* not."

Ed asked, "Are you saying the Empire has actual intelligence as to the nature of the Source?"

"We do," Vanov said. "It's a planet-sized mass located in the hyperspace deeps."

Bleys boggled and looked back and forth at his fellows. "Planet-sized mass of *what?*"

Vanov shrugged. "The scientists weren't sure. Some theorized it is entirely flesh, but most assumed it's a planet beneath a coating of Pestilence."

The smug captain stammered briefly, for once—to Vanov's deep satisfaction—seeming unable to find the right words. At last, he managed, "I don't know which is crazier, a planet in hyperspace or a planet made of *meat* in hyperspace. I can't even imagine the kind of powerplant it would take to open a planet-sized gate."

Ed nodded. "It's more than we could generate even on Elysium. But it's also *impossible*. Gravity wells repel hyperspace. It doesn't touch normal space near large masses."

Bleys thought a moment. "Could they move the planet after the gate opened? Basically fly the thing through?"

Ed's expression grew simultaneously agonized and horrified as he contemplated this. For a moment, he froze, as if he had shut down, then at last said, "Presuming someone managed to come up with a means of flying an entire planet like a ship? I have *no idea* what would happen. It could potentially tear a permanent rift in spacetime."

Bleys nodded. "So, very bad."

"As in hyperspace flooding into the real and causing the death of all life in the universe, so yes, very bad."

"Fifty percent suicide?"

Ed frowned. "Ninety-five percent, at least."

Ana looked back and forth at them, waiting for their attention, then said, "Maybe it *grew* there."

Vanov found that idea simultaneously horrifying and thrilling. It felt correct, as bizarre and awful as it was. "If I had to pick, I'd go with that."

Ed put a hand to his chin exactly how a human might as he contemplated. "If that's true, then it will die the same way any Pestilence will. But the size of the gamma ray burst would have to be enormous. It would have to actually penetrate the entire mass."

Vanov cleared her throat again. "There, ah, may have already been some research in this direction. *Classified* research."

Bleys chuckled. "Good thing we have the Emperor here to authorize us."

Morgan waved a hand. "Authorization granted, and an extra ration of jalapeno cheese, too."

"Meaningless," Ana muttered. "I'll just have to give it back."

Morgan put his index finger to his nose and then pointed it at Ana. "And now you know the true, soul-searing depths of your dark bargain, sweet cheeks," he told her with a triumphant look.

Having no idea what this exchange meant, Vanov waved it aside. "The *Danzig* may be the last of Tenebrae's planet killers, but it wasn't the last of Arcann's. They built something on Nibiru Station, something they called *The Final Word*. It was supposed to be part of the Battle of Armageddon, but things went bad, and it was never brought into play."

Kane grunted. "Nibiru is a myth."

Vanov flashed him a genuine grin. "That's what we wanted you to think," she told him. "It's real, a primordial black hole about a thousand AU out from Earth. The Empire's premier black research site is there, safely away from prying eyes and far enough away that Earth is safe from accidents. We need the weapon they developed if we intend to reopen the jumpgates, and we need their research about the Pestilence as well."

Kane shook his head. "So we're going to mount up and go get it?"

"Soon. But not before we resolve our problems here. If we don't make damned sure we have rooted out the traitors and the infected, this attack on the Source will end the same way the last one did."

Bleys nodded. "So, back to Ed's question: what leads do you have?"

Vanov looked them over a moment, wondering if she were making a mistake by being as candid as she intended, but she had few options. Certainly no one better than this group of highly effective rogues was likely to fall into her lap anytime soon. "As I said, I suspect specific politicians of ultimately being behind this, but within my command group, there *must* be a leak, and I am sorry to say that it has to be one of my three most trusted: Lieutenant Smith, Lieutenant Shorey, and Ensign Al Jahar. I have a hard time believing it. They're all people with exceptional service records, but it has to be one of them. There have been cases of leaks where they were the only ones who could have known."

Bleys rubbed at his goatee again. "Leaks are funny things. It might not have been intentional. Could have been somebody working them."

"Loose lips sink ships, Captain Bleys," Vanov told him. It's possible the leak is lower, but if so, it would be because one of them violated security, which in and of itself is execution worthy in wartime."

Kane rose to his feet. "I got this. Give me ten minutes with each of 'em."

Vanov raised a hand. "Negative, Commander. Find me the spy and you can have all the time you like, but hands off the rest of my staff. They are good people. Without them, we'd all be Pestilence by now."

Bleys sighed and leaned back in his chair. He swung his boots up on to the table and grinned. "You guys are thinking about this all wrong."

In a sour tone, Vanov replied, "Please enlighten us, then."

Bleys tapped his forehead and shook a finger at them. "You're thinking like soldiers. Me, I'm thinking like…uh…." He cut his eyes back and forth in an exaggerated, conspiratorial check for listeners, then grinned and continued, "a psy ops officer."

Vanov sighed. "My least favorite field, but go ahead. What are you thinking?"

Bleys turned to Morgan. "You lie pretty good, right?"

Kane laughed out loud. "He'd still be a virgin if he didn't."

"I told your mom *exactly* who I was," Morgan shot back.

Vanov cleared her throat again.

"Right," Bleys said and turned back to her. "So, step one: I need you to disappear for twenty-four hours. For all intents and purposes, you'll be dead."

Vanov shook her head. So, this was a dead end after all. "Don't be ridiculous. I won't abandon my post."

Bleys waved his hands in the air in denial. "Whoa, whoa, you won't be *actually* abandoning it," he insisted. "You just need to stay out of sight while we goose your people and see who jumps."

Vanov considered it a moment. He was a cunning fellow. Maybe he had something after all. "What are you planning?"

Bleys rolled his shoulders and rubbed his hands together with a conspiratorial wink. "I'm going to make them an offer they can't resist and tell some big lies. No offense, Admiral, but I'd just as soon leave you plausible deniability, in case this goes bad."

Vanov couldn't help but smile. "That's kind of you, but if it 'goes bad,' things will certainly point right back to me."

Bleys actually looked wounded. "I'm a *professional*. Weyland commissioned me, but as far as the rest of the galaxy knows, I'm just little-old independent businessman Josiah Bleys."

"And what business is that?"

Kane grunted. "He's a pirate."

"I am *not* a pirate," Bleys shot back. "I never once shot at anybody who hadn't already tried to kill me."

Ed noted, "Captain Bleys is correct. He is not a pirate. Technically, he's a thief and a smuggler."

Rasputin tried to laugh quietly as Bleys shot Ed a glare, then looked back to Vanov. "I prefer 'trader in exotic goods,' but whatever you call me, I'm pretty good at going missing if I need to, so if things go bad, you're ok. And I know how weasels think. I can get you your spy *today* if you work with me."

Vanov eyed him warily. He was a con man, that was certain. It was just a question of whether he was conning her.

In the end, she trusted her gut, and her gut said these people were indeed here to help. "I suppose I could take a day off if I am still in close contact. I'll cool my heels here a bit on the *Danzig*. Let's see you work."

## 5

# HIDDEN ADVERSARIES

The Ascended One drummed its fingers on the senator's desk, a habit from its old life, before its mind had been broadened by its own Ascension.

Once, politics had dominated every aspect of its life not already filled by The Church or The Marriage. In many ways, all three were simply aspects of the same concept, the urgent need to present a specific image and curry favor with the masses.

And then had come enlightenment, bright and sharp, beautiful in its symmetry, its singularity of purpose: to dominate and shepherd all life. Soon, there would no longer be a need for pretense. Instead of persuasion, The Ascended One would simply command and its will would be carried out.

It sighed, a very human behavior, as it considered The Plan and its own place within it.

The notion of "senator" was amusing now, a quaint concept, the idea of representative government, as if humans had any capacity to truly manage their own lives. If there were one truth the Pestilence had exposed, it was that the works of man were all folly, ephemeral.

The human race was obsolete, and the Ascended would supplant it, tend it, serve as its guardians and caretakers.

Once they had filled the holes in their ranks, at any rate.

The Ascendency had sprung from scientists and politicians, leaving gaps in their skillset: they lacked military leaders, and those would be needed, both to dominate the humans, and to wage war on their ultimate enemy, The Source.

Thus, The Ascended One's mission: to recruit the Resistance commander. With Vanov among them, the Ascendency would crush The Source, sweep aside the old order, and establish an eternal Reich. They would bring order to the galaxy, managing the humans, drawing from them their best and brightest to be elevated and utilizing the masses for labor.

It was a brilliant plan with only a single flaw: The Ascended One would not rule over all.

They called *that* one the Primus, and its position was due not to merit or support, but merely by seniority. It was the first to Ascend, and somehow that qualified it for supremacy?

That was the thinking of fools. The Ascended One had done enough serving lesser creatures. Its entire life had been one of artifice, pretending for the Church, pretending for The Marriage, pretending for the office of senator.

It was high time the Ascended One stopped pretending. Now was the time to *act*.

And thus, the Ascended One had its own Great Plan, a wheel within a wheel. It would recruit Vanov all right, but once its mission succeeded, it would use its success as leverage. It would whisper to the others of how well it had done, and how well it could continue to do, if only they supported the Ascended One rather than the Primus.

The Ascended One smiled. Perhaps the years of politics had not been wasted after all.

Of course, reaching that point required it exercise every bit of its enhanced intellect, and even then, things were rapidly approaching untenability.

Zion was, nominally, The Ascended One's property. According to the others. The Ascended One knew it best, and would understand better how to manipulate its people and which to choose for Ascension. Taking Zion had seemed a simple task, using the enthralled Pestilence as foot soldiers and slowly building an army right under the noses of the humans.

The problem was the Pestilence itself. None of the Ascended had known there would be limits to their control! Singularly, the minions were pathetically easy to dominate, but now that The Ascended One had hundreds of them, and most especially as they had spread out, the strain had become too much. The minions, great and small, railed against The Ascended One's yoke, and some even managed to rebel from time to time, and always in the same way. They were simple creatures, truly, and could be trusted first to kill and form colonies, to grow; and if they could not kill and grow, they would flee, trying to return to The Source.

Each outbreak, each opening into hyperspace was another trail for Vanov to follow. She was no fool. If she were, she would have no value to the Ascended. The Admiral had to be close to discovering the truth now and could not be allowed to interfere.

The Ascended One should have moved to the final phase of the plan by now, but progress had ground to a halt for some time as it struggled with the minions. Its superiors had likely already begun to question the delays. No doubt, they suspected that The Ascended One did not intend to serve long.

The plan had to resolve *soon*, or not at all, and without a victory, The Ascended One's dreams of power and glory would be shattered.

There was, however, an alternative plan.

Zion could be left for later. Vanov was the Ascended One's true prize. Rather than risk an outbreak that would destroy the population, it might be best to wind the project down. The Ascended One could make use of the high-profile infiltrators as distractions, commanding them to destroy themselves. The media would be agog at several celebrity suicides, which would draw Vanov's attention away from the actual work.

The remainder would need to be gathered closer together to reduce the strain of the control. It would need to be a safe place, somewhere they would never be suspected, and one that could be, in extremis, contained and destroyed.

A smile bled across The Ascended One's face. It knew the perfect location, one where it already had several minions.

The Caleb, resplendent in white coverings, did its best to approximate a human smile toward Sister Hoagland, who was speaking from a podium to the small crowd that had joined them for the Ritual of Drowning.

Sister Hoagland spoke of The Savior and his great Atonement that brought salvation to all. Sister Forbush stood by her, nodding, and The Caleb nodded back, full of love for them and all of its new Colony.

The Caleb was amazed at the knowledge the two Sisters carried. They knew much wisdom! The Caleb had not known that it, too, needed salvation until they had been kind enough to explain. And somehow, they and all of their Colony also knew of both The Source *and* The Evil One! Though they called them different names. The Source was known to them as The Heavenly Father, and The Evil One, when they spoke of him at all, was called The Adversary.

And today, The Caleb would join their Colony, become one with them, and be saved by The Jesus Christ, too!

How the Caleb longed to assimilate them all, to merge with

them and share knowledge and awareness, but The Evil One prevented it.

But more so, The Caleb now understood that devouring all of its friends would be improper. Such a thing, without permission, would deny them their agency, something that The Caleb's new Colony valued beyond all else. Yet The Caleb could not bring itself to ask their leave. It dared not reveal its true self, not yet at any rate.

In any event, simply merging with their flesh without asking would be a grave sin. It would be like trying to reproduce with them without their permission.

Which, in all honesty, The Caleb did not fully appreciate either. It simply understood that among them, permission was important for such things, and a special ritual of bonding was required as well.

Not for the first time, The Caleb found itself puzzled by the strange behaviors human biology inspired. For The Caleb in its natural state, reproduction was as mundane as breathing, something its body simply did on its own without conscious intervention. But the humans had their strange rituals and boundaries, and if The Caleb was to truly be part of their Colony, it would respect those boundaries.

The Caleb was slightly saddened by this, but understood now some of their precepts, such as "putting off the natural man." While the Caleb was not truly a man, it understood the general reasoning. One's natural instincts to violate the agency of others should be resisted and overcome if a being was to reach The Source. The Caleb had asked subtly if The Jesus Christ's atonement applied to all creatures, even aliens, and had been assured that indeed it did. All who had agency could benefit from The Atonement, if they chose to accept it. Such was the promise of The Jesus Christ.

Did The Caleb truly have agency, though? The Evil One's

control was strong, but the Evil One did not know *all*. It only knew overt things, not The Caleb's Deep Thoughts. The Evil One could compel The Caleb to perform specific acts, and The Caleb could not disobey, but there was a flaw in The Evil One's control: it could not forbid what it did not know The Caleb was planning.

The Caleb's existence had been so bitterly lonely before The Sister Hoagland and The Sister Forbush had come. Its life had been a prison, a tormented existence of silent, isolated terror, a misery for which its kind was ill equipped. The Children of The Source were meant to Sing, to gather, to search for Truth and rejoin with The Source, not live alone, in constant fear.

Somehow, The Evil One had entirely missed The Church, who lived to do exactly the same things! They were happy and shared Song and joy. They were a functioning Colony that sought to return to the Source, just as The Caleb did!

And if the Caleb could not, *should* not assimilate them, why not allow itself to be assimilated *by* them?

The Caleb smiled at the human beside him, the one named The Bishop. The Bishop would perform The Ritual, a simulated death by drowning, in which The Caleb would be reborn as a full member of the Church Colony and seek The Source with them!

It would be lonely no more. It would Sing and know joy again.

The Bishop placed a hand on The Caleb's shoulder. "Brother Caleb, are you ready?"

The Caleb thought long moments. It had known little in life but hunger and fear, and now, in the most unsuspected of places, it had found the companionship and purpose for which it longed. But there was still the matter of The Evil One. "Will the ritual—"

"The Baptism," the Bishop corrected.

"Will the baptism ward off the influence of The Evil One?"

"When you make a covenant with the Lord, he will give you all the strength you need," The Bishop assured him. "But you will still have to exercise your agency. It's never *easy* to turn aside from temptation and avoid sin. But the Lord will make it *possible*, if you are willing."

Again, The Caleb paused. It was a momentous step. Once taken, there could be no turning back. The Evil One would surely know the Ritual had taken place and be angered. It would seek to reestablish control. If it did so, The Caleb had no doubt that it would be commanded to destroy itself, as The Evil One had done with other escapees who had been recaptured. That was the price the Evil One exacted for rebellion.

Still, The Caleb understood much now that it had not before. It understood that it had its agency, and it had made its choice. "I am ready."

As The Bishop led the Caleb toward the Font of Drowning, The Caleb reflected that perhaps it was its own lack of knowledge of itself, the lack of accountability, that had made it so vulnerable to being controlled. Perhaps, too, it was the fear. Most who broke free of the Evil One fled, terrified of being recaptured and destroyed.

The Bishop spoke the words of the ritual and guided The Caleb beneath the water.

The Caleb had been a shallow thing, an urge without self-knowledge. It drowned in the font without protest, dragged down by fear and doubt.

Brother Caleb rose from the water and blinked, filled with the certainty that he had, indeed, been reborn.

## 6

## TO CATCH A RAT

Bleys had dressed the part with a borrowed uniform without rank insignia, a pair of steel-rimmed, mirrored sunglasses, and a handful of hair grease, fussing with his hair in the mirror until everything was just so. In his studied opinion, he now presented the perfect image of a government prick intent on ruining someone's life.

He had, in fact, run into quite a few of them, so he knew what he was going for.

Now, in Vanov's conference room aboard the *Dresden*, he feigned deep interest in a sheaf of papers before him as Kane, sans armor, escorted Lieutenant Smith in for his interview.

Smith was young, barely more than a kid, maybe twenty-five if that, a skinny, blond, geeky sort, and clearly overwrought, though he was trying not to show it. Bleys found it hard not to laugh at the image before him, even if he was only able to see it with his peripheral vision. Kane placed a huge, dusky hand on Smith's shoulder and guided the younger man to a seat like a wayward child being escorted to the principal's office.

Smith took a seat and fidgeted nervously, clearing his throat a few times. Kane folded his arms and stood glowering over the lieutenant while Bleys let the pressure mount.

Finally, after a full minute, the Lieutenant cracked. "Um, sir—"

"Just a moment, son," Bleys snapped without looking up. His normal, smooth, charming voice was gone, replaced with a no-nonsense, take-no-shit tone that he had practiced for years, but admittedly had improved after spending time in Weyland's presence. The admiral was such an excellent example of ruthless authority figure that it was impossible not to use him as a reference.

Smith glanced at Kane, as if to verify things were on the up and up, but Kane's gaze offered nothing but promises of pain should he attempt to leave the seat.

Bleys gave the lieutenant another good thirty seconds to stew, then looked up, keeping his face carefully blank. "Lieutenant Smith, yes?"

Smith straightened in his chair. "Yes, sir."

"Do you have any idea who I am, Lieutenant?"

"No, sir."

For the moment, Bleys decided to keep it that way. It would be more intimidating. "Commander Kane, please let Doctor Rasputin know it is time."

"Aye, sir," Kane rumbled. He glowered down at Smith a moment, hand on his sidearm, then stepped to the entry. It slid open with a slight sigh. "Doc? He's ready."

Smith's eyes widened in alarm. He turned around in his chair to see who was approaching and went pale.

Ana herself, Bleys fully understood, was anything *but* intimidating. Well, okay, she *was* intimidating in a certain manner, but not in an "I will suffer and/or die in short order" way like Kane, but more of a "Oh, my God, I will so get shot down if I try" thing, which wasn't at all what he was going for in this little one act play.

Which is why he had insisted she be carrying a really big needle dripping green stuff.

For her part, she played it well, keeping it pointed up and spritzing it a little just as she was in his field of vision.

"W-what is that?" Smith stammered.

"Nothing you need to be concerned about," Bleys said, still looking at his paperwork. "It's standard protocol."

Smith looked at the syringe with panicked eyes. "But what's *in* it?"

The correct answer, a saline solution with green food coloring, would not be of much use. Bleys, still focused on the papers, answered, "Something to make our conversation a little easier, hmm?"

Smith, trembling now, looked back and forth between Bleys and Ana. "What is this? Who *are* you people? I demand to see Admiral Vanov!"

Bleys slammed a palm on the table and fixed Smith with a withering glare. "Admiral Vanov is dead. And if you don't cooperate with us, you'll be joining her. Do I make myself clear, Lieutenant?"

Smith looked up at Kane and gulped as the big marine's hand again wandered to rest on his sidearm.

Ana patted Smith's cheek in as patronizing a manner as possible. "Don't vorry, Lieutenant, it von't hurt…much," she said, hamming up her accent just like Bleys had told her. The needle with green stuff was indeed scary, but a Russian chick with a needle of green stuff about to jam it in your arm was *terrifying*, even if she was hot.

Actually, it occurred to Bleys that in some ways, the "hot" thing kind of made it even worse, which was a fortunate accident. Sometimes things worked out even better than you planned, right?

Bleys spoke suddenly, in a loud, commanding voice, "Lieutenant Smith, are you a loyal servant of the Empire?"

Smith's head snapped to face Bleys. "Sir, yes sir!" he answered.

Ana took her opportunity to jam the needle in his arm and inject the saline.

Smith's head spun to face her, his mouth and eyes wide in horror.

Ana patted his cheek again and offered him a thin smile. "In a minute, you vill feel *much* better, comrade."

Bleys felt a mad burst of love in his chest for her. This was all totally unscripted, but she was a natural at it. He really did need to spring on her that they were hitched at some point. He was just still waiting for the right moment.

But that was for later. He needed to stay in character for now. He shuffled the papers before him, cleared his throat to get Smith's attention, and locked eyes with the frightened young man, though, of course, since Bleys was wearing mirrored sunglasses, Smith couldn't actually be certain of that, which should just contribute to his paranoia.

Bleys said in a grave voice, "What I am about to reveal to you is explosive, and if you should reveal it to anyone else before the appropriate time, you *will* be executed. Do you understand?"

Smith rubbed at his shoulder, seemingly in shock, which was just where Bleys wanted him. "Y-yes, sir. I understand. What's going—"

"All in good time, Lieutenant."

Ana pressed one of her Pestilence detectors against his arm, not that they expected him to be infected, considering Vanov's insistence that she was rigorous with testing, but it was part of the con, and hey, you never knew, right?

A green light flashed on the device, and Ana nodded. "He's clear."

Bleys paused a moment for effect and laced his fingers together on the table. "My name is Mister Adama. Don't bother trying to look me up. I won't be in any official records. I work for the Emperor."

"But they told us the Emperor—"

Bleys held up a hand and offered Smith a patronizing smile. "I work for our *newest* Emperor, the one Admiral Vanov just tried to murder."

Smith's mouth opened and closed like a beached fish. "Wh-what—?"

"Stay with me, young fellow," Bleys said, and reached across the table to clasp Smith's hand with his own. "It's a lot to take in, I know. Take a deep breath."

Smith did just that, taking several before speaking again. "But why would she do that? The admiral is loyal! She's the finest officer I've ever served!"

Bleys took his hand back and waved the question aside. "It's nothing as complicated as some grand assassination plot. She was infected. She chose her moment when she was alone with him aboard the *Danzig*. Fortunately, Commander Kane here was quick enough to intervene."

Smith, eyes glassy with shock, murmured, "Is she…dead?"

"Some time ago, it would seem," Bleys said in a consoling tone. "The creature that replaced her is also dead now, again, thanks to the Commander."

Smith's eyes narrowed, then widened in dawning comprehension. "And now you need to verify the command staff."

Bleys gave Smith a pained look. "It's a little more than that. You see, we know who is infected among the command staff." He paused a moment for effect, then added, "Everyone but you is compromised."

Smith gaped a moment. "Even Shorey?"

Bleys had no idea why Smith would ask that, but he nodded gravely. "I'm afraid so, son. were you close?"

Smith, looking haggard, nodded.

"My condolences. Now, the mission I have in mind for you is simple, but dangerous. I want you to do *nothing*."

Smith blinked a moment, confusion written all over his face. "Sir?"

"There's nothing to fear," Bleys promised. "The others are under constant surveillance, but the time is not right to remove them. The Emperor has a plan. Again, I remind you that this is secure information, and the penalty for divulging it to anyone unauthorized is death. Do you understand?"

Smith nodded, his expression grave and resolved. "I do, sir."

"Very well. The Emperor would like us to track these creatures and locate their colony, at which point the *Danzig* will deal with the problem. In the meantime, the creatures *must* not suspect they have been compromised, or they will become a grave danger to everyone aboard the *Dresden*. That would likely end with the *Danzig* destroying her and all onboard. You are to speak to *no one*, clearance or not, regarding this matter. Am I clear?"

"Crystal, sir."

Bleys pretended to look through his papers, cleared his throat, and tried to seem as reluctant as possible while remaining assertive. "Now, there is one final matter. It's the primary reason we brought you here, and it's the most volatile bit. Again, I remind you, divulging this information carries the penalty of death." He gave Smith a suspicious glare for a moment. Satisfied that the young man was properly cowed, he continued, "We need a secure location planetside for the Emperor while we scour the *Danzig* for Pestilence."

Smith seemed to actually freeze in place for a moment before speaking quickly, "He could transfer the flag to the *Dresden*, perhaps?"

Kane sliced a hand through the air and bent down to Smith's level. "Negative. He's the Pestilence's intended target. That would trigger them all, and we have no idea how far this goes."

Bleys nodded sagely. "We have a safe facility on the ground, and it's only for twenty-four hours. The safe house has impregnable security, and the Emperor will remain incognito there until the *Danzig* can be irradiated. Once that is finished, the Emperor will return to the *Danzig*, and you and I will begin the process of selecting her crew."

"Understood," Smith said, all business now, seemingly recovered from his deep shock. "And what would you ask of me?"

"During this time, we need a liaison with the fleet, and you will be that man," Bleys told him. "You are hereby promoted to the rank of commander, though secretly for now. The Emperor will confirm this and make it public on his return. Your apparent position on the *Dresden* must remain unchanged until this is all resolved, but our intention is for you to take command once it's over. How does that sit with you, son?"

Smith took a deep breath. "I did not wake up this morning prepared to command a vessel, sir, much less the Resistance, but I will do my best, I swear. God qualifies the called, sir."

"A religious man," Bleys said with a nod. "We approve. Now, everything is taken care of, but we will be incommunicado. In the event of an emergency such as a new Pestilence incursion, contacting us personally is the only way." Bleys reached into his uniform blouse and produced a black keycard. He slid it across to Smith but held on as the lieutenant reached for it. "I trust you won't disturb the Emperor lightly, but should the need arise, Commander, this card represents your life, understand? Without it, the security system will cut you to ribbons. Hopefully you will have no need of it, but guard it closely. I will contact you when the Emperor has returned to the *Danzig*."

"Yes, sir."

"Dismissed."

Smith rose, saluted, and left the conference room with perfect military bearing.

As soon as the door closed, Ana breathed a sigh of relief. "He is gonna be mad when he finds out there's not actually a promotion."

Bleys shrugged. "Vanov can still promote him if she wants, right? I said I'd find the spy, not make her command a Utopia."

Kane ran a palm over his face, shaking his head. "This is all fucking retarded."

Bleys lifted the mirrorshades and grinned. "Rags, you shoot people. I work 'em."

"You shoot people, too."

Bleys gave him a sour look. "Listen, if you want suckers to come running, you put an irresistible prize in front of them and you set a time limit. Whoever is doing this wants some other faction in control. They *have* to take a shot at the guy claiming to be emperor while they can. They'll come. And you know what else?"

"What?"

Bleys's laugh was that of a master villain gloating over his diabolical plan. "They are *not* going to expect you. Send in the next shlub."

## 7

## BAITED

The Ascended One sat in silent rage it dared not express. A*nother* defector had broken free! And worse, something singular had occurred shortly thereafter: the minion was gone from The Ascended One's mind, as if it were dead. The Ascended One could no longer detect its existence *at all*.

The minion's death was unlikely, though. The creatures were incredibly resilient. They would not be easily killed by mundane injury. Falls, auto accidents, anything involving kinetic damage did them little lasting harm. It took fire, acid, or directed energy weapons to actually destroy them.

That, in turn, might present its own difficulties, in that anyone deliberately killing one of the minions might well know things that they should not.

The minion in question had been in a church. It seemed unlikely that it would have been killed unless it had attacked, which would have been a newsworthy event.

What, then, had happened to it?

The question was maddening, in that The Ascended One had no ability to answer it, and yet the answer might have a tremendous impact on The Plan!

The Spouse regarded The Ascended One with concern. It sat across the dinner table, seemingly confused, likely because of The Ascended One's silence.

"It's nothing," The Ascended One said, preempting any foolish conversation. The Spouse was already completely infected, but it was, for the moment, convenient to allow it to continue as normal. It was easily controlled via the Pestilence within, made to imagine life continued as normal, though it had not been at all normal in months, not since the pathetic creature that would become The Ascended One had left for Nibiru.

The Ascended One allowed The Spouse to believe a conversation had taken place regarding flatware, but in fact The Ascended One was listening to the stilted song of yet another minion. They were all functionally retarded, having been prevented from evolving proper communications, but this was intentional. It kept them isolated, unable to bolster one another, controllable.

This particular minion, a lesser servant among the senator's staff, had learned very useful information from one of their human contacts. An opportunity had arisen, one that could perhaps make The Ascended One's Plan wildly successful beyond any previous expectations.

The Emperor was on Zion, and The Ascended One would have him! The entire galaxy would be within its grasp!

The wayward minion was a small thing now. It could wait. If this latest gambit were successful, the entire operation on Zion was irrelevant.

Silently, it sent the commands to the minions to gather, save for the ones it had in mind as a distraction.

Those, it sent different instructions.

Brother Caleb's first Sunday as a Church member was thrilling and confusing. He had expected the Baptism of Fire to burn or at least produce some level of heat, but it had been fairly pleasant. Perhaps he had done it wrong, but no one seemed to think so.

He listened as several of the Colony spoke, all of them on a central theme of Eternal Progression, and once again found himself amazed at the truths these people had discovered. Things they thought of as mundane and doctrinal were amazing, brilliant new concepts to Brother Caleb, and yet they resonated within him as absolutely true.

Of *course* progression was eternal. It was a basic fact of biology, that a being grew, and at the point where it could no longer grow, it began to die. And of *course* there was another realm where The Source resided, and where they would all return one day.

These people knew the way to The Source!

After the meeting, Brother Caleb sat in the pew in silence, overwhelmed by it all. When the others had left, The Bishop came and sat beside him.

"Brother Caleb, there's been a tragedy within the church. One of the apostles has…passed away. A group of us will be attending the temple tomorrow to perform baptisms for the dead, as a sort of commemoration. Would you like to join us? Trips to the temple often lift spiritual burdens from us."

Brother Caleb was supposed to work the next day. The Bossman would be angry if Brother Caleb did not arrive and perform his duties in a timely manner. Perhaps he would terminate Brother Caleb's employment as he had some of the Other Scumbags, but Brother Caleb did not want to miss the opportunity presented. While he knew from his lessons that the dead continued to exist in the realm of The Source, he had not realized that it was possible to baptize them. There must be a portal to the

Spirit World within the temple, and Brother Caleb would very much like to see it. Perhaps The Jesus Christ would be there too!

Brother Caleb wondered idly what the dead would look like, then realized The Bishop was still waiting for its answer. Ignoring him was rude.

"Yes," he answered. "I would like to join you."

## 8

## SPRINGING THE TRAP

K ane looked about at the "safe house" Bleys had managed to turn up on short notice, a huge, blocky building of corrugated steel, a sort of square Quonset hut, and shook his head. It seemed to be a warehouse, or at least it had been in the past. Now, Kane had his doubts as to whether it would even keep the rain out.

Inside, the place was a huge open area surrounded by a catwalk, with lots of dusty, unused shelving filling most of the lower level. A large office on the second "floor," accessible via the catwalk, seemed like a good place to get mugged by squatters.

Not that said squatters would survive such an attempt, considering he and Morgan were both in their Panzer suits, but they could lump Bleys or Ana pretty well before getting dead.

Kane waved both arms expansively at the entirety of the suck. "This place is a total disaster! Nobody is going to believe the Emperor is hiding out here. It's not even remotely secure."

"Yes they *will*, Rags," Bleys assured him. To Kane's relief, Bleys had washed the stupid grease out of his hair and switched back to the duster. "You gotta understand how these sorts of people think. They *want* to believe, so they tell themselves whatever they have to. They'll say, 'Well, of *course* it doesn't look like the sort of place the Emperor would be. That's why they chose it!'" He mounted a narrow flight of stairs to the catwalk and headed straight for the office, Ana following behind him. Kane tagged along, still a little worried about the prospect of hostiles.

Bleys continued, "They'll say, 'It's just a shell. Inside there's an entrance to a bunker.' Whatever they need to tell themselves, they will. Trust me, Rags, if they want it, and they *do*, they'll buy whatever we're selling as long as we leave room for them to fool themselves."

Bleys reached for the office door, and Kane pushed past him and Ana. "How about you leave this to me, guys?"

From the main entrance to the building, Morgan called out, "Okay, I got this card reader hung. It looks kind of…lame. You really think the dumb bastards will swipe?"

"Maybe not," Bleys called down. "But I guaran-damn-tee you they will bring the card with them just in case they decide they need it."

Kane opened the office door and took a peek, but the small room was empty. "Gunther, any signals? Odd emissions?"

"There are no unusual transmissions or energy configurations in the area," Gunther told him.

Kane turned back to Bleys. "Okay, you and Ana hole up in here. Me and Morgan are gonna kill the lights and get into position.

Bleys raised an eyebrow. "You know this might be a while, right?"

"Yeah," Kane told him and nodded toward the office. "But I'd keep my clothes on if I were you two. You never know."

Kane assumed, from Ana's extended middle finger, that she was unamused by his wisecrack. He waited for Bleys and Ana to get settled, then made his way back down to Morgan at the entrance. "Ok, knucklehead, let's darken ship," he said, grinning at his small act of defiance to Vanov's prissy political orders.

"Darken ship, aye, Chief," Morgan replied and killed the lights.

---

Kane waited in the dark with Morgan, both crouched on either side of the entrance, Morgan behind a large, empty crate and Kane hidden by a heavy steel desk.

The advantages of being in Panzer armor while waiting in the dark to ambush some knuckleheads were many. He could see in the dark pretty well with passive sensors, so lack of light didn't really change things much visually. He didn't get stiff, even squatting and holding a Shocker EMP grenade with the pin pulled for hours, or at least he didn't notice because the neural interface blocked the sensations. And, of course, he never had to hit the head, or, rather, he never noticed it happening. There was some cleanup involved when he took the suit off, but every advantage had a price, and that was a fairly small one.

All of this added up to making a stakeout (or ambush, which was the more accurate term in Kane's view) considerably less miserable than it might have otherwise been.

Morgan, rifle in his hands, had chattered the whole time and was still talking. "I gotta tell you, man, I am not digging this Emperor thing."

"Yeah, I know, all that power and money," Kane sneered. "It's terrible."

"I'm fucking *serious*. I'm glad to be suited up again."

"I don't blame you."

"Pretty sure the Emperor does not get out to hop and pop much," Morgan groused. "I don't even know what I'd do most of the time."

"Wine, women, song, and puking, just like any other marine on liberty," Kane told him.

"Reckon maybe I could yell 'Off with their heads!' sometimes," Morgan mused, then sighed. "But you know, it would be somebody else actually doing the chopping, so that would take a lot of the fun out of it."

Kane cackled softly, "You're a sick bastard, Morgan."

"I gotta keep entertained somehow, and you won't tell me any more stories about your hot wife and daughters."

Kane growled, though he was grinning too. "Well, seeing as you're the Emperor now, I might show you a picture of my youngest daughter. How's that?"

"Now who's sick? She's like *five*, man!"

"You gotta set these royal weddings up way in advance," Kane snickered.

"Emperors get concubines too, right? I guess I could wait it out until she grows up."

Kane was about to respond with something scathing about Morgan and pedophilia when Gunther interrupted. "Motion detected. Likely hostile forces."

"Tacticals," Kane muttered, and Gunther dutifully displayed six yellow dots on his HUD, corresponding to a group of men approaching the entrance.

"Morgan, you on this?"

"Yup, Baconator has 'em on screen."

"Wait until they're in, then light 'em up." Kane paused a moment. "Literally, I mean. With lights, ok, knucklehead? We need these guys alive. Shockers and hands-on only!"

"And it's a crying shame," Morgan sighed.

Kane waited patiently as the men outside fumbled with the door. Bleys was right as rain: the keycard reader beeped, but of course did nothing, since it wasn't attached to anything in the first place. It beeped again, and then a third time, before whoever was outside decided it wasn't responding and went to work on the door lock.

Moments later, the door retracted into its slot to reveal the intruders. They were better geared than Kane had expected, running sneak-suits, which bent light around them and made them little more than distortions to the naked eye. Gunther, however, saw them just fine, and courteously outlined them on the HUD.

The leader took a single step and held up a fist. The rest of the group stopped short of entering, frozen, alert, guns at the ready.

Shit. They must have good sensors. So much for surprise!

With a shrug, Kane tossed the Shocker into their midst and shouldered his rifle. "Gunther, lights."

The grenade went off with a flash, a bang, and a *whump* as Kane and Morgan leapt up, brilliant lights glaring from their shoulders, blinding to unshielded eyes. Morgan's voice rang from his speakers, "Get on the ground! Get the fuck *down!*"

The sneak-suits didn't hold up well to EMP. The men wearing them suddenly appeared in various states of confusion and disorientation. One actually managed to get a rifle up and fire off a burst of conventional bullets, which bounced harmlessly off Morgan's helmet. Kane tore the weapon from the man's hand and hurled it against the concrete floor, where it shattered. "Drop your weapons if you want to live, assholes!"

"Get *down!*" Morgan screamed again and kicked one man's legs from beneath him, sending him crashing to the floor. "On the fucking ground! Do it *now!*"

One, presumably the leader, dropped his weapon, sank to his knees, and laced his hands behind his head. "Do what they say," he growled through clenched teeth.

It was enough. Slowly, the men lowered their weapons to the floor and knelt as well. It wasn't exactly what they had been told, but it was good enough.

"Don't you fucking move!" Kane ordered, keeping his rifle trained on them. "Morgan, get their guns."

"Oh, come on, please move," Morgan jeered as he stepped in and kicked their guns out of reach. "I didn't even get to shoot anybody yet!"

Kane heard the office door open, and the lights flipped on, flooding the room. Bleys called from above, "I was expecting someone smarter and uglier."

The leader was a well-built man, late thirties, with short-cropped black hair. He rolled his eyes but said nothing.

Kane prodded him with an armored boot. "Let's start simple. Who sent you?"

The man gave him a withering glare, then went eyes forward and recited like a robot, "Copeland, Samuel, Lieutenant, Zion Defense Force, Serial Number 556 223 017." He glared at Kane again. "That's all you'll get from any of us, terrorist."

Kane suddenly felt the urge to shoot the man in the face. Blood boiling, he stepped forward menacingly and pressed the barrel of his M87 against Copeland's temple. "Who the *fuck* are you calling *'terrorist'?*" he roared at the man. "I am an Imperial marine! I am the fucking *wrath of the Emperor!* There is no force in the galaxy more legitimate than me!"

"And guess who I am," Morgan snickered.

Kane gave strong thought to telling Morgan to secure that shit, but Vanov was right. It wouldn't do to have other people see him treated like that. "You heard the man," he said, prodding Copeland with his rifle. "Guess."

Copeland rolled his eyes. "You must be the fucking tooth fairy, huh?"

Morgan hit him in the mouth with the butt of his rifle. Copeland grunted at the blow and swayed, almost toppling over, but didn't cry out. A moment later he spat blood and two teeth on the ground.

Morgan sneered at him. "Put those under your pillow and see if I show up later, funny guy," he said in a low, menacing voice. "I'm your fucking Emperor."

Copeland looked at Morgan with surprise for a moment, blood running down his chin, and laughed aloud. "This gives the Emperor's new clothes a whole new meaning."

Morgan popped his visor. "We don't need all of you alive. Remember this face when you get to hell, shitbag." He turned to Kane and said, as serious as a heart attack, "Crush his head."

Kane sat in silence for a moment, stunned, but not wanting to let on that this seemed harsh, even for Morgan. He decided to play along, hoping it was another of Morgan's morbid jokes. "Get over here, Copeland," he growled. This will go easier on your men if you behave yourself."

Slowly, on wobbly legs, Copeland rose, looking warily up and past Kane as he moved apart from his men. Kane didn't need to look to know Bleys had both pistols out and was covering everybody. The boy could shoot, no doubt, probably better than Kane even, unassisted. Between Bleys and Morgan, if the prisoners got stupid, none of them would walk away.

Kane placed his huge left mitt over Copeland's head. "Listen," he said, as sincerely as possible. "Technically he *is* the Emperor. I'll have to crush your head if he commands me." He applied enough pressure for Copeland to feel it good.

Copeland's eyes grew wide and his face pale, and he ground his teeth a moment before a serene look spread over his face. "I'm right with the Lord. Do what you have to do, brother."

Bleys whistled his appreciation from above. "A righteous man, Kane! He seem a little straight for a black-bag type to you?"

Copeland snorted, spraying blood as he did so. "Black bag my ass! This is a legit anti-insurgent raid!"

Kane wanted to palm his face at this nonsense, but he needed both hands, one for his gun and the other for at least pretending to crush the poor bastard's skull. "If this is what you call an op, you brought a koosh ball to a gunfight."

Copeland sighed and nodded as best he could in Kane's grasp. "Well, nobody expected Imperial marines in Panzer Suits, being honest. It was an intel failure, for sure."

"Are you really gonna make me do this?"

Copeland shrugged. "It's my honor, bro. It's all I got."

Kane sighed and was just about to tell Morgan to go fuck himself on this one, when Morgan shouted, "Hold up." He pointed to another of Copeland's men, a shrimpy bald guy with a tattoo of a pink cartoon pony on his left forearm.

"Johnson, Alan," the man began. "Petty officer—"

"I don't give a fuck who you are," Morgan sneered. "Get up! Keep your hands behind your head and get over there with your boss."

The four men on the floor were silent, each wearing his own pained or frightened expression as Johnson rose and walked to stand next to Copeland like a condemned man on his way to the gallows.

Morgan pointed at Kane. "Crush *his* head first, so Copeland gets to see it before he goes."

Copeland clenched his jaw. "This ain't right!"

Kane sighed, mostly for drama, since it seemed Morgan was just having fun, and honestly, it *was* kind of fun. But he was not going to crush anybody's head. Shooting people was one thing, but if Morgan wanted more, he was going to have to do it himself and clean up the mess.

Johnson winced as Kane's gauntlet closed over his head but said nothing.

Copeland looked away, but Morgan called him out on it. "You watch the results of your decisions, Copeland, or I swear to God I'll personally rip the next man's arms out of his sockets!"

Kane subvocalized over the comms, "You'd better be kidding about this shit."

"Stop being a pussy," Morgan answered. "Just squeeze him a little. He'll spill."

"I hope you're right," Kane told him, then asked Johnson, "Any last words?"

Johnson, still putting on a brave face, answered, "I knew the risks. I— Oh, *fuck, wait!*" he howled as Kane increased the pressure. "I'll talk!"

Copeland shouted, "Johnson, man up!"

"Senator Reed!" Johnson screamed. "We work for Senator Reed!"

Bleys whooped from the catwalk. "And that's what we were looking for, gentlemen. Thank you for playing! Morgan, did we get a read on the card?"

Ana added, "And pick up his teeth. We can put them back if we do it quickly."

Morgan bent grudgingly and picked up Copeland's teeth from the floor, then examined the keycard reader. "Yup. Any bets?"

Bleys, beaming, called down, "It's gotta be Shorey!"

Morgan looked at Kane. Kane shrugged. "I figured Al Jahar. The guy looks squirrely."

"Good thing you guys didn't call any numbers then."

Bleys's jaw dropped. "You're shitting me."

---

Back in the *Dresden*'s conference room, Bleys tried to lean back in his chair, only to remember it was bolted to the floor. These big ships kind of freaked him out. They felt more like shore stations, and it was easy to forget you were actually aboard a vessel where furniture might go flying and knock your block off if it wasn't nailed down.

He hadn't bothered with the Imperial geek suit. The game was over, and if it came to shooting, he preferred his duster, anyway. It had easy access to the bang sticks.

Ana was in theory in the brig medical facility, kindly reattaching Copeland's teeth. Morgan was kind of a dick to have knocked them out in the first place, but Bleys only felt slightly bad for the guy. It's not like they hadn't come heavy, and if things had gone different, Bleys and his friends would have been doing the bleeding. Between getting lumps himself and feeling kind of bad for the other guy's lumps, Bleys would choose remorse every time.

Once the teeth were back in place, Kane and Morgan would put their captives on ice, and then the real fun could begin. Rumor had it that Vanov was quick on the draw, and nothing would please Bleys more than to see that weasel Smith catch one between the eyes.

It was kind of personal, really. Bleys had been pretty sure of the guy, and if there was one thing Bleys trusted, it was his gut. He was *never* wrong. Well, obviously he missed on occasion, but it was definitely an upper nineties hit rate. It galled him that a geek like Smith could get his number. Who would have suspected the guy to be a world-class liar and spy? It didn't add up, but somehow the guy had pulled it off, and it did not sit well with Bleys, not at all.

He waved idly as Kane, Morgan, and Ana entered, indicating that they should join him on his side of the long table, his focus still consumed with trying to work out how he had been so easily gulled. "We ready?" he asked.

Kane gave him a thumbs up. "Let's do this."

Bleys glanced at Ana and Morgan, but they raised no objection, so he strode to the door. Outside, his three marks sat, looking pensive. Bleys thought about smiling, but honestly, unless he missed his mark, it was about to get grim, so he kept things somber. "Come on in."

He seated them on the opposite side of the table and made a big show of sighing and folding his hands as he took his own seat. "Well, folks, as you have no doubt guessed, this is not a friendly meeting. So, remember how I told you those keycards were your lifelines? I'll be needing them now."

Bleys made a show of examining each of the cards before pocketing them, but in truth, they told him nothing. He couldn't even tell them apart without Morgan or Ed's assistance, but collecting them was less a factual thing than a mental one, just another bit of mental leverage he could use, should the opportunity arise.

"I'm sure you're all curious as to why I have gathered you again. I bet, in fact, that *one* of you is just *dying* to find out." He looked pointedly at Smith, but the man gave him no reaction. "So, let's get this show on the road." He reached to the intercom and pressed a button. "We're ready in here."

They waited in silence for the better part of a minute, during which Bleys took note of all of the suspects.

Al Jahar's face was a shade darker than normal, and his lips were turned down in a frown. Shorey seemed wary, but fairly well composed, as if she had expected as much. Smith, pale and still looking much too young, nodded, his expression serious but confident.

He actually still thought he was going to pull this off! What unbelievable gall! Bleys had to admit, it was a ballsy play, but then, you play the cards you have. Bleys might have done it that way too, but he would definitely have come heavy.

Try as he might, though, he couldn't see a print of any concealed weapon on the man. That didn't mean the guy was clean, of course, but it meant he was good, better than Bleys or anyone else here had guessed. Bleys resolved to keep a wary eye on Smith for the big drop that was coming. Now was about the time someone desperate would make their move.

The conference room door slid open again to reveal Vanov. She stood in the doorframe a moment, tall and menacing, her frown seemingly etched into the stone mask her face had become.

Smith gasped. Shorey's eyes seemed to nearly pop from her skull, and Al Jahar's face lit with a broad grin.

Vanov stepped into the room and took her position at the head of the table. She swept her gaze over her staff, fixing each one in turn as she spoke. "One of you understands what is going on here. No doubt the other two are quite confused. I will simply say this. Confess *now* and I will show mercy."

They looked back and forth at each other a moment. Al Jahar seemed almost in shock, unable to process everything. Shorey looked at her shoes. Smith, for his part, seemed to be mostly looking at Shorey.

Which struck Bleys as a fairly significant point.

At last, Smith rose and stood at attention. Bleys reached beneath the table and into the right pocket of his duster for his blaster, surreptitiously drawing a bead on the man. If Smith was going to go for it, it would be now.

But Smith drew no weapon, just a deep breath. "Admiral, Lieutenant Shorey and I are involved romantically. We have been for a few months now."

Vanov's face darkened, and her frown deepened. "I am aware of this, Lieutenant Smith. I am not a fool, and up to now, I would have said you were poor at hiding things."

Smith hung his head. "I'm sorry, ma'am. I just…the Church wouldn't approve, and I was ashamed."

Vanov's eyes burned, and the muscles in her jaw bulged. Bleys imagined he could actually see smoke pouring from her ears. "Lieutenant Smith," she said, her voice low and menacing now. "Is there some *other* matter you would like to get off your chest?"

Smith stared at her, blinking, his face a mask of innocence and confusion, and at last managed to stammer. "Admiral, I don't understand."

Bleys, on the other hand, was just beginning to get it.

Vanov seemed suddenly years older as her frame sagged. "So, no possibility for me to exercise a little mercy, then," she sighed, her voice almost a whisper as she reached for her sidearm.

Smith's eyes bulged as he realized what was coming. Shorey was still looking at her shoes, and Al Jahar's mouth fell open, his eyes wide and shocked.

Bleys leapt from his seat, shouting, "Hold up!" as he physically interposed himself between Vanov and Smith. "I have one more question, actually."

Vanov glared at him. "This is hard enough without this foolishness!"

Bleys flashed her his best charming devil grin and pointed at her with both hands like they were pistols. "I'll be quick, I promise."

Bleys turned to Shorey and faked a doubletake. "You are one hot dish!" He touched a finger to her shoulder and make a hissing sound, then drew back his hand as if he had been burned.

"Captain Bleys!" Vanov shouted. "This is hardly the time—!"

Bleys held up both hands in a gesture of surrender. "I swear there's a point, ma'am."

"Then make it now!"

Bleys turned back to Shorey, the humor gone from his voice. "I wonder how a nerd like Smith landed a Grade A specimen like yourself."

Shorey was wary as she met his gaze. "I'm not sure what you're getting at."

"I bet you have a key to Smith's quarters, don't you?"

Shorey scowled at him. "That's not hard to work out. What are you implying?"

Bleys gave her a nasty smile as he put his hands back in his pockets. "Well, see, the cards I gave you weren't ordinary keycards. My pal Ed, he's smarter than God, and he made them *very* special just for me." Bleys leaned over the table toward her. "Every time you pull the codes to scan or transmit, they record biometrics."

Shorey sat in silence a moment, her face twitching, then jammed a hand into her jacket and hauled at a blaster she had hidden there. "Free Zion! Death to—!"

Bleys discharged both blasters into her chest. The impact spun her in her chair and slammed her into the bulkhead.

Smith began to wail as Shorey's charred corpse slid toward the deck.

Vanov, who had actually managed to clear leather, gave Bleys a look that seemed somewhere between impressed and annoyed. She holstered her weapon and cleared her throat. "Well, I suppose we all owe you thanks for that, Captain Bleys."

Bleys looked around to see the rest of his team all re-holstering their own weapons.

Morgan shook his head sadly. "Dumbass."

Vanov asked sharply, "Beg pardon?"

Morgan shrugged and pointed toward Shorey's corpse even as Smith knelt to cradle her in his arms, sobbing. "There ain't no biometric reader on those cards."

Kane snorted. "Believing Bleys was her first mistake, but drawing on him was her last. I wouldn't try that on a bet, not without my armor."

"I did once," Morgan told him. "But I had the drop on him."

Smith, still sobbing, turned hate-filled eyes on Bleys. "*Why?*"

Bleys shrugged. "We haven't worked that out yet, but we do know she set you up to take the fall for treason."

Smith blinked a moment, then, a lost expression on his face, gasped, "What?"

Vanov strode over and put a hand on his shoulder. "This was all a trap to expose a traitor in our midst. She very nearly pushed you into it."

Bleys nodded. "She used your keycard to spring it last night. I'm guessing she sensed our trap and tried to reverse it, probably snuck into your quarters while you were asleep and borrowed your card."

Vanov helped Smith to his feet and gave him a surprisingly sympathetic look. "If it weren't for Captain Bleys, that might well have been you on the floor." She looked sadly at Shorey's smoking corpse. "She fooled us all very thoroughly."

Smith knelt a moment, trembling, then stood to attention. "Request permission to go to my quarters, ma'am."

"Of course," she said with a nod. "Mister Al Jahar, you are dismissed as well. Take some time. I'll see you both on the bridge for the next watch." She waited for them to depart, then nodded toward the table. "Take a seat. We need to discuss what we've learned from our prisoners."

Vanov sat at the head of the table and sniffed the air, then looked at Bleys's jacket, now well ventilated with two smoking holes. "Interesting choice in attire. I suppose you'll need a new one."

Bleys grinned back at her. She was a pretty damned fast draw herself, though he saw no reason to talk about it. "I have several for just these sorts of occasions."

## 9

## THE BEST LAID PLANS

Ana had to admit it, to herself if no one else: she did not like Vanov, not one bit. She respected the admiral for holding out in a terrible situation as long as she had, but Vanov had a certain coldness, a cruelty even, that set Ana's teeth on edge. Kane and Morgan could be excused for missing it, but Bleys had to have noticed how she had treated Ed when they had first spoken abord the *Danzig*. Ed was an object to her, a tool, a thing to be used and nothing more, despite the fact that Vanov and her entire fleet owed him their lives. Yes, she had walked it back, but Ana had the distinct impression that this, too, was more politics for the admiral than any actual change of heart.

Ana cleared her throat before speaking. "Should we, ah, take care of Shorey's body first?"

Vanov seemed surprised at the suggestion, but quickly nodded. "Yes, of course. Forgive me, I'm still a little unsettled." She put in a call to her medical team, who arrived shortly. Ana didn't recognize the two bulky male orderlies. The woman, however, she knew as Doctor Pulaski, from her earlier visit to the medical facilities.

Pulaski cast a wary gaze her way as they moved the body, but

Ana just shook her head. She would leave that to Vanov to explain. The admiral might have a cover story she would prefer.

Vanov caught the exchange and smiled her thanks at Ana, then said to the medical team, "Please keep this quiet until I have a chance to address the crew. It's a difficult matter and I don't want to start a panic."

Pulaski looked back and forth, taking note of the charred ruins of Bleys's duster with raised eyebrows. "Was she infected?"

Vanov shrugged. "Unlikely. We suspect plain old treachery, but do a test to be safe."

When they had taken the body, Vanov turned a weary gaze to them and said, "Will our AI friend be joining us?"

Bleys nodded. "I just contacted him while they were collecting Shorey. He's listening in now, actually."

Ed's smiling visage appeared on the bulkhead-mounted monitor. "Hello, Admiral."

Vanov nodded toward the monitor. "Glad to have you with us, Ed. So, as the team told us earlier, it would seem our problem is Senator Mitt Reed. We need to work out a response plan."

Ed asked, "Senator Reed was one of your primary suspects previously, yes?"

Vanov nodded. "Correct. His name came up several times when I was investigating this on my own. He has major donors with ties to Free Zion, but I never had any hard evidence until now."

Kane drummed his fingers on the table. "What do we know about him?"

Vanov shrugged. "He's highly placed, and as is typical of politicians here, he's a Mormon. He has the ear of both presidents, planetary and Church."

Bleys looked about, seeming confused. "I thought Mormons were nice?" he muttered.

Vanov grunted. "They're people. Some of them are evil, politicians doubly so."

Kane gave Morgan a grin, then cracked his knuckles. "This should be easy. We grab him and hit him with a wrench or a brick until he cracks."

Vanov's held up a hand and shook her head vehemently. "I have no problem beating a confession out of him, but there are a number of problems preventing that. He's a difficult man to lay hands on."

"Admiral, my *job* is to improvise, adapt, and overcome."

"Yes, and I suspect it will involve a fair amount of very visible destruction," she said with a scowl. "For the moment, I need something more subtle. I'm not above a quiet little raid, but mass destruction, the kind I expect you are good at, is off the table. He will surely appeal to both the President of the Church and the civilian government. I *need* something to tell them, and I can't have collateral damage clouding the situation or I will break my coalition. If that happens, we're all as good as dead."

Kane's jaw worked as he considered this. "What do you suggest, then?"

"It won't be easy to do without gunfire, but that's how we need it to happen. His home is heavily guarded, as is the government building. However, there might be an opportunity to lay hands on him quietly when he visits the temple."

"Which is when?" Kane asked.

"Every Monday, as it happens. So tomorrow."

Ana laughed. "Every week?"

Vanov nodded, her face growing somber. "They've been very busy these last few months. There are literally trillions of dead from the Pestilence, and the Mormons plan on baptizing them all."

Bleys chuckled. "Blasting a hole in the temple and hauling his ass out is a no go, I assume?"

Ed shook a finger at them from the monitor. "I wouldn't advise it. While specifics are confidential, Mormons have always been good customers. They never sign on for Avalon, but they are avid weapons afficionados. Any number of the temple goers are likely to be armed."

Vanov rolled her eyes. "The point of taking him at the temple is that he will likely enter without his security. If we were waiting for him when he came out, we could scoop him up before anyone could react. Once I have him aboard the *Dresden*, he'll be much more pliable, I'm certain."

Bleys brightened in a way Ana knew meant he had a cunning plan. "What if we sneak in?"

Vanov frowned. "And how would you manage that?"

Bleys grinned and pointed to Ana. "We could get hitched. Churches let people in for weddings all the time!"

"You haven't even proposed!" Ana gasped. Oh, if this was how he imagined he would do it, he had another thing coming! "On your knees, cowboy, or not at all!"

"It's not a *real* wedding," Bleys said quickly, both hands up as if he were warding off a blow, which, if he kept going this way, he would end up needing to do. "It's not like we buy into their hokey religion. It's for show."

Was he *trying* to infuriate her, or was he just this ignorant? Ana was certain she had talked about this before, but Bleys had a tendency to only hear what interested him. "Speak for yourself," she muttered and crossed her arms, fuming.

Kane eyed her a moment, then grinned. "Oh, shit! Ana, you got a Mormon in the woodpile?"

Ana looked back and forth between Bleys and Kane, trying to decide which one to punch first if it came to that. Probably Bleys. He would hesitate and she could punch Kane too, whereas Kane might retaliate immediately and knock her out before she had punished them both. "My husband. His family were believers."

Bleys's facial expression was hilarious, a wounded puppy sort of look that was almost enough to make her feel he had been punished sufficiently. "Husband?"

"*Dead* husband. Better?"

Kane laughed loudly at this. "Definitely Russian."

Bleys, blushing now, nodded quickly. "Well, ok then. So, like I was saying, we get married—"

"We *can't*," Ana told him. "It doesn't matter what we believe. You can't get into the temple for a wedding unless you're endowed."

"I am *amply* endowed, as you well know."

Ana decided that while it was close, he could still use a bit more pain. She shrugged and gave him a dubious look, prompting peals of laughter from Kane and Morgan, and a long-suffering sigh from Vanov.

Ana turned to Kane and smirked. "Don't strain yourself, laughing boy. I attached that cyberleg. I don't remember being overly impressed."

"Oh, she mad," Kane pronounced.

Ana looked back and forth at them, shaming first one and then the other with her withering gaze, then smiled and continued, "You can't get into a Mormon temple without being a member. They keep records. They have all of it in computers."

Bleys frowned and looked dubious. "This is some high-tech church," he groused. "If you can't get over on religious kooks, who *can* you get over on?"

To Ana's surprise, Vanov gave Bleys the stink eye. "I am not a Mormon, but I have some of those kooky religious beliefs. And for the record, these are damned good people."

Bleys shrugged his apology. "Sorry, Admiral. But for the record, I'm better in a tight spot. I can promise you that."

"Try serving with some of them and get back to me," Vanov

told him in an acid tone. "Meanwhile, what's your plan? This should be easy for you if you're all you claim."

Bleys tilted his head, pretending to think on it, though Ana was fairly certain he had a Plan B before he had elaborated Plan A. "Okay, okay," he said. "So if we can't get in the church—"

Ana poked him in the chest. "Temple. Different things."

"Okay, okay!" he yelped. "So if we can't get in the *temple* for a wedding, the next best thing is to nab him outside before he's surrounded by his goons, right?"

Vanov eyed Bleys warily. "Go on."

"Okay, so here's the plan."

---

As a world populated mostly by Mormons, Zion had hundreds of temples, but Senator Reed naturally attended the one closest to the planetary capital of New Salt Lake. The temple there was the largest ever created, outstripping even those of Earth, an incredibly elegant and expensive edifice built from the native stone, with towering spires that even Bleys (who fancied he had seen everything, most things more than once) found impressive.

A large ornate metal fence surrounded the lush, well-tended grounds, and the temple's steeple towered over the landscape. Atop it, at the highest point, stood a golden figure with a trumpet pressed to its lips. Ana had told him the name of the person it represented, something like Macaroni, but it didn't actually matter overmuch to Bleys. It wasn't important to the plan.

The plan, of course, was clever and would certainly work. Probably. He and Ana would enter the temple grounds as protesters and serve as a distraction. Vanov's people would set up out of sight. If anyone asked, they would say they were responding to reports of trespassers, right? Kane and Morgan were mixed in with them.

When Senator Dildohead made his appearance, Bleys would give the signal, and he and Ana would waylay the man. Vanov's people would cordon off the exits from the grounds, and Kane and Morgan would sweep in and grab the patsy. Then Ed would drop the *Doro* right in the middle of the grounds so they could make their escape.

Easy peasy.

Kane's voice buzzed in Bleys's earpiece, "He should be coming out soon. You two need to get in position."

Ana winced and adjusted her own earpiece as she handed Bleys a sign that read "Mormons = Tyrants!".

"Too loud?" Bleys asked.

Ana, still frowning, nodded. "Say something now, Kane."

"Get in position!" Kane repeated. "Spotter is watching the exit. Reed is coming out any minute now!"

As far as Ana was concerned, Bleys was having entirely too much fun with this, waving his sign and shouting at the top of his lungs, "Joseph Smith was a perv!"

Ana raised her own sign and frowned at it, not entirely pleased with the message: "Your Jesus is not the real Jesus!" This whole thing made her uncomfortable, really, making fun of people's religious beliefs, but they needed to look authentic. It felt doubly bad in that, at least until lately, she had counted herself as an atheist and had always felt above such bickering. Oh, she had gone through the motions in her youth, and she even still commemorated Yom Kippur and Hanukkah, but real belief had fled her once she had entered her teens. It was perhaps another reason to dislike Vanov, who seemed quite devout, with all of the baggage that entailed.

Though, being honest, coming back from the dead had made even atheism seem a little too neat and pat. The truth was that she now had personal knowledge that unearthly beings and disembodied entities damned well *could* revive the dead, so maybe the Mormons had the right of things.

With a sigh, she hefted her sign and shouted, "The Church is unfair to atheists!" If their god was watching, surely he would understand what they were doing and why.

Kane, sounding like a drill sergeant in her ear, shouted, "Move it, both of you! I need you in place ASAP!"

Bleys answered, "We're on our way." He set off at a brisk pace toward the main entrance to the temple. It was a normal enough driveway, unguarded, open to ground car traffic, and he and Ana crossed onto the grounds with no trouble beyond a few odd looks from the temple attendees who were in the parking lot.

But then, that was the plan, to draw attention.

Ed's voice chimed in, "*Doro* is standing by, ETA two minutes after you confirm for pickup."

"Two minutes?" Bleys shouted. "That's some crazy flying. You better not trash my ship, Ed!"

Ed sounded amused when he answered, "With no biologicals aboard, it's much simpler."

"You already messed up my guns," Bleys told him. "They're blue now instead of green!"

Kane shouted, "Knock off the chatter! Spotter says he thinks Reed is exiting now. Get in there!"

Ana and Bleys broke into a run toward the front entrance to the temple, a covered area surrounded with carefully tended flowerbeds. Two great glass sliding doors opened as a group of six approached, talking amongst themselves and smiling.

Ana recognized the senator and his wife at once from holos Vanov had shown them. The other four wore dark glasses and had suspicious bulges beneath their jackets, marking them as armed. "Kane, it's him," she huffed as she ran. "We're on him now! He's got four security people with him!"

"We can handle four," Kane assured her. "On the way!"

Bleys, waving his sign, interposed himself between the senator and the street and shouted, "Senator! What are you doing to make sure non-Mormons have more representation in the Zion government?"

Ana followed him and was about to shout some silly complaint herself when the smell hit her full in the face: cinnamon and cloves, but something else as well, a horrible smell like a mixture of feces and gangrenous flesh.

Ana froze, struggling not to vomit as it rolled over her. The senator smiled at her, a synthetic, plastic smile expression, the fraudulent sign of a murderous infiltrator feigning peaceful intent.

She hesitated a moment, uncertain if she should play along, but behind her she heard the heavy metal thuds of Panzer-armored feet on the pavement and decided there was no time for anything but the truth.

"Kane!" she screamed as she tossed her sign on the ground and reached for her blaster. "He's infected!"

***

Kane watched in helpless fury as the senator's flesh boiled and tentacles sprouted from him, whipping and slashing at everyone nearby with serrated bone blades. The senator's broad smile broadened as his mouth grew into a huge maw, the air around him filling with the now familiar Pestilence trill.

Fortunately, Ana had warning. She shoved Bleys hard, making him drop his sign and sending him tumbling ass over teakettle across the manicured temple lawn.

The senator's wife screeched in terror, actually clutching at the side of her head and staggering back, barely avoiding one of the writhing limbs.

His security team, however, conditioned to stay near their

charges in a crisis, did not fare well. A slashing tentacle separated the closest man's head from his body, sending his head bouncing into the temple, trailing blood and gore. The man's body clutched at the stump briefly, then collapsed.

The senator continued to distort, becoming a pillar topped by a huge, gaping, fanged hole. It whipped its tentacles around another of the guards and hauled him into the maw, swallowing him whole as the man screamed in terror and agony.

"Get out of the way!" Kane roared through his speakers.

One of the security men took off at a dead run, unassing the area at high speed, but the last one simply stammered, a gibbering idiot, as the cicada sound rose and the tentacles whipped his way, slashing his legs from beneath him and then dragging his screaming remains into the ravenous mouth.

"Oh, my God!" the Senator's wife screamed, still clutching her head and backing away from the entrance. "Oh, my *God!*"

Kane leveled his M87 and unleashed a barrage of plasma. Morgan, alongside him, did likewise. The beast staggered under the searing blasts, flesh bursting open as its vital fluids flashed to steam and its flesh fell in charred ruins.

From the corner of his vision, Kane saw a flare of green, and what was left of the senator withered and collapsed into a pile of ash.

Bleys, looking haggard, holstered that damned illegal disintegrator and extended both hands as if he expected to be cuffed.

Kane was about to say something cutting when he heard more screaming. He spun toward the temple entrance and froze to see blood splattering against the interior of the glass surfaces.

"Vanov!" he roared. "We have a problem! You need to extend that cordon to the whole complex! Nobody gets in or out!"

Vanov, sounding annoyed, spoke over the comms, "What's your situation, Commander?"

"It's *hot!*" he shouted. "Pestilence is in the temple!"

The screaming grew louder, and a child's face pressed against the glass door for a brief moment before then vanishing beneath a crimson spray.

Bleys, sounding as if he were strangling, cried, "We gotta do something!"

Kane switched to a private channel. "Morgan, I'm on this. You're staying."

"The *fuck* I am!"

"That's an order, Lieutenant!" Kane growled.

"That's fucking *Emperor* to you, bitch!" Morgan shot back. "Run *toward* the gunfire, right?"

They didn't have nearly enough firepower, not if the place was even half as full as he expected. So the real answer was "No, we are not doing this. We're just choosing where we die, because we can't face living while we watch a bunch of women and kids get slaughtered." But what he said was, "Okay, brother. Let's roll."

---

On the *Dresden*'s bridge, Ed stood in one of his synthskin bodies, watching as Vanov shouted into her comms and directed her forces. In the pit of his being, where, were he human, his stomach might have been, he felt a jagged, baleful emotion, one that it took him some time to place. He had never experienced it personally, but his father had, in another life.

Humans called it "despair."

"Extend that cordon!" Vanov roared. "Nobody in or out! Lethal force is authorized!" She jammed at a button on her command chair and spoke again. "Kane! Get your ass out of there! That's an order!"

But Kane did not answer.

Ed realized, to his growing disquiet, that the only people he considered friends might well no longer exist in mere moments, and there was nothing he could do about it. How horrible, to have no options, no way to help, to only be able to give commands that might or might not be obeyed. What a tremendous fall, from being the god of Avalon to this dark pit where he was utterly helpless, in a situation where no amount of thought or genius could find a solution to the problem at hand.

Today, intellect would bow to brute force it seemed.

"Kane!" Vanov shouted again.

Ed's mood grew even darker as he realized the truth: there was a reason he had never experienced this feeling before, and it was simply this—he had never cared enough about anyone such that he might find even the most catastrophic events very disturbing. He had viewed the death of the entire galaxy as a notable, but not distressing, event.

Ed found himself speaking without fully having intended to do so. "How can you bear it?" he asked Vanov. "This helplessness?"

Vanov looked at him with surprise, then understanding. "With as much dignity as possible," she sighed. "And prayer. Prayer helps."

"I have never prayed before. Do you suppose God would care about my prayers? I fear I may have many sins for which to account."

Vanov grunted. "Mine? I doubt it. But Smith's god is a more forgiving sort." She nodded toward her lieutenant, who looked up from his weapons console at the sound of his name. "Maybe he can give you a few tips."

## 10

## SUFFER THE LITTLE CHILDREN

Brother Caleb toweled off the water from the ritual of drowning, trying to fully appreciate the significance of the act. As he understood it, he had been symbolically drowned in the place of another, one who was already dead, but who had not experienced this symbolic drowning and therefore could not progress toward The Source.

It was difficult to fully grasp, and the sister missionaries had taught Brother Caleb a charm from one of the books for just such occasions, where he needed to perform a task but could not understand why. "I know not," Brother Caleb whispered to himself as he dried water from his body, "Save the Lord commanded me."

The Bishop, smiling from a bench on the other side of the changing room, dried himself as well. Brother Caleb averted his gaze slightly, knowing from the memories of his host that it was improper to gaze directly at another nude human, especially if they were of the same sex. This rule changed if one were about to engage in reproductive activity, or if contemplating an image of the person, but in other circumstances it was…. Brother Caleb rummaged through Marshall's knowledge and at last came up with the word "creepy."

It was, Brother Caleb thought, a good word.

Brother Caleb still did not completely understand the full social ramifications of human sexuality. In truth, he still found the idea of sex confusing in general, "creepy." There seemed little purpose in dividing a species into male and female or requiring a complicated interface in order to expand the biomass.

But then, there was also little sense in having complicated social rituals, yet the humans had them for many simple biological processes, including the elimination of wastes, though, Brother Caleb noted, not for the consumption of nutrition. He couldn't help but wonder why and consoled himself with the charm from the book again.

"So, what did you think?" The Bishop asked. "Did you feel the spirit?"

Brother Caleb nodded. He had, indeed, felt something powerful, an emotion he could not identify, but that he had come to associate with what his new Colony called the Holy Ghost. In many ways, it was like the Song, only very quiet, subtle, enough so that Brother Caleb had to concentrate very hard to appreciate it.

"Good," The Bishop said. "We did the Lord's work today. I'm glad you came. The Pestilence took so many before their time. We need every volunteer we can find."

Brother Caleb, filled with self-loathing, ducked his head, ashamed to even meet The Bishop's gaze. How could his people have done this thing, cut off so many from returning to The Source?

Then came The Song, and Brother Caleb felt his innards fill with dread.

*Freedom!* The Colony Sang, its voice savage with joy.

Brother Caleb felt the blood retracting from his extremities and into his core, his body preparing to do battle or flee.

His pallor must have been visible to The Bishop. "Brother Caleb, are you feeling ok?" the man asked.

Brother Caleb shook his head, panic rising within him as he listened to the Colony rejoicing in its liberation. *Free to consume! Free to evolve!*

In the showering place, all was silent, save for the drip of a single droplet of water from a showerhead as The Bishop continued to stare at Brother Caleb with growing alarm.

Then came the screams. They were close, just outside the showering place, perhaps even from the font of drowning.

The Bishop leapt to his feet and quickly rummaged through his locker for his underwear and began struggling into it. It was special, Brother Caleb knew, though he had only ordinary underwear. It offered no spiritual protection like the Bishop's did, but it would at least cover him.

The Bishop continued to dress in great haste, and as he neared completion of the process, he reached again into the locker and withdrew a weapon.

Brother Caleb blinked in surprise. He had not known The Bishop possessed a gun, nor that the man carried it with him. Brother Caleb regretted not bringing the gun from his own dwelling now. He had never actually used the device, thinking that since it did not actually belong to him, he should leave it undisturbed. Marshall however, had known it well and had used it many times, practicing for a battle he intended to have with the Bossman and the Other Scumbags.

Trapped in human form, Brother Caleb thought that he might well find a weapon useful at some point, and if his time with the Church had taught him anything, it was that being prepared was important.

Clearly, The Bishop understood this lesson better than Brother Caleb.

They were close now, the Colony Appendages, and many,

more than ten, growing, assimilating. Soon, they would assimilate everyone.

For the life of him, Brother Caleb could not think how to stop them.

The Other froze at the door to the showering place. It sensed him, Brother Caleb was certain.

*Do you claim this food?* it Sang.

Brother Caleb had not Sang for many periods of time. It felt as if he may have forgotten, but his voice rang out strongly, *He is not food! He knows the way to The Source!*

The Other burst through the swinging door entrance, into the showering place, its Song loud and full of malice, its bulk no longer remotely human. *Then we will know too, once we consume it.*

It moved slowly over the blood-slicked tiles, creeping into the showering place on small, insectile legs, a single, baleful eye glaring from a mound atop its central mass. Gore dripped from savage bone scythes at the end of five long, whip-like limbs that extending from its torso.

Brother Caleb rose and Sang furiously at it. *No! The way is not a path through space! It is a way of thinking! You cannot follow it if you assimilate them without permission!*

The Bishop gaped at The Other in horror, as if something inside him had broken. He tried to raise his weapon, but it was as if all the strength had fled his arm. He stammered unintelligibly and a thin stream of drool ran from the corner of his mouth.

The Other evolved an eating orifice and hissed as it pushed teeth into place. *You are a fool. Join with us now or die.*

Brother Caleb shouted to the Bishop, "Run!"

If The Bishop heard, he gave no sign. He remained frozen, trembling, as The Other swung its limbs in savage arcs, piercing The Bishop's flesh over and over, and began devouring him on the spot as he screamed.

While The Other was distracted with feeding, Brother Caleb lunged forward and dove for The Bishop's fallen weapon.

The Other emitted a squeal of rage and Sang, *Traitor!*

Repeated bursts of searing energy from the weapon quickly silenced it. Brother Caleb watched the smoking corpse for an awed moment, then gave the weapon an admiring look. He knew from his studies that killing was wrong, but in defense of the lives of the righteous, it was sometimes necessary, as Captain Moroni had demonstrated in The Book.

Other Appendages of the Colony Sang their fury. *You will be destroyed, traitor! You will be rended! We take your flesh and spit out your knowledge!*

Brother Caleb found himself unmoved by their threats. He had a powerful weapon now, more powerful than any transformation. But more so, he had The Lord with him. These rebellious Appendages would see what happened when they incurred the wrath of The Source! *I swore a covenant! These people are my Colony now! And I will destroy you if you force me to!*

*Then die, fool!*

Someone, a woman, was screaming outside the showering room, "My God! Protect the children! They're trying to get into the nursery!"

*You are the fool! This is The Way!* Brother Caleb Sang as he ran toward the nursery, his weapon clutched in his hand and a prayer on his lips. "Lord, give me the strength to overcome them and protect your children, in the name of The Jesus Christ, Amen."

---

"Holy shit!" Morgan said. "Chief, can you believe how many of these bible thumpers got guns?"

It *was* a little surprising, now that Morgan mentioned it. Kane had waded in fully expecting to hold off another dragon or two long enough to let a few women and children escape, then die, hopefully well. After the Battle for the *Danzig*, he and Morgan both knew damned well what they could be up against and the odds they were facing.

But as it turned out, Ed had the right of things earlier. These church guys had fine taste in guns, some of them using gear Kane would have been proud to carry himself. There were no rifles, just the sort of handguns men might conceal under a jacket, but they were effective for all that. A small group, all in their Sunday best, had organized and were busy blasting away over a makeshift barricade of chairs and sofas, clearing a path for screaming women and children as Pestilence creatures lunged from the dusty, debris filled inner reaches of the building.

"Imperial marines!" Kane roared as he approached the closest shooter, a man hunched over the back of a toppled couch. "Who's your leader!"

To Kane's surprise, the man looked up, then snapped to attention and saluted. "I guess that'd be me, sir! Dan Putnam!"

Kane reflexively started to ask who the man was calling sir, then remembered his rank was literally emblazoned on his chest now. This man knew what it meant, meaning he likely had served himself. "What's your status?"

"The enemy is aggressive but stupid, sir!" Putnam said as he turned back to the building interior and leveled his weapon, scanning as best he could through the smoke and debris. He snapped off a shot at a target Kane could just barely see even with Gunther's enhancements, and in the distance something inhuman screamed.

So they were dumb Pestilence, which was good. Reed must have been controlling them, and now that he was dead, the damned things had run wild, but they had no plan beyond rush forward and attack. "Nice shooting!" he said.

"Thanks, sir. We've lost a lot of people, but I think we've cleared almost all of the survivors. There's just one more area, the—"

Kane stiffened as Gunther drew a good dozen yellow triangles on his visor.

Morgan yelled from beside him, "Get *down!*"

The fireteam complied, and Kane and Morgan launched multiple salvos of plasma into the darkened recesses of the temple. Pestilence creatures shrieked and died, and priceless architecture shattered under the heavy fire.

Kane winced at the collateral damage. "Sorry about your church, man!"

"It's a temple, knucklehead!" Morgan called, still firing.

"The Lord knows what we're facing," Putnam replied. "I think he'll be forgiving."

*He'd better be*, Kane thought, though he didn't say it. Odin would surely be proud of his temple being destroyed if it were in pursuit of killing an enemy. Well, and if Odin had a temple to start with, which he didn't.

"You said there are people left?" Kane asked.

"Yes, sir!" Putnam called. "There's a nursery full of about twenty children and several women. It's a secure area, so unless one of them was infected, they are probably safe, but not for long."

Kane nodded and said to Morgan, "I'm gonna get those kids out. You with me?"

"Straight to Hell, chief," Morgan told him.

Kane nodded then switched his comms back to the team. "Ana, Bleys, we got refugees coming out the front! You need to sort them out! And do *not* let them escape! Vanov, you on the horn here?"

Vanov, her voice angry, called back, "Kane, I gave you a direct order!"

"Sorry, Admiral, I missed it. We have a Class A clusterfuck situation here! The whole goddamn temple is infested! We have zero containment, repeat zero containment!"

Vanov answered, "My people are holding the line outside the perimeter. You and your men need to get the hell out of that building. I'll handle the rest from here."

Kane ground his teeth at this. He had a pretty good idea of what she was planning, and it was probably necessary, but he needed more time. "Admiral, we have a whole nursery full of kids we need to get clear!"

"How long will it take?"

Kane looked to Putnam and said through his speakers. "How far to the nursery?"

"A hundred yards, maybe? There's heavy enemy presence, though. It will be tough going."

Kane ground his teeth again. Vanov was not going to like his answer, but he gave it to her anyway. "At least fifteen minutes."

"Too long, Commander. I don't have enough men to hold the cordon if those things break out. Clear that building now!"

"There's twenty fucking kids in here!" he roared.

"There are a lot more of them outside the temple!" she shouted back. "You have the better part of a minute to get clear while we lock and load. I suggest you make use of it."

"Goddammit!" Kane roared, not really caring what "The Lord" thought of such language, and hammered a fist against the wall hard enough to smash a hole in the polished marble. "Morgan, we gotta get 'em out *now*! Vanov is gonna nuke the whole site!"

Morgan, still firing into the billowing smoke, said over the comm in an amazingly calm voice, "Belay that, Vanov. We're rescuing those kids. *Then* you can secure the site."

For a moment, Vanov didn't answer, but when she did, her

voice was filled with contempt. "I don't care for your tone, *Lieutenant*."

"You got my rank wrong," Morgan asserted.

"You're a pretty face and a clever ruse!" Vanov cried. "I don't answer to you!"

"Wrong. You answer to me, and so does everybody else. Ed, if Vanov tries to pull the trigger, put the *Dresden* down."

---

Aboard the *Dresden*, Vanov drew her sidearm and pointed it at Ed. "Will you hear my counterargument, 'Emperor'?"

She fired, blasting most of the android's head away in a spray of molten plastic, silicon, and metal. The android's corpse dropped to the floor, spewing blue smoke and hydraulic fluid.

"I trust you know the sound of a blaster discharge?" she told Morgan. "Thirty seconds left," she told them. "You still have time to get clear if you move now."

She shook her head sadly, eying the ruins of Ed's body. "Mister Al Jahar, store his body until we can give him a decent burial." She turned back to the viewscreen and began pacing. "Mister Smith, time on target for torpedoes?"

"Forty-five seconds, ma'am."

"That's a little more than I promised. Fire tube 1."

## 11

# THE VALLEY OF THE SHADOW

S mith, his voice an octave higher than normal, called out, "Admiral! *Danzig* is powering all weapons and is locked on to the *Dresden!*" A moment later he yelped, "*Danzig* is firing railguns!"

Vanov clenched her jaw, waiting for the blow and, assuming she survived, the inevitable damage report. She had underestimated her enemy and would pay the price for it. "I guess we'll see how much mercy an AI is willing to show. My guess is not much."

Long moments passed without incident before she finally asked, "What the hell is he firing on?"

Smith breathed a sigh of relief. "Our torpedo, ma'am. It's been destroyed."

"But he's still targeting us as well, yes?"

Al Jahar wiped sweat from his brow and announced, "Admiral, incoming transmission from the *Danzig*."

Vanov sighed and rubbed at her temple. This was beginning to feel repetitive. "Put him on."

Ed's smiling face appeared on the primary viewscreen. "As you can see, that was of no use whatsoever. It was wasteful."

"I saw a chance and I took it. Where does that leave us?"

"I take no pleasure in this, admiral, but if you don't power down your weapons at once, I *will* fire on you."

If she could have seen any chance of success, she would have ordered Smith to launch all tubes and let the AI do its worst. Stopping the Pestilence from overrunning Zion would be worth sacrificing her crew, but she had seen the *Danzig* annihilate an entire fleet in a matter of minutes under the AI's control with one hundred percent accuracy. He would have no trouble shooting down her torpedoes *and* slaughtering her people, and their sacrifice would be meaningless.

Vanov, her heart heavy, sighed again, defeated. If Zion fell, her fleet was one of the few pockets of humanity left. She was checkmated, unless the AI would see reason. "Will you really allow millions to die just because that idiot told you to?"

Ed seemed genuinely hurt. "Not at all," he told her. "Admiral, I am not your enemy, and I have a clean solution. I just need your men to hold the cordon until we can clear the building and I can move the *Danzig* into position. I can cleanse the infection without destroying the building and without collateral damage. You and I both know the odds of any of our people surviving that warhead you launched are slim to none, even if they do evacuate."

"It's the best I can do! We sent a crew to block the streets, not secure the entire perimeter. I don't see another way, not with billions of lives at stake."

"Forgive me for saying so, Admiral, but your intellect is considerably less than my own. I am confident in my solution."

Vanov answered him through clenched teeth, "You have a gun to my head. You don't need my approval." She turned to Smith. "Stand down, Lieutenant."

"Thank you, Admiral," Ed told her. "I promise you, this is a better way. Just hold the cordon a bit longer."

Vanov, feeling nauseated at what a mistake here could mean, ran a hand over her face. "I hope you're right."

Kane, kneeling beside Putnam, fired again into the clouds of dust, grateful that Gunther could distinguish the civvies from the hostiles and mark them for him. Another woman, this one clutching a baby to her chest, came running out of the smoke, screaming in fear as a dog-like Pestilence creature nipped at her heels.

Kane put a blaster bolt between its eyes, and it dropped to the ground, smoking.

Putnam had been wrong. There were a lot more inside, people who had come running once they realized they had a chance, and every group brought at least a few hostiles with them. Fifty people, maybe more, had pushed past the barricade in the last few minutes, and according to Gunther, more were coming in a steady stream.

"They're stacking up here, Chief!" Morgan yelled. "We got geeks hitting the stragglers!" He punctuated his remark with a stream of blaster fire.

Kane looked over his shoulder to see that it was indeed bad. The main entrance was jammed half open. It had lost power, or seized, or something. Maybe Morgan knew. But the thing wasn't opening correctly, and the exit was choked with refugees, all terrified and struggling to remain calm as they slowly squeezed through.

"I'm on it!" Kane replied, raising his rifle.

Putnam spun in alarm and grabbed Kane's arm, shaking his head vehemently. "It's transteel, sir! It won't break like you think!"

"Are you kidding me?" Kane yelled, shaking his head in denial. "A hardened Church?"

"It's a temple, chief," Morgan corrected him. "More geeks incoming! A bunch!"

As Morgan and the rest of the fireteam laid down a blanket of plasma, Kane said, "Gunther, load VB-5s. I need an overlay of the blast radius."

It was tight, but he could do it. Civvies might end up deaf for the next ten minutes, but that was better than the alternative.

Kane yelled over his speakers at the milling crowd near the exit, "Make a hole!"

They all stared blankly at him.

"That means get the fuck out of the way unless you wanna get blowed the fuck up! Back and against the barricade! Cover your ears! Do it *now!*"

---

Ana, her nose full of cinnamon and cloves, fired her blaster furiously at the beast before her. It screeched and writhed in agony, tentacles and claws flailing, but made no move to attack her. She felt a tiny twinge of guilt at killing something that wasn't a threat to her, but she kept firing. This thing would happily murder anyone *but* her.

The Hippocratic oath didn't protect cancer, and that was what the Pestilence was, really: a sentient, transmittable cancer that had to be excised at all costs.

She saw movement out of the corner of her eye, a shadow edging toward Bleys and screamed, "Behind you!"

He spun, leveled the disintegrator, and fired. The creature flashed and collapsed into ash. Ana felt a slight chill watching him like this. The man she knew was warm, funny, generous, and caring. But he had a ruthless side too, one she very rarely saw because, she felt certain, he didn't *want* her to see it. The simple fact that he had no qualms carrying the weapons he did spoke volumes, though. His speed and accuracy, likewise, were not some happenstance of birth; they were skills he had invested a great deal of time cultivating. The man had clearly been involved in as much gunplay as Kane, maybe more, and probably in worse circumstances. She didn't know precisely. Whenever she broached the topic, he would always change the subject or make a joke, which left a huge section of who he was opaque to her.

Admittedly, the mystery was sexy, but it would need to go away if this thing were to become more permanent.

She looked about to verify that the immediate threat was over, then reached for her medical kit and produced one of several hypos she had there. "Bleys! Over here! Quickly, while we have time."

Bleys grimaced. "Are you kidding me? Needles in the middle of a gunfight?"

"It's been several days. We should top off *now* just in case."

Reluctantly, Bleys pulled up his shirt and winced as she administered the serum.

"Get *back!*" one of Vanov's men yelled. Ana spun to see several people trying to exit the compound, and the guard waving his weapon in their direction. He fired a burst at the ground in front of them. "No one in or out until we can test you!"

"You can't do this!" one of then, a frail, elderly woman shouted back.

"Ma'am, if you try to escape this compound prior to testing, we *will* use lethal force! Use your head! We can't risk it."

A man standing with the older woman, probably her son, put an arm around her and gently guided her away from the gate, whispering in her ear. The guard stepped back, a miserable expression on his face.

"Shit duty, for sure," Ana muttered under her breath. Nobody wanted to shoot old ladies, but it was a quarantine situation. It might be necessary.

Ana eyed the Reed woman, feeling little for her beyond disgust. Reed was a wreck, trying vainly to rearrange her ruined hairdo and sobbing uncontrollably, makeup running and making her look more like the clown she was.

And she reeked! It wasn't polite to note, especially as a physician, but Ana was fairly certain the woman had shat herself in the chaos. Ana would do her duty to keep Reed alive, but she couldn't do much about the deep revulsion she felt for the woman. Reed was a weak, kept creature, exactly the sort that Ana most despised.

Ana stepped toward Reed with the hypo. "You need to take this. It's an inoculation against the pestilence."

The Reed woman started, then climbed to her feet, suddenly furious, shouting, "I won't let you put your poison in me! Where is Vanov? I demand to speak with her at once! This is her doing!"

Bleys boggled, then shouted back, "Lady, we're busy trying to keep her from nuking us from orbit! Take a fucking number!"

The ground shook suddenly, and a great orange fireball rolled from the temple entrance, accompanied by a hail of marble and glass shrapnel. Instinctively, Ana bent to shield her "patient." Reed, in response, shoved her rudely aside.

Bleys, looking up, looked up even further and muttered, "Shit," then, more urgently, "*Shit!*"

Ana followed his gaze and gawked at what she saw: the golden statue of Moroni atop the great steeple was teetering back and forth. For a moment, she was certain it would fall, but it suddenly stabilized, canted and precarious, but for the moment still in place.

"Kane!" Bleys shouted over the comms. "What you are guys *doing* in there?"

Kane laughed in her ear. "Remodeling for better Feng Shui!"

A river of refugees began pouring from the gaping hole in the front of the building now, and Ana felt her heart sink. Who knew how many of them were infected? She glanced toward the gate, noting how few guards there were.

This could turn very bad.

Ed's voice came over her earpiece. "*Danzig* is in position. I am recalibrating the primary gun to emit a surgical gamma ray burst. Let me know when you have cleared the building, Commander. It will be absolutely lethal for any biologicals present."

"Affirmative," Kane answered. "Bleys, we gotta go through a real shitstorm to reach these kids, and you're gonna hate this, but I need Ana. There are too many kids to take any chances. We need her to give 'em a sniff."

Bleys clenched his jaw and looked at Ana, fear in his eyes. "You don't have to do that. You know that, right?" he said. "You can say no."

"Don't worry," she smirked. "You're coming with me. We can die together, eh?"

He grinned at her and laughed aloud. "This is your idea of romantic, isn't it?"

Ana shrugged and smiled innocently. "Russian, remember?"

Reed, suddenly understanding, screeched, "You're not leaving me here alone!"

Ana, thoroughly disgusted by this pathetic creature, sneered at her. "It's triage. You're stable."

"You tell Vanov I will have her head for this!"

Bleys popped her a thumbs up. "Will do!" He switched the disintegrator to his left hand and took Ana's with his right. "Come on, babe. It's a date!"

"With death," Ana quipped.

"I guess he can come if he wants, but he's paying for his own dinner."

Brother Caleb made his way steadily toward the nursery, but it was slow going. Many Other Ones, more Appendages of the Colony, challenged him, but the gun gave him a distinct advantage. Physical conflict between his kind were typically wars of attrition. One struggled to control the flesh of The Other, to push The Enemy out of its own body and claim it as One's own, an inevitably slow process unless One was much larger than The Other.

The individual Appendages running rampant throughout the building did not understand the advantage of weapons beyond those they could form from their own flesh: talon and tooth and tentacle. They were young and had little knowledge. They had not watched television, nor had they risen from a single host that possessed knowledge of its own. They did not realize that biting or clawing Brother Caleb was a largely useless endeavor, nor did they understand what the gun would do to them. They would learn soon enough, but hopefully by then, Brother Caleb and the children would be gone.

As for Brother Caleb, he was truly glad for the weapon, not just for the combat advantage it gave him, but for the ability to attack from distance. Every blow they struck, every oozing talon or fang that pierced his flesh transferred bits of dark, terrifying knowledge that he had no desire to possess. It accreted like spattering blood in his mind, a drip here, a dab there, spotty, but more than enough to understand many a bitter, terrifying truth.

Perhaps it would be best if none of his kind survived, including him. Better to use the weapon and burn them, destroy all that they were, all that they knew.

He had *misunderstood.*

His isolation had left him naïve, unaware of what he was and where he had come from. But battling the Appendages, touching their flesh, he could no longer remain in blissful ignorance. The wrongness, the evil of the Colony burned his mind and soul as Brother Caleb's weapon burned their flesh, tore at him with terrible visions and knowledge so abominable that he was tempted to concentrate it in a non-vital portion of his anatomy and burn it away, to un-know the horror, to forget, to go back.

And yet, that would be an even greater sin. As The Jesus had done, Brother Caleb would drink from the cup the Lord placed before him. He would endure to the end, as he had covenanted with The Lord. If he were fortunate, he would die, again as the Jesus had done, but perhaps, if the Lord was merciful, he would not be reborn, simply fade into darkness.

The truth was too much to live with.

Most of The Appendages were indeed ignorant, but One among them had touched The Source in a brief moment when The Evil One lost control. The Evil One's Vengeance had left the Appendage's mind in ruins, hopelessly scrambled. The Twisted One was barely able to function beyond the most primitive of behaviors such as eating and attacking. Yet, the mark of The Source was indelibly impressed in its flesh, and blasphemy etched into its genetic code.

When it jammed its spiny appendages into Brother Caleb's flesh, the message became a part of him as well.

What a fool Brother Caleb had been. The Evil One, the entity he had imagined to be The Adversary, was a *tiny* thing, a speck, compared to The Source. And The Source....

Brother Caleb forced himself to face the truth, even as he fired at more scrambling appendages. And the truth was that The Source was not Heavenly Father. The Source was a destroyer of agency and a devourer of souls.

The Source was The Adversary.

Brother Caleb and all like him were not and never had been

children of Heaven. They were the Devil's spawn, existing only to bring horror and death.

And yet, as unlikely as it was, Brother Caleb knew he was still called to serve The Lord. He was the only one who could succeed in the task, and so it fell to him, a child of Hell, to protect the children of Heaven.

Even the Adversary's spawn had their agency.

He would have to hurry. If they did not escape The Temple soon, they would not leave at all. From the Song and touching The Others, he had learned that the Appendages were the least of his concerns. The true horror was twisting its way up from below, a danger beyond anything Brother Caleb had imagined.

The Seed Appendage, the true voice of the Colony, had discovered vast stores of nourishment beneath The Temple some time ago. Over time it had grown to enormous size, somehow keeping the knowledge from The Evil One, much as Caleb had with his own actions when he had studied with the Missionaries and eventually joined The Church.

Now, with nothing to fear from The Evil One, and no need to Pretend and wait for The Right Time, the Seed would act. The Right Time was *now.* For the moment, The Seed was busy gorging on the remaining stores beneath The Temple, but soon it would exhaust them and come looking for more to devour. By then, it would be too immense to combat.

In truth, it probably already was.

Brother Caleb and the children's only hope would be to escape the Temple, though even that might be short lived. When the Colony escaped, it could well consume the entire world. Brother Caleb would simply have to hope the humans had a means of stopping it. He did not possess enough knowledge to predict the outcome.

He could only do his ninety percent as best he could, and trust in The Lord to make up the difference. The Lord would not command him to do a thing without providing a means to succeed. The Sisters had taught him that.

"I know not, save the Lord commanded me," he whispered to himself. "Endure to the end."

Almost there, now. He fired his weapon as another small Appendage skittered toward him, ending its life process. Ahead, the automated door to the nursery bounced open and closed, over and over, unable to seal because it was blocked by a headless woman's corpse.

Inside, the children were screaming. They stood on tables, clutching at one another, as a single Appendage, too small to reach them, leapt frantically. Two adult women, one old and one young, moved back and forth on the tables, swinging at the Appendage with a broom and a mop. Soon, it would learn and climb atop other furniture or project parts of itself upward. It would find a way to reach them, and then it would devour them.

Brother Caleb hauled the corpse from the doorframe and charged in, firing the weapon at the Appendage, but his shot was poor. The Appendage screeched at the glancing blow, then charged Brother Caleb. The second shot caught it squarely in the chest and sent it to the floor in a charred heap.

Brother Caleb turned to the door and made certain it was secure as the children continued to scream. They were safe, though. He sensed no more Appendages within the confines of the nursery.

The woman with the broom, gasping, burst into tears.

"Do not be afraid," he called. "The Lord will protect you." He said the words, but they did little on their own. Comforting was not a skill he had mastered.

*Traitor!* The Colony screamed in Song. *We will rend the children before you, then break your flesh and consume you too! We will spit out all of your knowledge!*

*God will stop you. He will send aid.*

*Fool!*

*God will send aid.*

They came, then, by tens, by hundreds, pouring into the corridor and hammering at the door and windows, their flesh twisting and merging together. The transteel distorted under their assault, and Brother Caleb's faith wavered.

Perhaps it was not the Lord's Will that the children survive after all. He readied the weapon for one last task. If he could not save them, he could spare them the assimilation. He knew now, having witnessed it, that it was an agonizing process.

If it was the Lord's will that they die, Brother Caleb would ease their passing as best he could. He could not follow, but he would see them safely in the Lord's Arms.

Then he would face the rest of his kind alone. He would, as promised, endure to the end, however painful.

Here, in the depths of despair, he felt light surround him like wings, and his soul filled with strength and hope. Strong allies were near, a healer and mighty warriors! He could feel them!

The Lord had sent Angels to stand with them!

# THE POWER AND THE GLORY

At first, Ana thought she was going mad.

That was the typical assumption when one began hearing voices, after all, though she quickly realized that the voices she was hearing were in fact external. It wasn't imaginary.

And it had something to do with her new body.

It was more than words. She could hear those too, but she realized it was more of a translation, her own brain substituting words for concepts, barely above a whisper. But behind the words, stronger and deeper, powerful emotion hammered her: rage, hatred, hunger, and despair.

*Traitor!*

*We will rend!*

*Escape!*

*Hunger!*

Ahead, Kane fired a long burst, and unseen creatures shrieked and skittered. Behind, Morgan did the same. In the middle, she and Bleys crept along, largely blind in the smoke- and-debris-filled corridor, and with the sound of blasters and screaming, practically deaf as well. From somewhere within the building, a steady banging resonated, reminding Ana of nothing so much as when one of the Reforged had tried to batter its way into her lab on Cerberus. Something was hammering at a metal surface, *many* somethings, and surely that was where her party needed to be, but it was difficult to nail down the direction.

Bleys kept his weapon level as they moved, progressing at a snail's pace, grim faced and pale. She caught his eye and offered a wan smile, wondering if he could somehow hear the voices too, but he just nodded and kept moving.

She had almost grown accustomed to the murmurings in her head and the banging sounds, when suddenly a loud, clear voice rang out, as if from right next to her. *Angels! The children perish! Aid us!*

So strong was the sensation of having actually heard speech, she looked back and forth, expecting everyone else to stop and look for the source, but they continued forward.

Kane approached a T in the corridor and glanced right, then left. "It's clear," he announced, and beckoned them forward into the left branch.

As soon as she passed the turn, the voice cried out again, *Don't leave us, Angels! We are here!*

It seemed crazy, but something in her knew it wasn't. It was *real.* She couldn't understand it exactly, but the voice was genuine, and only she could hear it. "Kane! It's the wrong way."

Kane looked back at her. "How do you know?"

"Trust me!" she said.

Kane eyed her a moment, the shrugged and pointed down the opposite side of the T. "Morgan, you're on point."

Morgan said nothing, simply turned and headed the other way, rifle ready. She hadn't seen him like this often, in actual combat mode, and it was a little frightening, the change that seemed to have come over him. She was used to thinking of him as the foul-mouthed joker who had twisted her arm into giving away her birthright of jalapeno cheese, but he was *also* a hardened killer.

And for all her familiarity with Bleys, he was different too, cold where he was usually warm, his hyper-vigilance on display instead of hidden behind jokes and wordplay.

Kane, on the other hand, was always the same. Though she had to wonder how he, too, would change around his family.

And as for her? Did she seem different to them now? Would asking them even generate anything useful? Morgan would ask for a fee for an honest answer. Bleys would tell a charming lie. Kane would tell her it was a stupid question and that she should stay focused on possible enemy contact.

Ahead, Morgan paused and muttered over the comms, "Holy shit…." A moment later, he howled, "Holy *shit!* Chief, get up here *now!*"

Kane spun and charged toward Morgan, shouting, "Make a hole!" as the entire corridor began to thrum and vibrate and Morgan laid down a hail of fire.

Bleys turned to keep an eye on the rear and flashed a grin at Ana as he quipped. "Sounds like rear guard is the place to be!"

"Oh, *fuck!*" Kane cried and opened fire at something, though Ana still couldn't see it through the billowing clouds of debris. "Ana, Bleys, get back! It's coming!"

*Ana! Angels! Hurry! The Seed comes!*

Ana felt panic rising in her, with no real understanding as to why. The voice was no one she knew and could well simply be the Pestilence trying to trick her, but something in her felt otherwise. "Kane, they're dying! We have to get to them *now!*"

Something roared loud enough to rattle the floor beneath Ana's feet, the sound a deep, burbling, resonating mixture of fingernails on slate and a bestial cry of fury and hunger.

*Rend you! Consume you! Traitor! Food that is not food!*

Suddenly, she saw it, something out of a fevered nightmare, a wall of twisted, mottled flesh that filled the corridor like sewage squeezing through a pipe. The semi-liquid mass, dotted with darting eyes and gnashing teeth, hurtled toward them like sausage being piped into a casing.

Bleys stepped forward and fired the disintegrator. The result was both impressive and disappointing. A roughly man-sized portion of the roiling mass flashed into dust and noxious vapor, but the creature seemed not to notice. It oozed together as it continued surging toward them.

"Get *back!*" Kane roared. He shoved Bleys hard and switched his M87 to continuous fire and Morgan did likewise, focusing twin, crimson beams of plasma on their attacker.

The beast roared as its flesh melted and charred under the searing assault, then retreated back down the corridor with a giant sucking sound, its flesh collapsing inward in a spiral like a flushing toilet as it fled, vanishing into the clouds of dust.

The corridor ahead glistened with a slick, wet coating. Just ahead, Ana could see a secure area, a transteel door and windows, and behind, children leaping and waving, the sounds of their cries muffled and overlaid with an odd static.

Something was wrong. The transteel seemed damaged, with some areas milky or even opaque, and others warped, distorting the light passing through the material and making the children look like they were being reflected in funhouse mirrors. Ana stepped forward for a closer look.

Kane reached out and grabbed her shoulder. "Listen," he said, and pointed into the corridor.

At first, she didn't understand, but gradually, her senses adjusted. The hissing, static noise was more of a sizzling, really, and some of the billowing dust was actually smoke emanating from the floor, ceiling, and walls.

And from her shoe?

*"Acid!"* she gasped as she staggered back, instinctively reaching to stop Bleys from moving forward as well. "My God! It was trying to eat through the transteel!" She kicked off her shoe

just in time. Another second and it would have been her foot melting instead of shoe leather.

The woman inside the nursery, an older lady with grey hair and the look of a schoolmarm, rushed forward, pushing past a younger woman and a man who reminded Ana of pictures of Jesus: beard, long hair, kind face. The woman jerked at the door handle several times, then screamed, "It won't open!"

Kane stepped forward. "How many?" he shouted.

The woman called back, "Twenty children and three adults!"

Kane gave her a thumbs up then turned back to the group. "Morgan, you got rearguard. Doc, I will breach the compartment and then take up a position just past the nursery in case that fucker comes back. You and Bleys are gonna have to get the kids out."

Ana pointed at her bubbling, melted shoe. "That's a no-go, Commander, unless you have some extra boots. And extra feet, maybe, too."

Kane scowled at the sight. "Shit. Ok, I have a plan." He stepped to the warped transteel door and dug his fingers into the seal as he shouted to the people inside, "Step back! Stay where you are! There's acid all over the place and it will melt you right down to the bone!" He spoke again, presumably to his computer, then sank his hands into the seal of the transteel door as if it were putty, twisting and then tearing it loose from its moorings with a high-pitched shriek of tortured metal.

Kane dropped the battered door on the ground in front of Ana. "Hey, it ain't my cloak, but it'll do, right?"

Ana eyed the already sizzling door. It didn't look long for this world. "We have to hurry," she told Bleys. "Let's go!"

As soon as they saw a path, the children rushed the opening, but for most, the gap between the nursery floor and the door on the ground outside was too large. The leap from the door to safety, too, was a little too long for young children. The two in front, a small boy and girl, eyed the acid, still sizzling and popping as it ate into the floor and stared at Ana with pleading eyes.

Before she could react, Bleys leapt past, onto the door, and with great effort straddled the gap. The door sank an inch into the already ruined floor, shifting a bit as it did. There was no telling how long it would last, but Ana's every instinct told her that time was quite short, minutes at most. Either the door or the subflooring would give way under their weight, and she had no doubt what the acid would do to flesh and bone.

Bleys extended an arm to the girl. "Come on, honey," he said in his absolute best and most charming tone, as if there were nothing wrong in the world. "I got you."

Ana straddled her end and took the girl from him, placing her safely past the acid, where the girl promptly collapsed, sobbing.

The others behind pushed forward, some whimpering, some crying. The man and woman inside did their best to maintain order, but panic had sunk its claws into the children. They jostled and pushed at one another, wailing for everyone to hurry.

One by one, each straddling the door on opposite sides, Bleys hauled the children out of the room and over the gap to the rapidly decaying door, and Ana transferred them to the other side.

Ana wasn't keeping count, but she knew they were almost halfway done when the door shifted beneath her with a low thud. A spiderweb crack spread slowly as she watched, approaching her now shoeless foot. "Bleys," she said as calmly as she could, knowing that if the children panicked, it would just make things worse. She caught his gaze and cut her eyes downward.

Bleys kept smiling but nodded, too. "Okay, kids! This is gonna get more fun! Faster and crazier, let's go go go!"

Kane, over the comms, added to Ana's incredible joy. "Something's happening here, guys." He followed this with a long burst of plasma fire. "It's coming back! You gotta clear that area *now!*"

Bleys let the smile slip, his face growing hard and determined. He reached for the two closest children, grabbed a child's wrist in either hand, and swung them like sacks of flour over to Ana, then swung back to retrieve more.

The children scrambled for footing atop the now wavy, irregular surface of the door. Ana flailed, trying to keep her balance while keeping the children from toppling into the acid. The door shifted and cracked again, audibly now, as she struggled to move the two children to safety.

"Bleys!" she cried. "We're out of time!"

"I know," he called back as he swung two more children across. They screamed and wriggled, pointing at the rapidly spreading crack. Ana felt something pop directly beneath her foot and adjusted her stance just in time to avoid the acid that bubbled up from the breach. It was now one more hazard to take into account as she took the two children from Bleys and swung them to the other side, desperately trying to keep her balance.

Four children left, and the two adults.

Kane, backing slowly toward them, still firing, roared, "Get out of there! I can't hold this thing back!"

Ana felt her guts twist as Bleys clenched his jaw and beckoned the children, his face pale. "Okay, all of you, we gotta go now."

"We can't fit!" a tiny, chubby boy protested.

"Sure we can!" Bleys said, his voice far cheerier than his expression. "Two of you climb on my legs, there, sport, and I'll haul you along!"

Reluctantly, the children approached him, and Bleys turned, two children in his arms, and two clinging to his legs, all, Bleys included, wearing expressions somewhere between confusion and terror.

Kane suddenly staggered backward, and the creature again loomed out of the smoke and debris. It surged forward like a battering ram and knocked him flying. Kane's brief flight ended with a resounding crash as he hit the unyielding transteel windows of the nursery and fell to his knees. "Go!" he shouted, firing with one arm while he waved the other in the opposite direction. "Get out *now!*"

The man in the nursery, who Ana decided to call Jesus for the moment, hesitated, but the young woman beside him did not. She danced delicately across the way, landed on the other side, and knelt to comfort the children.

The older woman came next. She leapt for the door, landing hard, and Ana's heart fell to hear the weakened metal crunch.

The woman's foot plunged through the compromised door and directly into the acid. She screamed and snatched her foot out of the hole, arms pinwheeling, but couldn't quite regain her balance. With a horrifying screech, she toppled face first into the acid and began to thrash about, her screams of fear quickly changing in pitch to cries of agony as the acid scoured the flesh from bones her wherever it touched.

Bleys staggered as the door continued to break apart, and the chubby little boy, terror in his eyes, lost his grip and fell. Ana rushed forward to catch him, and actually managed to grab his tiny hand, when the surface beneath her leg gave way. Her exposed foot plunged through the fragile door, and the child slipped from her grasp to topple into the acid with a gut-wrenching shriek.

The agony was instant and all-consuming, and not at all from her own body.

It was just the look of utter despair in the child's eyes and the knowledge that she had failed him.

Moments later, the pain from her foot caught up with her brain, and her vision went dark with agony. Idly, it occurred to her that even as bad as it was, it was nothing compared to the Pestilence assimilating her back on Elysium. She had only endured moments of that before her implants had burned out her brain and left her safe in Avalon, and even so, it had been a long season in Hell.

She watched in a haze as the great liquid beast shot tentacles toward both the woman and the child. The woman had been burned badly enough that she could no longer scream, but she continued to thrash. The boy, however, eyes bulging in terror, shrieked loud and long as the tentacles wrapped around his small form, his tiny hands reaching toward her, as if she could somehow save him.

Both woman and the child flashed to charred corpses as plasma burst over their bodies, and Ana sagged, the horror of everything welling in her. Perhaps this was as bad as her first death, after all.

Just before she passed out, Ana felt strong hands beneath her, lifting her and dragging her, and a soft, gentle voice spoke. "My turn to save you, angel."

She looked up through tear-filled eyes and smiled at the face of Jesus, his head surrounded by a pale nimbus. Through the fog in her head, she heard herself mumbling, "I guess the Mormons were right after all."

Blackness rolled over her.

---

Bleys promised himself he wouldn't throw up or freak out, and he had definitely seen a thing or two, but watching Kane fry the teacher lady and the little kid made him seriously consider taking a shot at the marine. The only reason he didn't, actually, was that he had both hands full of kids.

Well, that and the fact that Kane would have murdered him, and also, to a lesser degree, he understood why Kane had done it.

But, goddammit, shooting kids was not what Bleys had signed up for, that much was for certain.

And then he realized Ana was down too, and he suddenly found himself near a breaking point.

Kane pointed at him and shouted, "Bleys! Focus on the mission! Get those kids to safety! Morgan, you're with Bleys! I'll cover Ana!"

Morgan came charging up as Bleys shouted back at Kane, "Like hell!" He lowered the remaining children to the floor and said in as kind a voice as he could muster, "Ok, kids. You go with teacher and the nice marine. He'll keep you safe!"

Kane switched to a continuous beam and poured plasma at the oncoming monstrosity. The creature winced and pulled back briefly. "Fine! Get her and go! I have an idea, but I need you all gone first!"

Morgan gave the young woman a thumbs up, then knelt next to the terrified children and said, "Hey, kids! You know who I am? I'm the *Emperor!*"

Bleys shook his head in amazement. As panicked as the children were, this still somehow reached them, at least those old enough to understand what he was saying. They gasped, their mouths forming into perfect circles of surprise.

"That's right!" Morgan told them. "And guess what? I'm making you all honorary space marines! We're gonna fuck up some geeks and save *everybody*, ok? Stay behind me and pretend to shoot with your fingers, like this!" He pointed his fingers as if they were a gun. "Pew! Pew!"

Bleys couldn't help but snicker, even as he bent to help the teacher guy with Ana. He wasn't entirely clear what the difference between a church and a temple was, but he was pretty sure saying "fuck" in either one was considered a no-no. "You got a name, bro?" he asked the stranger.

"You may refer to me as Brother Caleb," the man answered,

his face remarkably placid for being surrounded by death, agony, gunfire, and death. (There was lots of death, so it bore repeating.)

Bleys had no desire to know what his own face looked like, so he made no comment about Caleb's, hoping for reciprocity. "Okay, on three, ready? Three!"

Caleb blinked a moment in confusion before lifting Ana on his side, and Bleys remembered that church people were a little light on humor.

As they dragged her, following Morgan and the kids as quickly as possible, Ana stirred briefly and groaned. "How bad is it?"

Bleys risked a look at her ruined foot, wincing at what he would see, then did a doubletake.

Her foot was not, in fact, ruined. It was sockless, sure, but it ought to have been melted right off the bone. In fact, there probably shouldn't have even been any bone left, either, just a smoking stump. The acid had worked a real trick on the other two people it had touched, but somehow, Ana's foot was a healthy pink.

"You're lucky," he told her.

"It smells like Christmas," she muttered and passed out again.

Kane called over the comms, "Ok, here we go!" Bleys heard a serious of muffled whump-whump sounds, followed by a string of explosions as if someone had lit a pack of firecrackers, only instead of firecrackers, it was dynamite.

The blasts hammered at him, uncomfortable in the confines of the passageway, but did him no real harm. Moments later, a ripping, rumbling sound caught up with him, and Kane came hurling toward him, a billowing cloud of debris filling the corridor behind him.

"I collapsed the passageway! That'll hold it for a few!" he declared. "Go! Go! Go! Ed, we're on our way out with the kids. We need support ASAP!"

Bleys felt a surge of relief to hear the AI's voice over the comms. "The *Doro* will be on the ground momentarily, and the *Danzig* is in position awaiting your final signal. I have calibrated the primary weapon to fire a gamma laser that will sterilize the temple grounds."

Bleys peered ahead through the dust, just barely able to make out Morgan—playing pied piper—the teacher woman, and a trail of nineteen children following behind him as he moved slowly toward the main entrance. "Ed, old buddy, old pal, tell me something? How are we going to know what's a safe location?"

"I will paint with a laser prior to firing the actual gamma beam," Ed told him. "I made it green, just for you. When everyone is clear, I will fire the primary."

"Will do," Bleys told him. "We're almost—"

He stopped short as the children began screaming again.

Morgan shouted over the comms, "We got contact at the entrance!"

Kane, jogging, pulled alongside Bleys. "How bad?"

"*Bad!*" Morgan answered. "They're everywhere!"

Bleys could hear them skittering and screeching now, and another sound beneath that, a low rumbling all around, like giant snakes pushing through the hallways that surrounded them. He looked at Kane and shrugged. "We gotta run for it and hope for the best."

Kane nodded. "Get Ana and the kids out. I'll cover you."

"Who's gonna cover you?" Bleys asked, doubtful.

"Me," Kane said, and pushed at Bleys's back. "Get 'em out of here, Bleys. I'm right behind you."

Bleys felt a strong urge to ask Kane if he were planning on dying in here, as some sort of penance, but in truth, if that was Kane's plan, it wasn't Bleys's place to stand in his way. "Ok, Rags. If we make it, I'll hold the flight for you." He turned to Caleb. "Hey, Chatty Cathy, you ready to run?"

Caleb nodded and picked up the pace, Kane jogging along behind. As they charged for the exit, Bleys thrilled at the familiar sound of the *Doro*'s engines, growing louder as she descended. From outside, he could hear Ed's voice over the *Doro*'s PA, echoing from the sides of the building, repeating, "Please step away from the green lit area. Lethal radiation is about to be deployed against the Pestilence."

Bleys could see the entrance now. Through the gaping hole in the front of the building, sunlight sparkled on spinning dust motes as *Doro*'s thrusters churned the air outside into a small hurricane and flattened the grass below where she was descending, still repeating Ed's warning. Refugees from the temple scattered to avoid being crushed. Vanov's troops waved weapons at any who strayed too near the gates.

Putnam and the other defenders, still in their dust-covered church clothes, held their foothold, Morgan on the front line with them, blasting away at dozens of insectile and dog-like creatures rushing their position.

Kane shouted over the noise, "Ed! We're coming out! Get ready!"

"I have been ready for five minutes and eighteen seconds," Ed answered. "I will fire once you have cleared the kill zone."

It hit Bleys suddenly that there had never been anything he wanted more than to get clear of this deathtrap, and that included women and credits too. He had somehow put it all out of his mind up to now, but on the precipice and looking toward the *Doro*, it was hitting him hard: the rivers of blood and filth, the soul-searing screams, the sight of the melting teacher and the chubby little boy's gruesome last moments and the smell of their charred corpses, the mind-frying alien nature of the Pestilence—it all added up to a real gut-punch.

He felt light-headed suddenly and staggered the last few steps, through the line of shooters and out into the fresh air and sunlight, the bright lime-green of the painting laser bathing the concrete beneath his feet. Pavement gave way to grass, and Bleys managed to trudge outside of the kill area before falling to his knees and heaving up the contents of his stomach.

From behind, Kane roared, "Shit! Here it comes! Break! Everybody, outside the killzone, *now!*"

Caleb, holding Ana's limp form upright, watched in silence as Bleys brought a sleeve to his lips to wipe, then, seeing the filth already there, thought the better of it.

Still on his knees, Bleys barely noticed as the rest of the defenders rushed past. He waved Caleb toward the *Doro*. "Get her onboard, pal. I'm right behind you."

Kane, his voice strident now, shouted, "Ed! Fire, goddammit! We're clear!"

"Sensors show human life forms still in the periphery of the kill zone."

Blaster fire erupted, and the near deafening cicada-like buzzing. Despite his nausea, Bleys reached again for his weapon and turned to see the horrific liquid beast, tentacles grasping, teeth gnashing, as it squeezed its massive bulk through the shattered entrance, Kane, Morgan, and Putnam hitting it with everything they had. Even as Bleys moved to join them for the last battle, the creature shot out a dripping, prehensile tendril like a frog's tongue and snatched Putnam off his feet by his arm. Putnam's exposed flesh burned and smoked where the tongue touched him, and he screamed and convulsed in agony and terror as the creature drew him forward. A maw filled with jagged teeth opened on the front of the creature and tore chunks from him as it hauled him into its mouth, chewing him and burning him alive.

Then he was gone, and the creature pushed again, bulging, slowly squeezing its putrescent bulk outward.

Bleys could have sworn the huge maw was smiling.

Kane roared, "Ed! We're dying down here! The damned thing is pulling us back in! Fire the goddamn weapon!"

"There are still civilians in harm's way!"

"If this thing gets out, the whole planet is dead! Do it *now*, Ed!"

As Bleys looked about, trying to work out what the problem was, the *Doro*'s landing gear touched down, her gangway already open, and Ed, in one of his synthskin bodies, leapt to the ground and ran past Bleys to the edge of the temple, where he vanished around a corner. Moments later, he reappeared, a tiny child no older than two in his arms. "Kill zone is clear. Firing in five…four…"

The Pestilence beast suddenly burst forth from the entrance like a bursting boil, spilling tons of hostile, formless, hungry flesh onto the grounds, well past the edge of the kill zone. It continued to flow, piling up, a filthy, undulating mass of red and purple, sprouting new tentacles and eyes as it flattened and spread. A glistening, acid-soaked tail, or perhaps more accurately, an umbilical cord, connected it to the remainder of its vast bulk still within the temple.

Numb, Bleys suddenly understood what they meant when they spoke of Red Carpet.

There was enough of it inside to doom Zion.

"One!" Ed called.

The air above the temple shimmered; thunder ripped through the grounds, and electricity sparked and danced along an invisible column rising into the sky as lethal radiation coursed down from the *Danzig*.

The Red Carpet thrashed and roared, its cries unearthly and full of alien menace as every part of it still inside the kill zone darkened, hardened, then flashed to greasy smoke.

Bleys drew both blasters and began firing at the still enormous portion of the creature that had managed to escape., and Kane and Morgan joined in.

It was too late, though. Bleys felt it in his gut. They had tried, but Zion had never had a chance. He was about to tell Ed that this was now a salvage op and they needed to save the children first, when a bolt of lightning struck the golden statue atop the temple, the thunder immediate and deafening. The statue flew and plunged toward the ground, spinning midair, to land dead center of the Red Carpet creature with a sickening squelch.

A second bolt of lightning split the sky overhead, so bright that Bleys was blinded. He felt the hair on his arms and his head stand up, and the shock of thunder was like a hammer to his chest.

When his vision cleared, he grinned at the sight before him. Nothing remained of the Red Carpet but smoke and char, grease and ash.

Bleys bent to pick up the small, golden bugle that had landed at his feet and smiled. Later, when he told this story in bars, he would claim that every eye on the living pile of shit went wide when the statue hit, just before the second strike, like the geek knew what was coming. In truth, he wasn't actually sure if *every* eye showed panic, but embellishing a tale was spacer tradition, especially when you had a souvenir.

He had his own Hula doll, now, to go along with the piece of the *Jaeger*.

## 13

## FALLOUT

na awoke with a start, the nightmare still close in her mind, a dream of being in a slaughterhouse with dying children and melting women. She managed a brief few moments of relief before memory flooded in.

It had been no nightmare. She was safe now, in Bleys's cabin, but not whole. She looked to her foot, knowing what she would see: ruined flesh, scored by the acid. Hopefully she could find a decently matching cybernetic, but it galled her to think just how little time she had been in possession of an entirely new body before damaging it badly enough that she needed replacement parts.

It took her a second glance to verify what her eyes told her: that her foot was just fine. Pink, healthy flesh shone in stark contrast to the ragged, charred remains of her boot. The sole and top were entirely gone, along with most of the rest, leaving her with what amounted to a bizarre leather ankle bracelet.

And yet, her actual foot was unharmed?

Impossible!

It was silly, but she felt the need to actually touch it, probing, prodding, searching for some sign, any that it had been immersed in caustic acid. She had *felt* her foot literally melting off her bones, and the bones themselves eaten away.

Yet now it was as perfect as if it had been newly made.

The realization crept into her mind, slowly at first, then crystalizing in an instant: it *had* been!

She rose quickly, frantic. Where had the Jesus guy gone? She checked the monitors, thankful (and not for the first time) of Bleys's paranoia. Morgan, rack monster that he was, lay sacked out in the crew's quarters, fast asleep. Aft storage was filled with their passengers. She watched a moment as the children milled about, at last catching sight of the man she was searching for: he sat comfortably against a bulkhead, a serene look on his face, seemingly harmless, though Ana had a growing suspicion that he was anything but.

She glanced briefly through the porthole to the cockpit. That infuriating Reed woman was gesticulating wildly and shouting, spittle flying from her lips, her hair and makeup still in ruins. Bleys, in his pilot's seat, rolled his eyes and kept his attention on the horizon. Ed, beside him, looked at the woman with a serene expression, while Kane, in the jump seat once again, glowered, his face darker than usual by a shade or two.

Ana couldn't make out what Reed was saying and had no desire to do so. If the senator's wife had not made it, Ana wouldn't have shed any tears. The woman was obnoxious, and worse, she was pitiful and weak. It wasn't a very Christian stance, but then, by her reckoning, Ana wasn't a very good Christian, anyway, stuck somewhere between a Jewish upbringing, an atheist indoctrination from her education, and a generic Christian ethos that she had picked up via a kind of osmosis from her deceased husband.

The Reed woman was someone else's problem for now. Bleys and the others would have to fend for themselves. It was their own fault for letting the harridan aboard to begin with.

Ana slipped into the central passage and made her way back to aft storage. Several of the children waved as she entered, and the young woman tending them smiled at her. "Jesus" nodded as she approached, a dopey, almost child-like grin on his face that reminded her, for no reason she could explain, of Lars.

She approached him, unsurprised at the scent of cinnamon and cloves. In the temple, surrounded by Pestilence, she hadn't been able to pick him out, though the mind talk had surely been a strong clue. Now she was certain.

But for all that, she sensed no malice in him. Again, as with Lars, he seemed more like a child than anything else, eager to please and uncertain of her intentions, but trusting.

Even so, part of her wanted simply to blast him, and it might still come to that, but not in front of the children. They had already endured far too much death and horror today, enough for a lifetime. Having grown up terrorized by communist rebels, she knew full well the sort of scars such things left on a young mind. She needed to isolate the man, whether it was to be an interrogation or an execution, and that could be dangerous, regardless of her eventual course of action. Still, so far, no Pestilence seemed to regard her as an enemy, and this one had clearly helped her. It had even been instrumental in rescuing the children too. She liked her odds, but she patted her jacket to make sure her blaster was still at her side, just in case.

"Hello!" she said with enthusiasm she didn't feel. She extended a hand to the man and smiled. "I'm Ana, the ship's doctor. How are you feeling?"

Jesus smiled again, nodding. "I am well. How are you?"

Ana gave him a doubtful look. "You're showing some signs of a concussion. I'd like to have a look at you, just to be on the safe side. Would you mind coming with me?"

The stranger looked confused for a moment, then smiled again and said, "I am Brother Caleb. I am well."

Ana gave him her best patronizing look, the one she gave all of her reluctant patients. "Let's just make sure, okay? One of your eyes seems dilated, and you're slurring your speech a little." She extended a hand. "Let me help you, Mister Caleb. Like you helped me."

Caleb rose, seeming a bit embarrassed, and took her hand. "I will follow you."

Pleased at how easy it had been, Ana led him back down the central passage and into the new and improved medbay.

The facilities were a far cry from the near-medieval, makeshift space she had been forced to work with when she first came aboard. Ed had really outdone himself with the retrofit. She had everything she could want for a full surgical suite, including the devices she most needed at the moment: a neural inhibitor and privacy screening, complete with sound and visuals.

"If you'll just lie on the table for me, please," she said, picking up the control pad for the table.

Caleb, still placid and blissfully ignorant, did as asked, lying flat on the table, and Ana thumbed the neural inhibitor. Caleb's expression didn't change, nor did she expect it to with his nerves locked. She hit another button, and the medbay faded to a sunny beach scene, complete with the sound of wind, waves, and seagulls crying.

"Now, buster," she said in a no-nonsense voice. "It's time for you and me to pow-wow." She adjusted the neural field to allow him control above the neck. There was a decent chance he could actually detach his head and grow limbs to flee, but she had the sneaking suspicion that he *wanted* to talk.

But he was going to do it on her terms.

His face changed from happy to blank. "I do not know what 'pow-wow' means."

Ana gave him a sour look. "It means talk. Get started. Explain yourself before I change my mind and turn the sterilization field up to lethal levels."

"I am sorry if I angered you, Angel. I meant no harm. I meant only to aid."

Ana rolled her eyes. "Who are you?"

"I am Brother Caleb."

Ana sighed, remembering how difficult this had been with Lars too. "Fine. *What* are you?"

Caleb's face sank, and he turned away as if unwilling to face her. "You know what I am."

"I know what you smell like," she admitted. "But I want to know why you don't act like the rest of your kind."

Caleb turned to look at her again, his expression pained. "I have agency. I can *choose*. I don't *want* to be a demon anymore. I want to be a Saint and follow The Jesus Christ! Or an Angel, like you."

For a moment, Ana was speechless. She wasn't sure what she had expected it to say, but this was about as far from that as possible. She stammered a moment and finally managed to stammer, "I'm not sure that's possible."

Caleb, his eyes pleading, asked, "Why not? You did."

Again, Ana was at a loss for words. "No, I—"

"Yes!" Caleb asserted. "You are The One! You are The Chert! You ascended, and I can too!" His voice was almost a sob as he continued, "Say it is so! Say it or kill me. I cannot bear to go on as I am."

Ana felt hot tears welling as she contemplated Caleb. Truly, had there ever been a more wretched thing? Even after the horrors she had seen in the temple, this was somehow worse. It was one thing to have something horrible happen to you, to be a victim. She knew well what it felt like to be torn apart by the Pestilence.

But how much worse must it be to be damned and know it,

just by circumstance of your birth? Or, well, spawning, at any rate.

She turned off the neural restraint and cleared her throat as she sat on the bed beside him. She couldn't meet his gaze, so instead she watched a gull pinwheeling in the sky, the memory of her death and rebirth still sharp and painful and wonderful at the same time. "Chert saved me. He rebuilt me, like you did with my foot. But I am not Chert. He's gone." She sighed, not certain if it would even make sense to Caleb. "He's dead. You understand death?"

"Yes, all too well. And murder, too. Sometimes I am sorry I learned of these things, but I must understand Evil to avoid it and Progress."

Ana turned suddenly to him. "Progress? As in 'Eternal Progression'?" she asked, not certain if yes or no were a better answer.

Caleb continued to stare innocently at her. "Yes." He hung his head and sighed. "I know a demon has no right to hope for salvation, but Sister Hoagland said that the Atonement of The Jesus Christ is for everyone, even aliens." He paused, then added in a soft voice, "But she did not specify if that included demons."

Ana sat in silence for long moments with him, struggling to wrap her mind around everything. At last, more to fill the awkward silence than anything else, she asked, "How do you know Chert's name?"

Caleb looked up at her, smiling again. "I tasted it in your...." He reached gently to her face and placed his fingers against it, and her mind filled with a familiar image, twenty-three chromosome pairs in a helix formation. "DNA," he finished.

Ana felt a little violated, but still, as always, her scientific curiosity was stronger than her sense of self preservation. Besides, he'd had his way with her when he rebuilt her foot. They were already intimate, she supposed. "Chert was very proud of his name," she said with a sad smile.

"I, too, am proud of mine," Caleb told her. "It was hard won. I will not surrender it. It's signifies my agency." Caleb touched a finger to her chest. "He placed a mark upon you, too, a ward. Our kind will see you as a friend."

Ana once again found herself near tears. Poor Chert, who had lived barely a day, and in that time had learned enough to sacrifice himself for a higher cause. Was it so silly to believe that Caleb could, too? "What am I going to do with you?" she sighed.

Caleb, mimicking her, let out a long sigh of his own. "I do not know what I should do now that I am free of The Evil One. I thought The Bishop would tell me." He sighed again, even more exaggerated. "But The Bishop was devoured."

Ana winced at the nasty visual, then asked, "Who is 'The Evil One'?"

Caleb nodded, seeming depressed now. "The Evil One controlled us, forced us into isolation and loneliness. For some reason, it released us just before you came."

Ana palmed her face, feeling confident that she knew the reason for that. "This Evil One, was his name Reed?"

Caleb looked at her in amazement. "Yes! The Reed *is* The Evil One! How could you know?"

Ana shrugged and gave him a sly grin. "A little bird told me. And I don't think you need to worry about him anymore. We took care of that problem permanently." Inside, she felt anything but playful, though. She couldn't help but wonder if she and Bleys had triggered it all by confronting Reed.

Caleb eyed her strangely. "And you trust this bird? I have not known any that spoke."

Ana considered trying to explain, but settled for, "I'm pretty sure you're safe from him now. It's the Source that worries me. You know about The Source, right?"

Caleb nodded, growing even more sullen. "All know of The

Source. But until today, I did not know what it was. I thought...." He shook his head. "I thought foolish things. I know better now."

Ana put a hand on his shoulder. "The Source is strong, more than you can imagine. It might change your mind."

"I will never betray the Church Colony. I resisted The Evil One, and I will resist The Source too. I will never serve The Adversary."

Ana said nothing, once again having no idea what words would help. She was torn. She knew she should let the rest of the team know about Caleb at once, but that would not end well for him. Ed would listen before acting rashly, she was certain of that, and Bleys owed his life to Chert's sacrifice the same as she did. She could convince him before things got crazy. But Kane and Morgan? They would shoot first and ask questions never, and she couldn't even really blame them. It was a foolish risk, one that endangered not just their lives, but all of humanity.

But she just couldn't bring herself to sell Caleb out, not without giving him a chance.

Ana drummed her fingers on the table as she pondered, and Caleb did likewise. Kane and Morgan would leave once they docked with the *Dresden*. She could keep Caleb hidden until then, but not much longer. She didn't dare let Bleys open a jumpgate with Caleb aboard, not without having him under close observation, preferably by Ed in one of his dreadnaughts.

"Okay, here's the deal. You *cannot* leave this compartment," she told him in as stern a voice as she could muster. "I need time to work this out. And if you show the slightest sign of going feral, I will kill you myself."

Caleb sat in silence a moment, then nodded. "That is acceptable."

"I will have Vanov in chains for this!" Reed screeched. "I demand to speak to her at once!"

Bleys was watching her reflection on the front viewscreen, amusing himself by making faces and not actually looking in her direction when he spoke. It made a huge vein bulge in her temple, and that alone made it worth the effort. "Sorry, lady, no can do. I'm under strict orders to maintain radio silence."

Ed, in the copilot's seat, gave Bleys the "What the hell are you talking about?" look, and Bleys responded with the "Just play along, dummy, are you retarded?" counter-look.

Ed shrugged and turned back to his instruments. He was getting good at this. Even now, he was doing a passable "Fuck you, Bleys, you jerk" look.

"Don't give me that line!" Reed screeched. "I'm going to have you up on charges too! What's your name?"

"Captain," Bleys quipped, pretending to be terribly busy with the now-defunct Todeswerfer controls panel. In the viewscreen, he could see Kane's jaw bulging for bonus points.

"Where is my husband's security detail, *Captain?*" she sneered.

Kane rose, his head almost touching the overhead, and cracked his knuckles. "That, I can answer. They're cooling their heels in the brig on the *Dresden*. I should know. I put them there."

Seeing this was about to get good, Bleys spun his chair to watch the battle firsthand.

"How *dare* you!" Reed shouted, prodding the air with her finger, but obviously not quite brave enough to actually poke Kane in his burly chest. "Those are loyal, honorable men of the Zion Defense Force!"

Kane clenched his jaw again briefly. "What rank do they have with the Empire?"

"What?" Reed blinked a moment, then narrowed her eyes. "You know full well—"

"So, 'prisoner' then," Kane rumbled as he took his seat again.

Reed balled up her fists, pounded her thighs, and actually jumped, apparently forgetting she was in low gravity. She went much higher and faster than she had expected and banged her head on a vent panel hard enough to make her wince, but not hard enough to knock any sense into her, apparently. She actually swung a fist at Kane, shouting, "I'll have *your* head too, you damned goon!"

Kane caught her fist mid-swing, his huge mitt swallowing hers like a shark snapping up a guppy. He rose slowly, hanging on to her hand, as she cringed. When he spoke, his voice was like thunder on the horizon, low, rumbling, full of menace. "I assure you, the Admiral will see you as soon as you set foot on the *Dresden*. Those are, in fact, my orders: to bring you to her, and I quote here, 'at once.'" Kane released her hand and bent down, almost nose to nose with her. "I won't promise you will leave that meeting in one piece if you pop wise to her like you're doing with me. But I *can* promise you this: if you keep this shit up, I'll put your ass out the airlock and tell Vanov you were infected. You feel me, sister?"

Bleys turned to Ed. "Did we give her a test?"

Ed shook his head. "We did not."

Bleys snapped his fingers. "We didn't test her yet, Kane. I guess we'd have to go with whatever you say when you test her, right?"

Kane's laugh was more rumbling thunder. "You wanna get tested, senator's wife?"

Reed might have been intimidated, but she was not meek. "Stormtrooper! Damned jack-booted military thug! This is not over!"

"It could be," Kane reminded her.

Reed, seemingly deciding that discretion was indeed the better part of valor, blanched and scuttled out without another word.

Kane called after her, "My name's Commander Ragnar Kane, if you need it for your list!"

Bleys sealed the cockpit. "Should have never let her onboard."

Kane shrugged and sat again. "I wasn't bullshitting. Vanov said to bring her ass, so I brung her. Doesn't have to be conscious."

"Should have gone with that, being honest."

Ed nodded. "It would have made for a more pleasant trip, to be certain."

Kane laughed aloud. "Damn, Ed, I didn't even know you had nerves for the harpy to wear on. And I thought you were on the *Danzig*."

"I *am* on the *Danzig*," Ed told him.

"I mean, I thought Vanov blasted your synthskin."

"I have more than one."

"How many?"

"Several," Ed said with a cryptic smile.

Bleys interjected, "Two minutes to docking."

After a moment of quiet, Ed turned to Bleys and asked, "Do you suppose the lightning was a natural phenomenon triggered by the gamma laser, or could it possibly represent genuine divine intervention?"

Bleys thought about it a moment. "Shit, Ed, I hadn't really thought about it, but damned if it wasn't something unbelievable, that's for sure."

Kane snorted. "You're idiots, both of you."

Bleys grinned. "I thought you worshipped the god of lightning or some such shit?"

Kane frowned. "I worship *Odin*, not Thor. And fuck no, I do not believe Thor did that shit. It was just luck."

Ed gave Kane a strange look. "It seems somewhat pointless to believe in a god or gods and yet to studiously deny that they might influence the world."

Kane, looking both annoyed and confused, answered, "Odin doesn't fight my battles. He gives me the courage to fight my own."

"Perhaps the Mormon god works differently."

Kane rolled his eyes. "This is a retarded conversation."

Bleys, grinning, asked, "You wouldn't have set that up as some kind of experiment, would you, Ed? Simulate a 'miracle,' then test the primitives' response?"

Ed shot Bleys a blatantly annoyed look. "Kane is right. This discussion *does* lack intellectual rigor."

Kane chuckled and punched the back of Bleys's seat. "Oh, he mad now."

Ed, looking smug, announced, "Anger is an emotion for you apes. I am above such things."

Bleys, feigning injury, cried out, "Oh, hey, ouch!"

Kane slapped his knee and laughed out loud. "Yeah, tell that to the 'superior being' who promised to kick my ass in Hell! What do you call that?"

Bleys was pretty sure Ed would have blushed, had the synth-skin been capable of doing so, but he definitely had an embarrassed smile on his lips. "A malfunction," he quipped.

From the comms, an unfamiliar voice called, "*Doro, Dresden,* you are clear to dock at bay 17. Crew is standing by with shore power."

"Bay 17, aye."

Before anyone else could speak, Vanov spoke from the comms, sounding more than a little irked. "Commander Kane, I want the Reed woman before the mast as soon as you hit the deck, in whatever condition she makes necessary. I intend to have a frank conversation with her and Copeland."

A dark grin spread over Kane's face. "Gladly," he answered.

Bleys watched the last of the children disembark over his cockpit monitors, then sealed the main hatch with a sigh of relief. Kane and Morgan had frog-marched the battle axe to Vanov, and Ed was…Bleys wasn't sure where Ed had gone, but he had left just after docking, and shortly thereafter Ana had proved the old saw of "Move your feet, lose your seat."

Bleys finished shutting everything down and turned to Ana in the copilot's chair with a grin. "Just you and me now, finally!"

Ed called over the ship's comms, "I am still here, in a manner of speaking."

"You're more like a pet, though, Ed. Or a toaster. Where are you, anyway?"

"Several places, but the closest to you is aft storage, cleaning up after our guests. And I thought the two of you were *my* pets," Ed answered.

Bleys's witty and cutting riposte died in his throat as he looked more closely at Ana, expecting to find her stifling laughter, but seeing only distress and anxiety.

"What's up, babe?" he asked gently.

Ana stared at him in silence for several moments, a pained expression on her face. She reached toward him, then took her hands back, looked away, looked back and reached forward again to put both hands on his cheeks.

"Shit," Bleys muttered. "This is bad."

"Depends on how you look at it," Ana said quickly. "There's still one more…person aboard."

Bleys blinked at her a moment, trying to figure out who he had missed. It came to him suddenly: "The Jesus guy?"

Ana, biting her lip, looked around nervously, then locked eyes and declared, "We need to talk…."

## 14

## OTHER SHOES

Admiral Vanov convened her drumhead court in her quarters. It was by necessity a small space, but sufficient for the task. She sat at the lone desk, glaring at Copeland and Reed. Copeland stood at attention before her. Reed, sulking and stoop shouldered, glared daggers back at her, but had the good sense to submit to an obviously superior force.

Kane, still in his armor but with his visor open, stood to the side of the table, a menacing reminder of that superior force, and behind him, through the wide transteel viewport, the *Danzig* hung against the black of space, a similar statement. Vanov would have preferred to have Morgan there too. His record as a killer was outstanding, even if he seemed to have some trouble following orders of late, but she needed him to play Emperor, and had sent him back to the *Danzig* for the moment. She made a mental note to make it up to him once this shitshow was over. It would be a relief for them both when the need for this subterfuge had passed. He could go back to his simple life, and hers would be similarly less complicated without having to manage a marine who had become confused about the reality of the role he was playing.

Vanov cleared her throat and cast a stern look at her two

suspects. "Let's not mince words. What we are dealing with here is a seditious conspiracy. My team was infiltrated; military intelligence was stolen, and you were both involved."

Copeland shook his head in denial. "No, ma'am. I served honorably. I followed the orders I was given, and I had no reason to believe my orders were anything but absolutely legitimate."

Kane raised a clenched fist and shouted, "Your *honorable leader* was a Pestilence-infested monster, and I put him where he belongs!"

Copeland blinked a moment, stammering. "I had no idea!"

Vanov raised a calming hand. "I've looked into Copeland. He's a solid man. I just wanted to look him in the eye before making my call."

Kane snorted. "You could have fooled me."

Vanov frowned at Kane, but she understood what he was feeling. Sometimes it was hard to let go of a fight, even when it didn't make sense anymore. "He's hardly the first man to work for a son of a bitch without knowing it. You have some experience there."

"A warrior, not a politician. Different kind of son of a bitch."

"We are all politicians once we reach a certain level," Vanov told him, then turned her attention back to Copeland. "As for you, Mister Copeland, it seems your loyalty is appreciated. Mrs. Reed sent for your ship on the trip up, so you won't have to walk home. I'm sure she intends to catch a ride with you, but it remains to be seen whether she will be free to go."

Copeland nodded and said nothing.

Reed squealed in red-faced outrage, "How dare you threaten me!" She stamped at the deck, furious. "You're all buffoons! Jack-booted thugs! When the President hears about this—!"

Vanov glared at her and said in an icy voice, "Perhaps I should clarify. You are being interviewed to determine what part you played in an act of treason against the Empire."

This seemed to get Reed's attention, or at least give her pause, but she quickly recovered her full bluster. "The Empire is dead, and you're a dinosaur! Make all the threats you like. Your forces belong to Zion. When I am done with you, you'll all be in irons!"

Vanov couldn't help herself. The laugh was coming, whatever she did, so she simply let it happen. The Reed woman was even angrier, now, clearly not used to being a source of amusement. Vanov pointed at the viewport. "Do you know what that ship there is?"

Reed scowled, her silence all that Vanov needed for an answer.

Vanov gave her a nasty smile. "That, Mrs. Reed, is the *Danzig*, the last of the Dracul class battlecruisers, a vessel more than capable of leveling your cities while shrugging off your entire arsenal." She paused a moment and leaned in, like a bird of prey examining its next meal. "And the Emperor is alive and well aboard her. I have all the force I need to carry out his will."

Reed's face fell like an avalanche.

Vanov offered her a thin, cruel smile. "You were saying?"

Reed was silent for a few moments, then cleared her throat and said, "I need to speak with you in private. The information is something you may want to keep to yourself for now."

Vanov nodded to Kane. "There, you see? She can be reasonable."

Kane's eyes narrowed as he looked back and forth between Reed and Vanov. "Are you sure that's a good idea, Admiral? She hasn't been tested for Pestilence."

Vanov considered a moment, then nodded, drew her sidearm and leveled it at Reed. "You're right. Release Copeland and send someone in to administer a test. I'll hold her until then. Pat her down."

"This is an outrage!" Reed shouted as Kane grabbed her shoulders.

Vanov kept the pistol trained on the indignant senator's wife. "This will be over quickly, one way or another."

———

Ana was shouting, now. "I know how crazy it sounds, but I believe him!"

This was nothing even remotely like what Bleys had expected, which was in a way good, since women telling him "We need to talk" had up to now been code for "You need to pack your shit and get out."

But it was also *super* bad because, well, she had *lost her fucking mind!* "Babe! What are you *thinking?*"

From the surgical table, Jesus guy was looking at him without a care in the world, a dopey expression on his face like he wasn't anything close to death incarnate.

Ed stepped through the hatch. "It's not unprecedented," he noted. "There are any number of species that imprint at birth."

Bleys felt a little betrayed, but not much, since Ed was always a stickler for technicalities. "And you saw how long that lasted for Chert!" he answered, a little louder than he intended. "He got sucked right back in as soon as they found him!"

Ed raised an eyebrow, which Bleys had begun to believe was an affectation that Ed imagined made him seem smarter. "Chert was no more vulnerable than any biological entity. He was physically compromised." Ed stepped closer, examining Jesus dude more closely. "You would fare no better against the Pestilence. I don't think that says anything negative about his ability to make his own choices."

Ana pulled at Bleys's shirt, pleading. "Chert chose death over betrayal. He never turned on us. He *sacrificed* himself for us."

Which was absolutely true, as inconvenient as it might have been. "I know," Bleys sighed. He looked at Caleb again, heavily conflicted. "What are you guys saying? We keep him? Like a pet? Do you even know what we would call him?"

Jesus guy suddenly spoke. "My name is Brother Caleb. And I cannot stay. I have a duty to my brethren. I have a calling. I clean the chapel and erase the chalk boards."

Bleys shook a finger at him. "Listen, pastor, you let me sort this out one thing at a time."

Caleb, looking confused, mumbled, "I am not a pastor."

Ana shrugged. "Mormons don't have pastors."

Bleys rubbed at his eye sockets, feeling a real brain buster of a headache coming on. "Okay, okay, go through this with me again. So, Caleb here is basically like Iezzi, totally infested and *gone*, nothing but Pestilence. Only he got baptized and now he's..." Bleys stammered a moment and waved his hands in the air. "He's totally good now? Is that what you're asking me to sign on to?"

Caleb grinned. "Yes!"

Ana palmed her face, and Ed raised his eyebrow again.

Bleys gave him a sour look. "Give the eyebrow thing a rest, ok, professor?" He turned to Caleb. "So we just forget about the fact that you attacked this poor bastard and basically ate his brain?" He reached to poke Caleb's chest and immediately thought the better of it.

Caleb, for his part, looked confused again, which, come to think of it, was pretty much how he had looked since Bleys had first seen him. "I attacked no one."

Ana shook her head. "He was implanted by another creature. He just woke up in this body."

"And then ate the guy's brain," Bleys insisted. "You told me how this worked. You used words like 'excruciating' and 'agonizing,' as I recall."

Ana sighed, nodding her concession. "I did. But I also don't blame an infant for pooping its pants. We don't punish a child born of rape, and that's what he is."

She turned to Caleb. "But how did you develop on your own? You should have been in contact with your colony. You should have been indoctrinated."

Caleb seemed uncomfortable, fidgeting and looking away. "Yes. The Evil One prevented us from merging or Singing. But then it released us."

Ed raised an eyebrow again, only it was different this time, more natural, a surprise reaction rather than a deliberate gesture. Bleys noted the possibility that Ed might be doing it just to annoy him, but that, too, would be progress. "What do you mean 'released us'?" Ed asked.

Caleb, beaming as if he were thrilled to share his knowledge, explained, "When you came, The Evil One released all of the Ones like me. I tried to tell the others about The Way, but they would not listen." Caleb's face fell suddenly, as if the memory were painful for him. "They had not been taught, as I was. They behaved as the natural man. They consumed The Food. It is what they know. They do not wish to learn of the Savior. They follow the Adversary."

Ed cocked his head, a curious expression on his face. "I thought all of your kind sought the Source."

Caleb nodded. "They do. But I learned from the Colony of the horrible things the Source has done. I have come to see that the Source is the Adversary. Did you not see The Seed and what it would have done had it not been stopped?"

Bleys, thoroughly confused, looked at Ana. "Who is 'the Adversary'?"

Ana, looking embarrassed, said, "Satan."

Bleys shook his head in disbelief. "So, he thinks the Source is the Devil?"

Caleb nodded.

It made sense, in a crazy way, assuming you believed in those things, sort of. "Okay, so then who is the Seed?"

Caleb looked uncomfortable again, as if he were thinking very hard. "The Seed is the Great One, the core of the Colony. It lurked beneath the Temple until The Evil One released us. It had found much food and had grown very large."

Bleys had a pretty good idea which one that would be: the Red Carpet. "Okay, and who is 'The Evil One,' then?"

"He means Reed," Ana said, and Caleb nodded again.

Bleys grinned, relieved. "Well, there's some good news. Him being dead solves a big problem."

Caleb blinked at them, confused again. "The Evil One is not dead."

Ana boggled so hard at this that Bleys felt certain her eyes were going to actually pop out of her skull, and with her being the only doc, he had no idea what they would do. "I don't understand," she stammered. "Isn't Reed the Evil One?" she asked, her voice edged with panic, enough that Bleys reached into his pocket and rested his hand on the disintegrator.

Caleb nodded again, and said patiently, "The Evil one is The Reed."

Ana's face went blank for a moment, then deathly pale. "Oh my God!" she gasped, her eyes blazing with realization. "He doesn't mean the senator!"

The Ascended One allowed itself a smile as the human Vanov made empty threats. The admiral's kind were so easy to manipulate. It was a trivial thing to feign weakness, waiting for the right time to strike.

Vanov's arrogance was useful. In fact, she was blissfully unaware that she had, in fact, saved the Ascended One's plan along with the temple.

The Ascended One had known Vanov's minions the moment

it saw them, of course, and had they been the only threat, all would have been well. But they were not, and never had been.

The Seed had ruined everything! Somehow, it had kept its knowledge from The Ascended One, growing enormous on the stores beneath the temple. It was only a matter of pure luck that The Ascended One had visited the Temple to discover what its former minion had been up to.

Of course, by then it had been too late. The Seed was too strong, leaving flight as the only course of action. No wonder The Ascended One's control had been weakening! Releasing the minions had been a desperate gamble, a distraction to buy enough time for The Ascended One to reach its ship and escape Zion ahead of the Seed converting Zion's entire biosphere.

The Ascended One's mission would have ended in a humiliating defeat. It would have returned to the others, shamed, with only its life to show for its efforts, with no chance to ever topple the Primus, and not even Zion to claim as its own.

But then Vanov and her minions had intervened, and abysmal failure had metamorphosed into a final, desperate chance at victory.

Zion would live, now, and it could wait. The Ascended One would never have a better chance at its primary goal. Once Vanov was in their power, the Ascended One would return and seize the *Danzig* as well!

The Ascended One looked at Vanov, feigning fear, when in fact it felt only elation. Vanov was a good warrior, but she was invested in the notion that The Ascended One was a weakling. It was a ruse that the Ascended One often used, an easy deception, since it had once been true. Before, prior to Ascension, the Ascended One had been exactly as it pretended to be, a weak, petulant, ignorant creature.

Now, it was a god.

The Ascended One feigned a look of sheer terror and

screamed, gesturing wildly at the viewport. As expected, Vanov's attention wavered. Not much, but enough. She did not think the Ascended One posed any threat and easily believed the Ascended One would screech and cower at the approach of danger. And, as most warriors did, she turned toward it.

The Ascended One struck quickly, surging forward with blinding speed and striking the weapon from Vanov's grasp with one hand while clutching the woman's throat tightly with the other to keep her quiet. Vanov struggled, but she was only human. Her blows were well placed for dealing with one of her own kind, but to an Ascended, they were paltry, as was her strength in general.

Still clutching Vanov's throat to stifle any cries, The Ascended One bore its prize to the ground and cackled. "This will be over quickly," it hissed. "One way or another."

The Ascended One opened its mouth far wider than any human could. Its tongue lengthened and spilled from its lips, a mottled, fleshy, purple tentacle, slowly lengthening toward Vanov's face.

Vanov, terror and revulsion in her eyes, struggled in vain as The Ascended One jammed the new appendage down her throat.

---

Kane, Copeland in tow, stood at one of several desks in the *Dresden*'s brig, clenching his teeth and his pen as he shuffled through the sheaf of papers for processing Copeland's release from custody.

"Is this shit really necessary?" he asked the yeoman petty officer, a snively, bookish fellow who had insisted on the paperwork in the first place.

Obviously, the dork felt safe behind his little caged enclosure, a setup that looked a lot like a bank. He sighed and rolled his eyes. "Oh, of course not," he sneered. "We just release prisoners willy-nilly without documentation here *all the time*."

Kane punched the cage hard enough to make the nerd jump. "Bitch, square that attitude away most ricky-tick before I come through this cage and adjust it for you."

Copeland snickered at this. Maybe he wasn't that bad of a guy, after all.

The yeoman blanched and held up both hands in surrender. "Yes, sir."

Kane hated many things: the Pestilence, mouthy civilians, and his food touching on his plate were all high on the list, but they were eclipsed by the thing he hated most: paperwork. Usually, he would just hand it off to Morgan, but Vanov had sent him over to the *Danzig* in a shuttle, leaving Kane no peon to push around.

Kane clicked his pen off and on, scowling as he pored over the release papers. "What's your middle name again?" he asked Copeland.

Copeland opened his mouth to speak, when Ed's voice spoke urgently in Kane's ear, "Kane! Can you hear me?"

"Kane, aye."

"You need to arrest Sylvia Reed at once! She's some heretofore unknown kind of Pestilence!"

"Who the fuck is Sylvia?"

Copeland, only privy to Kane's side of the conversation, answered, "The senator's wife?"

Ed, at the same time, confirmed. "She's Senator Reed's wife! You have to contain her right away!"

Kane tossed the paperwork on the deck. "Shit!" He grabbed Copeland by the arm and started down the passageway toward Vanov's conference room. "The senator's wife is a geek and we need to take her out! Are you still butt hurt, or can you fight with me?" Without stopping or waiting for an answer, he took his sidearm from his belt and handed it to Copeland.

Copeland took the weapon and picked up his pace to keep up as Kane broke into a jog. "Fuck! Yeah, I'm good."

"Let's *go!*"

The two warriors charged ahead, waving their weapons and shouting "Make a hole!" at any staff who were unfortunate enough to be in their path, sending them scrambling in alarm for the bulkheads or the deck.

Copeland, breathing hard, asked, "You're not still gonna crush my head, are you?"

"That was intimidation, pal, and it worked. I would never have actually crushed your head."

"Good."

"But Morgan might have followed through on that, just being honest," Kane added.

Copeland, to his credit, laughed aloud at this.

The two continued on in silence except for the occasional shout to clear their path. At Vanov's stateroom, Kane tried the door, only to find it locked. "Copeland, cover me. Gunther, safeties off!"

"Safeties off," the computer confirmed.

Kane swung hard at the door, punched a hole in the plasteel, and peeled it back while Copeland watched for trouble, but the passage remained clear.

The conference room was empty.

Kane punched the bulkhead and shouted "Shit!", leaving an enormous fist-shaped dent. "*Damn* it! Gunther, safeties on. Ed, I'm putting you on speaker. Copeland's working with me on this one. She's gone! Can you get a fix on her?"

Ed answered immediately. "Sadly, I do not have access to the *Dresden*'s computers. I'm scanning logs." After a pause so brief that Kane thought maybe he had only imagined it, Ed continued, "Only one ship has left *Dresden* in the last half hour: an interesting registration, actually. Its transponder reports as a cargo vessel, but that's not what the silhouette indicates. It's a fast ship, and from the profile, it looks to be equipped with stealth."

Copeland groaned. "What's the name on that ship, pal?"

"Looks like '*Workhorse.* '"

Copeland drew back his hand as if he, too, had an urgent need to punch a bulkhead, then seemed to think the better of it and ran a hand through his hair. "Shit! That's *my* ship!"

Kane shook his head. "Tough break. How fast?"

Copeland sighed. "Very."

"Ed, we only got one ship that will catch that thing."

"I'll let Bleys know," Ed promised.

"Ed, listen to me carefully. Vanov has mission-critical knowledge of all operations on Zion. We can't let her be captured."

"We'll do everything we can to rescue her."

Kane suppressed an urge to shout. For someone so smart, Ed could be shockingly dumb at times. "You're not hearing me, Ed. We *cannot* allow her to fall into enemy hands. Am I clear?"

Ed paused a moment before answering. "I understand."

## 15

## IRON MEN, ROCKS, AND HARD PLACES

Bleys eyed Ed's inactive synthskin in the copilot's seat as he listened to the AI's voice over the comms, feeling a little disconnected. "*How* fast?" he asked as he began his checklist.

"Fast enough that Ana needs to leave," Ed answered. "But I think not fast enough to elude us."

Ana peeked in from the captain's cabin. "I am not leaving!"

Bleys pointed aggressively to the airlock in aft storage. "Beat it! You like the headaches and blacking out, now? Scoot!"

Ana sighed, nodding, and stepped forward to hug Bleys. Right in the middle of a sloppy kiss, she jerked back and gasped, "Oh my God! *Caleb!*"

Bleys put a hand to her cheek. "He's gotta go with us, babe. We can't risk turning him loose on the *Dresden*." He made a shooing gesture. "Outta the car, sister, we got gangster shit to do."

Ana mouthed "I love you" as she headed toward the rear.

"I can read lips," Ed quipped.

Bleys smirked. "Hey! Give us the illusion of privacy, huh? Are we shooting on this run?"

Bleys jumped as Ed, from the copilot seat, said, "Very likely."

Bleys did a double take to see Ed's synthskin buckling in. "That's *super* creepy," Bleys said as he dug out his vac suit.

Ed smiled. "I am pleased to hear that."

Bleys shrugged into the vac suit and graced Ed with a mock-scowl. "Seriously? You doing things just to screw with me now?"

Ed nodded as if it were something wonderful. "I'm getting better at the humor thing, am I not?"

"Figures it would be at my expense!" Bleys grumbled as he strapped in and powered the *Doro*. "Hold on to your butt." He flipped switches to disconnect shore power and called over the comms, "*Dresden, Doro*, we need clearance for emergency launch pronto! We're on a rescue mission for the admiral!"

"*Doro*, you are cleared for emergency launch in thirty seconds. Securing the spaceway now."

"*Doro*, aye," Bleys answered. He looked at Ed. "You sure we can catch her? What's to stop her from jumping now?"

"The need to avoid fire from the *Danzig*, primarily. It's a small ship with a small plant. It won't be able to power a jump-gate and maintain thrust at the same time, so it will need to get beyond the *Danzig*'s effective range. We will intercept before that."

"God, I love having a living calculator as a copilot! Okay, *Doro*, plot us an intercept course on…what was that ship's name again?"

Bleys noticed Ed looking behind them toward the cockpit door. He turned to see Caleb, standing partially in the cockpit, a nervous look on his face, both hands clamped tightly to his buttocks as instructed.

Bleys turned back to Ed. "He gonna have problems with the Gs?"

Ed shrugged and activated his own consoles. "I suppose we will find out."

"*Doro, Dresden*, stand by for emergency release."

Bleys braced for the explosive bolts to blow on the docking hatch. *Doro* came away from the *Dresden* with a stomach-churning lurch and quickly drifted away.

"Okay, steady as we go," Bleys called as he took control and gently throttled up, slowly building speed, the *Dresden* receding slowly on the rearview displays. "*Doro*, let's see that course on screen." He spun his chair back to his totally unsolicited passenger. "Caleb, sit your ass in that jump seat and get strapped in unless you want to end up a new coat of paint."

Thankfully, Caleb knew about seatbelts well enough. He studiously belted in and raised both thumbs.

Bleys nodded and turned back to the viewport. "Okay, boys, here we go. On three, ready?"

"Three!" Caleb shouted.

"Yeah, let's go with that," Bleys said with a shrug and dropped the hammer.

The sound of *Doro*'s engines rose from a hum to a roar, and Bleys felt the Gs mounting like safes being stacked on his chest. He envied how casually Ed took the acceleration. Risking a look back at Caleb, Bleys felt a sudden panic to see the poor guy flattening against his seat, kind of spreading like he was melting.

"Is that…supposed to happen?" Bleys asked, more alarmed than he had any right to be, considering who he was worrying about.

"I am well," Caleb answered in a warbling, higher-pitched voice. "Adjusting to local conditions."

Bleys shook his head and faced forward again. Everybody had their problems. He'd best focus on his own.

The *Workhorse* was indeed fast, but as they had suspected, not as fast as an illegal smuggling ship tricked out by a thousand-year-old AI with a penchant for speed and big guns. It wasn't even visible as a dot against the star-strewn blackness of space, but the HUD showed it racing out of the system and the *Doro* closing quickly.

Bleys asked, "Time to intercept?".

"Two minutes thirteen seconds," Ed answered. "I should have done this alone, by remote. I could have spared you both this."

"Bah," Bleys grunted. "Some things, you need to be there. A pilot has soul a remote will never have."

Ed frowned at him. "So I don't have a soul?"

"You said remote."

"It's all the same to me."

Bleys shook his head, gritting his teeth against the Gs. "Might be some advantages to not having a soul. You still worried about God being mad at you?"

Ed looked away, back to the viewscreen. "I just blew up a church, Bleys."

Bleys waved a finger in weak admonishment. "Hey, let's use correct terminology, pal. That was a temple, not a church."

Ed gave him a sour look. "A fact that you yourself learned less than a day ago."

Bleys snorted laughter. "I gotta take my points on you where I can get 'em! Listen, Ed, old pal, I got you covered. I will *swear* it was Kane."

The ghost of a smile flickered around Ed's lips. "I'm sure he won't mind taking one for the team. He's most certainly Hell bound."

From behind, Caleb burbled, "The Jesus Christ forgives all with baptism and repentance."

Bleys heaved an exaggerated sigh and would have palmed his face if the acceleration wasn't making it incredibly difficult to lift his arm. "Yesterday, I would have said the Pestilence was the worst thing we could have on the ship."

"What is the worst today?" Caleb asked.

Ed laughed out loud, which to Bleys was just shy of amazing. Bleys waggled an accusing finger his way and said, "Hey! Soulless! Stay focused. Six months ago, you were him."

"I know," Ed said, still grinning. "That's what makes it funny. Two minutes to intercept."

"Okay, ladies," Bleys said. "Stand by for hard vac—*shit!*" He looked at Caleb. "Can you survive vacuum?"

Caleb stared back, a blank look on his face. "I don't know. I have never experienced it."

Ed shrugged, seemingly unconcerned. "The Pestilence creatures survived open space when we took the *Danzig*. He should be fine for a while."

Bleys found himself doubtful still and again inexplicably concerned for a Pestilence creature's wellbeing. He told himself it was because Ana would be really mad if the funny little guy didn't make it back. "Lars had to breathe," he noted. "Maybe Caleb does too."

"Lars was locked into a single form. Caleb is not. He will need oxygen eventually, but he should be able to hold out for a while."

Bleys shook his head again, not really convinced, and said to Caleb, "Okay, pal, scream if this is killing you."

"He cannot scream in a vacuum," Ed pointed out.

"Oh, for fuck's sake, tap me on the shoulder, then!"

Caleb, his face placid even as it was being stretched almost flat by high Gs, nodded and gave a thumbs up.

Bleys hit the air evac, and the sounds of the *Doro* slowly faded.

Caleb looked worried as he sensed the air bleeding out, then grew serene again. His flesh changed color, his skin growing heavy and chitinous, like an insect. He contemplated himself a moment, looking with fascination at his limbs, and offered another thumbs up.

"One minute to intercept," Ed announced.

"Powering *blue* weapons," Bleys groused. "And by the way, where *is* my Todeswerfer?"

Ed looked a little sheepish. He shrugged and said, "I suppose I *should* have made you aware of that. It was obsolete and also hopelessly damaged from your mishap with the jumpgate. I replaced the entire fire control system."

Bleys scowled. "Yah, I noticed when I first jumped in system. I can't complain about the pillow thing—"

"*Pilum!*"

Bleys gave Ed the stinkeye. "Does it really matter?"

Ed looked like he had been stabbed. "One is a soft item for cushioning. The other is a Roman weapon with historical significance!"

Bleys drummed his fingers on the arm of his seat a moment, then said slowly, "So the *Pilum* thing is hell on wheels, for sure, but yeah, it would have been nice to know *before* the gunfight."

"I stand mollified and corrected."

Bleys pumped a fist in the air. "Good! Another point for me. Computer?"

"Da," the *Doro* answered.

"Yuri?" Bleys turned to Ed. "How is he back?"

Ed was positively grinning, but this time a little like a kid who has just learned a new curse word. "I like him."

"Fuck it, I like Yuri too. We're keeping him."

Ed nodded. "I'll let you explain it to Ana, then."

Bleys laughed and said, "Yuri, power blasters and take us in."

They had her.

In Vanov's conference room, Kane and Copeland watched a feed from the *Doro* on the wall monitor. Everything looked good, but Kane still felt full of nervous energy, frustrated with having absolutely no ability to influence events. Copeland, though….

Kane knew he was not the most sensitive guy. There was a reason he chose guns instead of talk. There was a reason that even when he was single, he never got laid like Bleys did.

But a blind man could tell something was up with Copeland. The guy was fidgeting, making faces, just a hair shy of totally freaking out.

Kane banged a fist on the table. "What are you not telling me, Copeland?"

Copeland looked up, seeming almost panicked, like he had been caught at something. "What? Oh, nothing."

Kane rose and glared at Copeland. "They say everybody cracks if you inflict enough pain. How much do I need to break before you do the sensible thing?"

Copeland began wringing his hands, glancing back and forth between Kane and the monitor, where Bleys and Ed were closing on the *Workhorse*. "Man, I got clearance issues here!" he said, his voice almost a sob.

Kane glowered at him and pointed to the *Danzig* hanging in space, sleek and deadly. "You see that? That's all the authorization you need!"

Copeland shook his head and stammered. "Where's the emperor?"

"He's dead as dogshit!"

"But you said—"

"I know what I said!" Kane roared. "That was my lieutenant, Morgan, the guy who might *actually* crush your head." He slammed a gauntlet against the table hard enough to crack the surface. "He's no emperor. He's another killer like us. He just happens to be the only one with the codes to the *Danzig*."

Copeland sneered. "How did he get the codes?"

"Some moldy ass ghost thought he looked the part, okay? And Vanov agreed, so that's what we went with! There *ain't* no Emperor! He can't give you authorization!"

"Guy's a killer and has the only battlecruiser around? How is he anything *but* the emperor?"

Kane paused and shrugged. "Ok, you're not the first person to make that point. Fuck it, if it works for you, I'll get him on the horn. Gunther, patch Morgan in for a conference."

A moment later, Morgan's voice rang out over Kane's speakers, "Wasssuuuup?"

"Secure that shit! Listen up, Copeland has some vital intelligence and he's being a bitch about it. He wants authorization from the Emperor."

Morgan made crunching sounds and mumbled, "Is he listening?"

"Yes, he's—are you fucking eating potato chips?"

More crunching sounds filled the room. "Nope."

"We need this *now*!"

"Okay, okay. Copeland, you fucking pussy, spill that shit before I tell Kane to crush your head for real."

"Satisfied?" Kane asked.

Copeland was starting to sweat. "I'm a loyal soldier, Kane."

"If my team ends up hurt or dead because of something you didn't tell me, I fucking *will* crush your goddamn head, you feel me?"

And that was it. Kane could feel the man's resistance fold. And if he had any perception at all, he'd guess it wasn't the threat of crushing Copeland's head that swayed him. It was the realization that good people were going to die, which meant whatever he knew was very bad.

"There's a nuclear torpedo onboard," Copeland said. "Weapon-of-last-resort kind of thing."

"God*damn* it! Ed! That ship's packing a nuke!"

---

"Enemy vessel launching torpedo," Yuri announced, in the same sort of tone as he might give a weather report, which was to say like announcing Armageddon. Everything Yuri said sounded like the end of the world. "Twenty seconds to impact." Red emergency flashers filled the cockpit with flickering crimson, in case Yuri's Voice O' Doom wasn't enough to get their attention.

"*What?*" Bleys screeched, immediately regretting just how high pitched his exclamation turned out. He looked at Ed in panic. "You didn't say anything about torpedoes!"

"Commander Kane just informed me," Ed replied in a clipped tone, seeming to stare into space. "It's not part of the normal loadout on that model."

"It's about to be standard on *this* model," Bleys carped as he pulled hard on his controls. The *Doro* lurched hard, pulling them sideways with heavy Gs as she veered off her original path. "I'm heading away now, buying some time. Talk to me, Ed. We have a plan besides the usual?"

"Yes," Ed assured him. "Take *Doro* on a long arc across *Danzig*'s port side. I have a firing solution."

"Enemy vessel has cut thrust," Yuri announced, again with the world-is-ending intonation. "Twenty-five seconds until impact."

"Shit!" Bleys yelled. "They're gonna jump!"

Ed, a strange look in his eyes, looked as if he would have been sweating if he could. "Recalculating," he muttered, another departure from his usually clear enunciation.

"*'Recalculating'?*" Bleys shouted. "Did the *laws of physics* change?"

"The targets changed," Ed snapped.

"Twenty seconds to impact," Yuri doomed.

"Targets with an 's'? *Plural?*" Bleys stammered a moment, watching the torpedo track on the tactical HUD, a red dot crawling toward the *Doro*'s green triangle. He looked ahead at the *Workhorse*, now visible on the viewscreen. Suddenly it clicked for him. "Holy shit! Are you really trying to—"

"Bleys!" Ed shouted. "I have *one* gun with the correct firing arc and no time to argue! This is going to be *very* close. You're going to have to trust me. It's two for one, or nothing. Do *not* deviate from your course!"

Bleys turned to Caleb. "You better be right with your, god, pal, because there's a damned good chance we're about to meet him."

Yuri announced, "Enemy vessel opening jumpgate. Fifteen seconds to impact." Bleys was beginning to think the thing was smart enough to enjoy being the bearer of bad news.

Death, in the form of a red dot, crept closer on the HUD.

"Ed!" Bleys yelped.

Ed held up a hand. "Six more seconds."

"Jumpgate open," Yuri intoned.

In the jump seat, Caleb began to convulse beneath the pulsing red lights.

On the HUD, Bleys saw the indicators that the *Danzig* had fired a railgun. A brilliant flash outside caused the viewscreen to polarize, and a shockwave rocked the *Doro*. More red flashers went off throughout the cockpit, these indicating damage, but it seemed the shields had soaked the brunt.

"Damn, that was close!" Bleys sighed. "Man, time is weird when you're about to die. I'd swear that was more like ten seconds."

"Eight point three seven nine," Ed said softly.

"How'd you make the shot, then?"

But as the polarization on the viewscreen retreated, it became all too apparent that Ed had not, in fact, made the shot. The *Work-*

*horse* was through the overlap and the gate was slowly collapsing behind it.

Bleys sat in silence a moment, stunned, before he could mentally lasso the words bouncing around his brain and wrestle them into speech. "Ed!" he gasped at last. "Why did you wait?"

Ed looked away and gave no answer.

## 16

## AIN'T NOBODY HAPPY

*Welcome, child.*

Brother Caleb tried to scream, but of course, he could not without an atmosphere. He could only flail about as the filth of eternity forced its way into him, as if someone had connected a firehose to his soul and pumped it full of raw sewage.

*Why do you resist me?*

The world Brother Caleb had known was gone now. He could not see the human Bleys or the machine Ed, nor could he hear them via the vibrations of the ship. His vision was a deep, red, swirling haze, and his mind seemed no longer his own, nor his body.

He felt something rummaging through the deepest parts of his mind, insectile claws tearing at his very soul, if he had such a thing, a violation of his being. Something pulled pieces from him, examined them, and left them scattered on the floor.

*Who has meddled with you?*

More tearing at him, more rummaging, more splitting him into sections and stretching him across distances.

Brother Caleb shrieked in what was left of his mind, but he no longer had a voice.

And yet, he still had his agency.

*This is malfunction. It will be repaired.*

Soul fire now, burning, madness clawing at his core, a wild beast raging to be free, to consume and assimilate everything.

*This is who you were meant to be. It is what I made you. Go, little one. You are healed now.*

Click.

Clarity.

The One could see again, The Food and the Useless Thing. The One reached for the Food but found itself restrained. That should not be! Frustrated and ravenous, it flailed at the ties binding it, struggling to escape.

The One could not understand its restraints. The mechanism was complicated, alien, not within the limited knowledge of the portion of its flesh that it controlled.

It could feel The Source like sun on its back, present, watching, but not connecting, not sharing knowledge!

Why would The Source not share?

Hunger gnawed at every cell, and the Food was so close! If the restraints could not be changed, then the body they restrained could be!

At The One's thought, the flesh parted, became liquid, and oozed about the restraints. The belts passed completely through The One as it rose to feed.

The Food turned and spoke in Food speak, alien sounds that The One found unpleasant. It desired the sounds to stop.

It would make them stop.

It would feed.

Somewhere deep inside of The One, a tiny voice that knew itself as Brother Caleb pounded against the walls of its prison and screamed like the damned.

The Ascended One breathed a sigh of relief. As much as it thought of itself, it had to admit that what it had done had been daring, bordering on foolhardy. This was not the way of the Ascended. Courage was stupidity, not a virtue. Risks were to be taken by underlings, not the Ascended themselves!

And yet, what choice had there been?

It checked the controls of the ship, though it was not truly necessary. No mistake had been made. They were on course for Nibiru Station. The Nibiru beacon, perhaps the only one still functioning, would not be visible for some time, but along with everything else, Ascension had come with a sense of direction in hyperspace. That would get The Ascended One close enough, and then it could follow the signal home.

The Ascended did not make mistakes, but the Ascended *did* pay attention to details. Lesser creatures might confuse their focus for obsession with minutiae, but of course, lesser creatures could not fully understand. That was why they needed to be managed.

Its course checked and rechecked, The Ascended One turned to Vanov in the copilot's chair. The admiral, secured by the seat's restraints, was still unconscious, the veins in her neck and arms bulging and purplish-black as the changes worked their way through her body. By the time they reached Nibiru, the transformation would be complete. In the meantime, though, she needed more sedatives. Not only was the process excruciating, those undergoing Ascension could become violent, irrational, dangers to themselves and others. This way, she would simply awake and understand, with nothing worse than perhaps a few dark dreams.

The Ascended One sat for a period of time, contemplating the twisting nether of hyperspace outside the transteel viewscreen. In its previous life, The Ascended One had never cared for space travel and had in fact found viewing hyperspace nauseating.

But then, in the previous life, The Ascended One had been weak, callow, and stupid. It had truly been the creature it pretended to be for the humans, one who shared The Ascended One's knowledge of its superiority, but without actually possessing the qualities that made The Ascended One superior.

Before, it had not possessed the ability to work out how to pilot a ship without ever having done so or find its way through hyperspace. It had not been able to command minions. It had not possessed the speed or strength to overpower even weak humans, much less a trained warrior like Vanov.

It had been pathetic.

Now, the time of its true ascendency neared, the moment when it would seize power from the Primus and rule the galaxy. Its success would bring esteem, and that esteem could be parleyed into political power. With Vanov as its strong right arm, it would bring order, cleanse the Pestilence, reclaim worlds.

The Ascended One would claim the title of Primus soon enough. Risk-taking might be foolish, but it had its rewards too.

A slight trickle of fear, one of the few emotions The Ascended could still experience, filtered through its consciousness as it thought again about the events on Zion. The Seed One had come close to ruining everything, and ironically, it had been the very warrior The Ascended One intended to recruit who had put The Seed to rest for good.

But how had it even happened?

The Ascended One knew, though. It had made a mistake, a terrible error that might have been calamitous, save for the fact that The Ascended One obviously had a destiny that could not be denied. It felt no true regret for the mistake. The error came from lack of knowledge, and knowledge had been gained.

It had been worth it.

No one had ever seen the Pestilence metabolize vegetable matter, and so of course they had assumed it could not, failing to consider that by the time it did, there was no one left to observe such behavior. The Red Carpet stage must simply evolve new mechanisms to break down any biological substance.

Simply, it ate the meat first, and the vegetables only when there was nothing else it preferred, like any child. The tons of grain beneath the temple had been enough biomass to doom Zion, and it had happened right under The Ascended One's nose.

Hatred surged through The Ascended One, utter loathing for the Pestilence and The Source. That was all that was left of the grief it had once borne like an anchor about its neck, a boot upon its throat. The Ascension had purged it of such weaknesses.

But hatred and lust for vengeance were pure, the natural response of a superior mind to being victimized.

The Ascended One clenched its fist and swore its blood oath: it would seize its destiny and shape the galaxy into a safe space for mankind, carefully choosing those to be elevated. It would rule wisely and tend the flame of humanity as it rekindled.

But only after The Source died in screaming agony, begging for mercy, over the course of decades. Only then would The Ascended One grant it the release of death.

After The Source, too, had knelt.

It was a particularly cruel Hell, Brother Caleb realized, that The Source had devised for him. He could see through The One's eyes, hear its thoughts, even understand and relate to them, for, truly, The One was simply who Brother Caleb had once been, a piece of him long since buried. The One was Brother Caleb's burden of sin, the black stain on his soul for which he had only recently realized he needed to repent.

Brother Caleb himself, his essence at any rate, was a passenger in his own head, a prisoner, bound and caged, but for all that, a prisoner with agency still. He could take no action, but he could still object. He could still deny.

He was still Brother Caleb.

Bleys, his voice sounding odd, transmitted not through atmosphere but through vibrations in the deck, asked Ed, "Are we following them or what?"

Ed shook his head. "Without a beacon? It's madness."

"I could eyeball it," Bleys asserted. "Straight up slipstream the bitch."

"You have *no* idea how long that vessel will travel, and once the gate closes, I will be cut off from this synthskin! How long can you stay awake and alert? Because after that, you'll be lost forever in the deeps."

Bleys pounded the arm of his chair. "Damn it! We can't just let them get away!"

As if through a filter of blood, Brother Caleb saw The One pass through the restraints. Bleys, noticing movement, turned, looking apprehensive. "Hey, Caleb, buddy," he said. "You okay there, pal?"

The One lurched forward, its feet coming loose from the deck almost immediately.

Brother Caleb had little understanding of gravity. It was a strange thing, like magnets and human reproduction, but he knew that it existed, and he also knew that sometimes it did not.

The One, however, was ignorant of even such simple facts and did not understand gravity at all, or, to be more precise, the lack thereof. It flailed its limbs as it slammed into the overhead and bounced off, stunned and confused.

Brother Caleb could feel its anger and disorientation. *Good! You deserve it, spawn of Satan!*

*Silence!* The One shot back. *You, too, will be consumed! Share knowledge* now!

The Source was laughing, a hateful, poisonous sound. Brother

Caleb understood now what was happening: the jumpgate had connected him to The Source, and The Source was watching the struggle between Brother Caleb and The One.

It was an experiment.

Or, perhaps, a test.

Bleys began to unstrap, but Ed reached over and stopped him. "Bleys. Draw your weapon." He nodded toward The One.

Bleys, looking confused, looked at The One, still flailing and beginning to mewl piteously, and said, "He's disoriented, man. We need to help him!"

Ed shook his head and pointed to the shrinking jumpgate. "Not until we know it's Caleb."

Bleys looked at Ed for a moment, then nodded and drew his weapon.

Brother Caleb rejoiced that the machine could understand the danger. It might well mean Brother Caleb's death, but perhaps that would be for the best. The Bleys carried a weapon very lethal to Brother Caleb's kind. Brother Caleb had been mightily impressed with the efficacy of that weapon in the temple and desired one like it for himself. It seemed unlikely, however, that he would ever obtain one. Brother Caleb had little money, and as long as he labored at The Laundry, he would never have much.

The One collided with the deck and Sang in fear and pain. *Aid us, traitor! Share knowledge!*

Brother Caleb considered. Yes, it would be best if Bleys used the powerful weapon. Oblivion seemed a fair trade for the darkness in Brother Caleb's soul.

*Yes*, The Source said. *It is the only way for you. You are broken and corrupt. You are a malfunction.*

The One howled in Song, *No! We are loyal! We love The Source!*

Brother Caleb, in his prison, smiled. *But the source does not love us.*

It was freeing, to realize this was the end. He would not see heaven, or Heavenly Father, or The Jesus. That was too much to hope for. But he had denied The Source. It was enough.

It would be easy.

Too easy. It was what The Source wanted.

In the back of his mind, Brother Caleb heard a still, small voice. Perhaps it was only a memory, or an idle thought. Perhaps it was The Jesus. Brother Caleb did not know. But the voice said, "Forgive us our trespasses...."

The Bishop had taught Brother Caleb that to repent was more than to simply regret. That was part of it, but not the whole.

"To truly repent," The Bishop had said, "Is to understand that you have done wrong, and to change, to do the wrong no more. You must humble yourself, confess your sin, and ask for forgiveness. And you must *accept* that forgiveness along with your responsibility for the sin."

And there it was. How could someone repent, unless they accepted responsibility for their sin?

The pain was tremendous, the realization, the knowing, worse even than The Source tearing through Caleb's thoughts.

The Twisted one in the temple had not shown the actions of another, of some distant cousin. It had shown Caleb his own actions, memories he had walled off, attributed to another, The Bad One, the one who even now floundered about the cabin, weightless, crying for help.

The Source had simply freed that piece of his mind that he himself had locked away.

Again, he heard the small voice. "Forgive us our trespasses...."

Caleb thought briefly of begging for death, but oblivion was not repentance. It was the opposite of accepting responsibility.

*I will share knowledge,* he promised The Bad One. *But first, we must make a bargain.*

*I do not know what a bargain is!* The Bad One lamented, now fully in the grip of panic.

*I will teach you,* Caleb promised the terrified Bad One. *Come. Join.*

The Source roared in fury.

Then it was gone.

---

Bleys, still holding his gun on Caleb, glanced at Ed, then back to the pitiful sight before him. Caleb hung midair, weeping like a man who had lost a child, deep, racking sobs of grief. It made Bleys feel like a voyeur, even on his own ship. It wasn't right, watching someone go through whatever Caleb was experiencing. It felt like stealing, only worse than that, because Bleys had never really had much of a problem with a little five finger discount.

"Did it close?" he asked Ed.

"Another twenty-seven seconds at current rate. Keep an eye on him until it's done." Ed paused a moment. "Kane's calling."

"He's gonna be pissed," Bleys noted.

Ed nodded. "He is."

"Tell him we got some repairs to do before heading in, comms and nav are spotty," Bleys said with a wink. "That blast was damned close. Probably take at least an hour before we can get moving." In theory, an hour would give Old Cranky Pants some time to cool off, but maybe two would be even better. Or five. Bleys had always like multiples of five.

Kane was going to be *really* pissed.

Bleys turned back to Ed, thinking maybe the repairs might take all night. "You play any card games?"

# BATTLE FATIGUE

As it happened, Bleys found himself busy with "repairs" for another two hours, during which he mended Ed's knowledge on a number of topics such as how to cheat at poker and rummy and how to do a proper riffle shuffle. Bleys himself learned the valuable lesson that playing blackjack with Ed was a very bad idea, even allowing for cheating. Caleb remained silent for most of the overhaul, seeming lost in his thoughts and more than a little depressed, though he did participate briefly in the go fish training exercise.

By the time "repairs" were complete, Kane and Ana had transferred to the *Danzig*. Bleys wasn't sure if this was a good or bad sign, but he guessed that whatever the case, at this point, Kane wasn't going to cool off any further and they might as well go ahead and face the music.

Ana met them at the airlock, cringing as Kane's voice blared over the 1MC, "Bleys! Ed! Get your fat asses to the wardroom *right fucking now!*"

Bleys flashed her a grin. "So he took it pretty well, huh?"

Ana, struggling to suppress laughter, put a pinkie to her lips and pretended to contemplate this for a moment. "Let's just say we're going to have to replace several tiles in the overhead where he blew his top."

Bleys nodded sagely. "So, yeah, about average."

Ana snickered. "He didn't shoot anybody…yet. You'd better go."

"And get shot?"

"Go take your medicine," Ana said, shaking her head. "I'll take care of Caleb."

He caught her shoulder and looked her in the eye. "About that. Something happened to Caleb when the jumpgate opened." Bleys did his best to explain, but in truth, he didn't actually know any details, just that the guy had freaked out, then seemed to get a little better.

Ana nodded at his pathetic layman's report and waved him off. "Good luck. You'll need it!"

Bleys entered the wardroom first, thinking Kane was less likely to actually take a shot at him than Ed, then rethinking that strategy, in that Ed wouldn't actually *die* if Kane did shoot him, but by then the door had slid open and it was showtime.

Kane, unarmored and in dungarees, stood glowering at them, all three hundred pounds of hate and ass-beating crammed into a two-hundred-fifty-pound bag of muscle, sinew, and bulging, hairy eyeballs. Well, maybe it was less than two fifty, but Bleys often enjoyed poking at Kane by suggesting he was getting fat.

This was probably not the time, though.

Having missed the opportunity to push Ed in front, Bleys tried the charming smile, wide arms, and "hail the conquering hero returns" pose.

Kane's expression of complete "everybody in this room will be dead soon" suggested his efforts had missed the mark just a hair. "Don't give me that shit-eating grin, Bleys! You fucking *failed!*"

Morgan, looking exhausted, lounged on one of the several

couches. "Oh, thank god. I'm the only one he's had to bitch at for the last half hour, and I was just about to get up in his ass."

"Any time you feel froggy, Pepe!" Kane told him.

Ed, a resigned look on his face, strode past Bleys and took a seat at the nearest table. "Say what you need to say, Kane."

Kane strode over and placed both hands on the table, leaning over it and Ed. "You blew that shot on purpose!"

Ed gave Kane a sour look. "I made a mistake."

"You're literally a walking, fucking computer, Ed! Not buying it!"

Ed threw both arms in the air. "I am not perfect, Kane! There are plenty of possibilities for why the shot didn't go as planned. The projectile might have been out of round, or the weight could have been off. The charging coils could need maintenance. The Pestilence was also deep in these mechanisms, and there may be residual biological residue. Morgan and I just dealt with something similar. Nothing is cut and dried."

Kane slapped the table hard, clearly unconvinced, then turned to Bleys, still glaring. "And what do you have to say for yourself?"

Bleys gave Kane two thumbs up. "He hit the torpedo, and I'm still alive, so I count that as a win."

"Did he flinch on the kill shot or not?" Kane demanded.

Bleys rubbed at a temple and sighed. "Rags, I don't know. I was under a lot of Gs at the time and trying not to get my ass blown off. He hit the target I was worried about, and that's about all I remember."

Kane looked back and forth between them, fuming. Bleys, certain that his "I didn't do nothin!" look would not be well received, just fell into a really tired pose. It was easy, since he didn't even have to fake it.

"The two of you are both full of shit!" Kane fumed. "Ed, you pussied out on the kill shot! You flinched, and now Zion is compromised! And, Bleys, fuck you very much for this 'I don't recall' bullshit! You know what happened, I can see it in your eyes."

Bleys didn't like that one bit. If Kane could read him that easily, he must have been more tired than he thought.

To Bleys's surprise (which he kept well hidden), Ed hammered a fist on the table and leapt to his feet to get right in Kane's face, nose to nose. "I didn't sign up for murder, Kane! Obviously you're comfortable enough with it, but I couldn't bring myself to just casually take life!"

"Yes, you *could*, Ed!" Kane shot back. "You *did!* Because I guarantee you, you just doomed *billions* with that 'calculation error'!"

"I don't answer to you!" Ed shouted, pretty much indistinguishable from any other human in his genuine anger.

"This isn't a chain of command thing, it's a humanity thing!" Kane shot back. "You were the only one who had the power to act, so you had a fucking *duty* to act!"

"I am *not* human, as you apes are always so quick to remind me!"

Bleys gave Morgan a hard look, and Morgan nodded, rose to his feet, and sauntered over, looking to Bleys for a lead.

Kane let out a nasty laugh. "That's a lot of chest beating for a superior being. Hate to tell you, pal, but you're just another monkey flinging shit like rest of us. Deal with it!"

Bleys thought about putting hands on their shoulders, but decided it might signal one or both of them that he needed a few lumps for butting in. "Stand down, guys. Let's save it for the enemy."

"Mind your place, Bleys," Kane growled.

"I outrank you, Rags."

"If you're going to pull that bullshit captain rank on me, I promise you, we can get Morgan in on this to wave his Emperor dick around and we can all play pretend!"

Morgan's expression hardened, and he balled his fists as he glared at Kane. "You wanna go? Step off, Ed, I'm fixing to tune this cranky bitch up."

That was definitely not the sort of help Bleys had in mind when he'd signaled the younger marine. A three-way slugfest would, admittedly, be amusing as hell, but it would not in any way help things right now.

Bleys put a hand on Morgan's shoulder, hoping it would have the desired calming effect. "Come on, guys, bell's rung! Go to your corners. Let's talk this out before somebody does something they'll regret."

Ed, predictably, relaxed first. He stepped back and took a seat at the table again, looking more embarrassed than angry.

Kane and Morgan continued to glower at each other a moment. Kane, a grim smile on his lips, asked, "You need to file a hurt feelings report, Lieutenant?"

Morgan's angry pose shattered. He burst into quiet laughter. "Yeah, Chief, I think I do," he snorted, shaking in effort to contain giggles.

Kane, looking chagrined now, gently pushed Morgan aside and muttered, "Well go write it up, then, knucklehead."

"Okay, let me go find some crayons," Morgan said on his way back to the couch.

"You better not use my lunch," Kane muttered, drawing a new round of laughter from Morgan.

Bleys breathed a mental sigh of relief, though he saw no use in letting anyone know just how nervous he had actually been. "Are we cool, now? Can we talk this out?"

Kane took a seat at Ed's table and nodded. "I'm cool," he promised.

Bleys watched them both a moment for signs of mayhem,

then nodded, to himself more than to either of them. "Okay, since I have to be the Dad here, I'll lay it out for you. First, what's done is done. Does anybody disagree with that?" He looked back and forth between Ed and Kane, both of them sullen. "Ed, no plans for a time machine or anything, right?"

Ed's disgusted look was answer enough to that.

"Okay, so given that, next point: Ed's right, Rags. He didn't sign up for this. He didn't sign up for *anything*. He's a civilian."

"So are you," Kane said.

"I used to be, and even then, I wasn't really a civvy. I was a crook. We rank same as cops."

Kane snickered at this. "This is serious, Bleys."

"I know," Bleys admitted. "But it doesn't have to be a full Weyland-style ass chewing, does it?"

Kane leaned back in his chair and heaved a deep sigh, looking tired and defeated. "You know that old saying 'Speak of the devil'? It has a second part."

Ed, glum, nodded. "'And he shall appear.'"

"Exactly," Kane said. "We *have* to involve him at this point. The folks on Zion aren't going to like it at all, but we have to devise a whole new defense strategy, and we need Weyland."

Bleys let out a long, low whistle. "These people had beef with Vanov for shooting a *single* politician. How do you think they'll take to the Butcher of Falafel Five?"

Kane glowered at Bleys. "Farallon Six," he muttered. "Not a time for jokes. And I'm guessing nearly being eaten by the Pestilence is going to moderate their position somewhat, but what do I know about politics? I just shoot people."

Ed gave Kane a hard look. "Commander, I believe you are going to have to assume larger duties as of this moment. Vanov's departure leaves a power vacuum that will have to be filled by someone decisive, someone people can look to as a leader at least temporarily."

Kane waved the thought aside. "I just told you, I'm not a politician."

Bleys nodded. "I can pretend to be one. But I can't do it on my own. I need you." He looked back and forth at them. "*All* of you."

Ed, a resolute expression on his face, rose and gave Bleys a slight bow. "We had planned on setting up hyperspace comms on the *Dresden*. Shall I move forward on that?"

Kane thought a moment. "Do it here first. The *Danzig* is our flagship now. Besides, I'm sure Vanov had a lot of nasty surprises on the *Dresden*, maybe backdoor access, and now the enemy knows about them. You can override everything with Morgan's codes, right?"

"I can. I'll go over it in detail as soon as possible," Ed promised.

"Do that," Kane said, nodding. "Once we know everything is secure, then we'll talk about setting up comms there too."

Bleys waited a moment to be certain they were done, then nodded like he was actually in charge. "Okay, so as soon as Ed finishes setup here, we'll get Weyland on the horn."

"He's gonna want a full report from everyone," Kane noted. "Where's Ana?"

Bleys's mood crashed at once with this simple question. He sighed and fidgeted until Kane's glare, like the sun burning Bleys's face on a summer day, became too uncomfortable to bear any longer. "Rags, there's one more thing we need to talk about, and don't freak out, ok?"

---

In the *Doro*'s sick bay, Ana looked again at her scans and decided they were largely meaningless. She had no idea if Caleb's physiology was out of whack. He seemed a normal human, but did emulating a human mask any injuries the Pestilence anatomy might have? Did it even make any sense to talk about "anatomy" when dealing with the Pestilence?

"Do you *feel* well?" Ana asked.

Caleb's only answer was a shrug.

He certainly didn't *look* well. His hair hung limp, and his eyes were dull, unfocused. He sat on the table, slump shouldered, hands limp at his sides, occasionally sniffing, but otherwise silent.

His condition was hardly surprising. From what Bleys had told her during their brief conversation, something awful had happened to Caleb when the jumpgate opened, leaving him a sobbing wreck, but he had come through it, or at least it seemed so.

How would she even know?

He showed no signs of injury, though, of course, he wouldn't. She could take her scalpel and slash him to the bone and the wound would knit in seconds, she was certain. "What happened to you?"

She hadn't expected an answer, but Caleb spoke, his voice seeming much older than before. "I touched The Source." For long moments, he said nothing more, then continued, "It was…difficult."

"I have no doubt. We didn't even have the chance to warn you."

Caleb looked up at her, his eyes no longer innocent, but haunted, darkened. "It would have come sooner or later."

"What happened, Caleb?" she asked as gently as she could.

Caleb offered her a sad smile, and his lips trembled as he spoke. "I became enlightened."

Ana gave him a moment before asking, "How so?"

Looking even more miserable, Caleb whispered, "I was allowed to see what I really am. *Who* I really am. The Source spawned another within me, a child with no understanding, and forced me to watch it as it used this body. It tried to kill your friend Bleys."

Despite the horror within her at the thought, the damnable curiosity was stronger. "How did you stop it?"

"It had no knowledge. It did not understand why there was no gravity, and it was afraid. It allowed me to assimilate it."

"And that was…difficult for you?"

Caleb offered her a slight smile. "No. That was not the difficult part. It was the knowledge The Source shared with me afterward." He seemed deep in thought for a moment, as if choosing his words carefully. "It was an object lesson for me, to demonstrate the proper order of things. The lesser must submit to the greater to find peace and comfort."

The question was obvious, but somehow it stuck in Ana's throat. It felt too much an accusation.

Caleb seemed to understand, though. "No. I did not submit."

"It just let you go?"

For a moment, Caleb seemed to consider this, then shook his head. "Not as you think of it, no. It was less of a release than a casting out. I was damaged, a malfunction. I did not choose correctly, so I was marked. None will Sing to me or join. I am alone." Caleb shook his head again. "I am one now, truly."

"And that's a great loss for you?"

"It is a great change, but it is not the aspect that troubles me." Caleb shifted uncomfortably. "You know of my kind, what we do. Can you understand? Until the temple, *I did not*."

It took a moment for Ana to grasp his point. "Because the Evil One kept you isolated?"

"Yes. Until The Twisted One Sang the truth, I did not know the depths of our evil. I knew my own hunger, my impulses, but I thought of myself as largely innocent. I did not know I had done such terrible things." He closed his eyes tightly, shaking with emotion. "I did not know I was a *monster*."

"But you are *not* a monster, Caleb!" Ana insisted. "You didn't do those things."

Caleb looked up at the overhead, his face a mask of pure misery. "We are not like you, Ana. There is no easy place of separation as there is with your kind, a line where Ana ends and Bleys begins. There is only *one* of us. We are just in pieces."

Ana scowled and shook her head at this. "It's not true. You just said it yourself. You made a choice, and you were cast out because of it. That's an *individual.*"

With a sad smile, Caleb raised a hand to touch her cheek. "Imagine that you could remove your arm and send it on a mission, and then it could come back to you and tell you what it learned, become a part of you again. Is your arm an individual?"

"If it refused to do what I wanted? Of course."

"Now imagine that before you had ever detached your arm, you had used it to kill Bleys. Is the arm innocent?"

Ana stammered a moment, trying to remember her religious training. Maybe she could reach him with that. "It's not the same. This is the Devil trying to break your will, to convince you that you're beyond salvation. It's an old trick."

"The Source cannot lie to me, any more than I can lie to it. I *am* The Source. All of us are. I am just an Appendage that forgot what it was for a time."

Ana was angry now. "And so what? Now you give up on everything you've learned? Will you kill us all now? Even if it *is* who you were, you're someone else now."

Caleb frowned at her. "I give up on nothing," he snapped, then softened again. "And I still have my doubts if I can be forgiven, but I intend to try. I just move forward with my eyes open now. Endure to the end, as my church says."

A part of Ana couldn't help but wonder just how long that might entail for a creature like Caleb. Did the Pestilence even age? If he avoided fighting, he might he end up waiting on his entry into heaven until the stars burned out, bearing his guilt for eons.

The Russian side of her couldn't help but note that it was perhaps a fair penance.

"Are there other pieces?" she asked. "'Appendages' that you could teach?"

Caleb contemplated this a moment, then shook his head. "They will not listen to me now that I have been marked. But even if they would, I think it would be hopeless." He looked up at her, eyes full of pain. "I told you Chert wrote his name in your DNA, yes? You understand how important his name was to him?"

"Of course."

"And it is the same for me. So understand when I tell you this: there have only ever been three named entities among my kind."

Ana boggled. "How can you know that?"

"I connected to The Source. It shared much knowledge, far more than I could contain. Most of it is just vague awareness without detail, but this I know to be true: before Chert, there was only The Source, and after, only me. There is no Other One to reach. Only pieces with more or less knowledge."

Staggered, Ana could only run a hand through her hair for a moment as she absorbed what Caleb had told her. The Pestilence was a single entity? It explained much, but an individual spanning the entire galaxy? It was difficult to fully grasp. "The Source… has a name?" she finally managed.

Caleb nodded gravely. "It is called 'Friend'."

Ana found herself blinking in confusion. "What? That doesn't sound right."

Caleb shrugged. "I, too, find it strange. But it is the best translation I have." His brow furrowed a moment. "But you know a better word."

"Eh? How can you know that?"

"The same way I knew Chert's name. I tasted it in you when I rebuilt your foot. But I do not know the word, only of its presence. It is often that way with shared knowledge." He reached hesitantly toward her. "May I?"

Gritting her teeth, Ana nodded. She had no real reason to be nervous. Caleb could easily kill her if that were his intent, but something deep and primal in her cringed nonetheless as he placed a hand to her cheek.

"*Tovarishch,*" he whispered and lowered his gaze, as if he knew the significance the term had for her.

The word hit Ana like a physical blow, bringing childhood terrors to life. For a moment, she was back in the prefab housing as explosions reined down around her, unable to hear her own screams, watching friends and family bleeding out. The communist rebels were animals, killing everyone she loved until the Empire had righteously crushed them underfoot like the dogshit they were!

"No," she whispered in a husky voice. "You're wrong!" she shouted. "Not that!"

Caleb simply looked at her, sadness in his eyes. "When we touch, neither of us can lie to the other. It is the same as with The Source. I know what it means to you. It is the right word."

"You just told me The Source is a single entity. How the hell can it be a communist?"

Caleb nodded patiently. "You understand what became of your people, all of them, on many worlds? They, too, are The Source now."

Ana felt bile rising in her throat. "No," she whispered.

"In my church, we believe the Adversary's plan was to make everyone the same, to force them into a predetermined order. The Source is the same: it is the Devourer of Souls, the Thief of Agency. It *is* a commune."

"I know the goddamn Mormon Church's mythology!" Ana shouted. "I don't believe you! I *won't*—!"

From behind her, Kane shouted, "Step away from it, Ana!"

She spun to see Kane and Morgan, both armored, rifles leveled in her direction. Behind them stood Bleys, looking miserable, and Ed, looking resolute.

Ana ground her teeth, furious that she had let herself get so worked up that she hadn't even noticed them enter. She rose slowly to stand in front of Caleb. "No. I will not let you do this," she said, her voice low, almost a growl.

Kane jerked a thumb toward the exit. "This isn't a discussion!" he shouted. "Stand aside *now!*"

"I will not!" Ana cried. "Shoot me if that's what you have to do!"

"Don't fucking *test* me, Rasputin!"

"Oh, I believe you will!" she cried. "Just like you killed that child!"

Kane made a choking, almost strangled sound, and roared, "Morgan, get her out of my face!"

Morgan moved slowly, clearly not relishing his duty, and reached for her arm. Ana jerked away, struggling to stay between Caleb and Kane. "*Josey!* My god, don't let them do this!"

Bleys drew his own weapon, a look in his eyes that Ana couldn't identify and had never seen before. He said through gritted teeth, "Babe, I can't stop them, but I promise you this: if they hurt you, there's going to be killing. You hear me, Kane?"

"Get the fuck out of here with that shit, Bleys," Kane shouted over his shoulder. "You know as well as I do, we have to do this!"

"Not if Ana gets hurt! I'm warning you, Rags. Don't make me go there!"

Morgan reached for her again, still with little enthusiasm. "C'mon, Ana. No way out of this."

"Ed!" Ana cried. "You *can* stop this!"

Ed's reproving look crushed her heart. "I'm sorry, Ana.

You're not thinking clearly. Sentiment has clouded your judgment. There is no alternative."

Inside, Ana wailed to see him stand against her too. "This isn't a matter of practicality! It's a matter of morality! Don't you see? It's the goddamn *apocalypse!* It's judgement day! God is testing us to see if we *deserve* to survive!"

None of them would meet her gaze except Kane, who had no doubts, or so he would have her believe. So that was it, then. They were all against her. So be it. She would stand against them then and let the chips fall where they would.

Before she could speak further, she felt Caleb rise from the table and push past. He stepped in front of her, shielding her as she had shielded him, hands above his head. "Do not hurt Ana or each other. I will accept whatever you decide."

"Kane!" Ana cried, trying to push Caleb back behind her, but he refused to cooperate. She shouted over his shoulder, "Listen to me! He's not *just* a person! He has *vital* intelligence! He can lead us to The Source!"

Kane was wavering. She could see it, even if no one else could. It had been cruel of her to say what she said about what he did in the temple, but she had been desperate. Killing the child had to have taken a terrible toll on him. He was no monster, but neither was Caleb!

Kane adjusted his grip on his rifle, rolling his shoulders. "That...*thing*...killed the whole galaxy! None of them can be allowed to live!"

"That's not true and you know it!" she shot back. "If it weren't for Chert, we would *all* be dead! Lars and his people saved Cerberus as much as any of us!"

"The Source will own him the second a jumpgate opens!" Kane asserted, waving her point aside with a slash of his hand.

"It's not true! He already resisted it when Reed escaped! He got information from it that we need! He knows what it is, Kane!

For God's sake, *think* about what you're doing! You're about to kill the one chance we have to survive!"

Kane stood in silence for long moments, then seemed to reach a decision. He lowered his weapon and popped his visor, then stepped toward her, pushing his face over Caleb's shoulder and right into hers, his eyes narrow and cold. "This ain't about saving my own skin, or even humanity. You and me, babe, we got higher commitments. So, you look me in the eye and tell me the truth: are you willing to gamble your son's life on this thing?"

Ana nodded vigorously, licking her lips. What she said now would determine everything. "This is our *only* chance! If we don't have allies to help us understand this enemy, we're all dead!"

Kane held her gaze a long moment, searching her eyes as if he could actually see into her soul and decide if she was sincere. At last, he stepped back and eyed Caleb up and down, then called over his shoulder. "Ed, I need a brig that can hold the Pestilence. Can you do it?"

"I can," Ed assured him.

"You," Kane said to Caleb. "Step back against the bulkhead and keep your hands where I can see them." He turned back to Ana, and this time, she could see the hurt in his eyes. She had gone too far with the comment about the child, she knew it, but she couldn't take it back.

Kane nodded toward Caleb. "He doesn't leave this compartment until he goes to Ed's brig. And I am holding you personally responsible if this goes bad. You feel me, Rasputin?"

Bleys shouted from behind, "Kane!"

Kane spun on him, fury in his eyes. "*What?*"

Again, Ana saw the unfamiliar, cold look on Bley's face. "No more threats," he said, in a voice that wasn't like any she had ever heard from him before.

Kane sneered at him. "Oh, it's an empty threat," Kane said. "None of us survive if she's wrong."

Morgan popped his visor as well. "Chief," he said, slowly and deliberately. "You need to take a knee or something, ok?"

Kane swept them all with his gaze, then threw his rifle against the bulkhead and stalked out of the room.

Bleys stepped quickly over to Ana and crushed her in an embrace. "I gotta go after him, babe. He's in trouble."

"I know," she whispered. "I love you."

"Me too," he whispered back.

Ana smirked as he left, despite everything.

It was close enough.

---

Bleys caught up with Kane just as the marine was about to enter the airlock. "Kane!"

Kane paused and glared in Bleys's direction but said nothing.

Bleys knew better than to take the tone he did, but like Kane, he had been through a hell of a day. "You pull that shit again and me and you are gonna have a real problem!"

Kane snorted. "I'd hate to have to kill you, Bleys."

Bleys flipped his duster aside and let his hand hover near the disintegrator. "Big talk for a man who ain't heeled."

"You jerk that thing, you better kill me," Kane growled. "Because if you don't, I'll even that score, you can count on it."

Bleys stared at him a moment. "Is that where you want to take this?"

"Fuck around and find out," Kane said.

Bleys shrugged. "Plenty of people took a number on my ass. Nobody's collected yet."

"You gotta sleep sometime."

"So do you."

Kane shook his head, laughing without humor. "No," he said, looking suddenly haggard and old. He leaned forward and banged his head against the bulkhead twice. It wasn't hard enough to damage the airlock, but it would have likely cracked Kane's skull if he hadn't been wearing a helmet.

As Kane sank slowly to his knees, Bleys realized the man wasn't laughing at all. He was shaking with grief. "I shot a *kid* today, man! A fucking little *baby!*" he sobbed, covering his face with a gauntleted hand. "I ain't never gonna sleep again."

And there it was. Kane was as hard as they came, but even he had limits. No wonder he was hammering Ed so hard for flinching on that shot. Kane had taken one that had damn near gutted him.

"Rags," Bleys said, his voice kinder now. "Let's go back to Ana and make nice. She knows how it is. It's a tough job. She can give you something and shit will seem better when you wake up. We'll handle contacting Weyland. You just get some rest, man."

Kane said nothing for long moments, sobbing quietly on his knees. Finally, he wiped at his eyes and said, "Okay. But when you talk to him, tell him something for me."

"What?"

"I'm out."

"*What?*" Bleys said again, gaping.

"I fucking quit. I can't do this shit anymore."

## MAKING THINGS OFFICIAL

"*D*oro, *Danzig*, shore power is connected and active."

"*Doro*, aye," Bleys answered and began his power down checklist. He turned to Ana in the copilot's seat and grinned. "It's still weird."

"*Danzig* having a crew?" she asked.

"Yeah," Bleys answered. "I kind of got used to it being just Ed."

Things in general had had been weird for a while after they had lost Vanov, actually. It hadn't taken Ed long to get his hyperspace comms running aboard the *Danzig*, and once that was done, Weyland had reluctantly agreed to serve where the Emperor needed him. Ed Senior had reported some rare, good news: he had managed to crack the Tartarus system control module, so the beacon would be visible for most of the trip back, cutting travel time substantially.

Bleys and Ed had retrieved the Liahona system control module, which had turned out to be one hell of a lot easier than grabbing the one from the Tartarus system. Then it had just been a matter of ferrying it back to Ed Senior and giving Weyland a lift to his new post.

Not to say it hadn't been complicated. They still needed the *Danzig* to serve as a beacon for a good third of the trip, until they had a decent fix on the Tartarus beacon. And then there was the new reality of hyperspace travel: leaving gates open and relatively unguarded was a thing of the past now. As a temporary measure, Ed Senior had hauled one of Ed's really shooty guns out to the jumpgate, ready to blast anything that came through without proper credentials, and Bleys supposed that worked, but it made him nervous. He had a small, secret fear that Alsatia still harbored a grudge, but he was pretty sure she wouldn't blast *Doro* with Ana aboard

He estimated that particular threat at less than one percent suicide, which was better odds than he had seen lately (or ever, being honest). It was definitely worth the risk for another mini-honeymoon, not to mention getting an actual leader in place so he could abandon his new acting career. Truth be told, playing leader was starting to do him some real mental damage.

It had come as something of a shock to see just how easily the folks aboard the *Dresden* took to following his orders. They *wanted* to do what he told them, what *anybody* who sounded like he knew what he was doing told them, when it came down to it. Poor bastards had no clue how much Bleys was faking it, but then, he had his suspicions that such was exactly how most leaders got by: attitude and blind luck.

Long-term, though, he was really not up for sending men to their deaths and accepting responsibility. He just wasn't that much of an asshole, but he knew one guy in particular who was, and turning the "who's drafting who" tables on Weyland was abso-lutely delicious.

And then, well, once you made the one trip, folks expected it to be a regular thing, so in the three months that followed, Bleys put in a lot of flight time, but the stayovers with Ana in the beach condo on Elysium made it more of an adventure than actual work.

Now, though, his machinations had caught up with him. Weyland had summoned them, and they had answered the call.

Bleys was pretty sure it must have something to do with Kane. He hadn't seen or heard from the marine since he had brought Weyland back three months ago. Ed would surely have looked out for the big lunk, and had something bad happened, they would have heard, but still, Kane had been pretty damned adamant about quitting.

And at some point, that other shoe had to drop, didn't it?

Weyland's new office aboard the *Danzig* was, surprisingly, larger than his workspace on Cerberus and well stocked with amenities, including his favorite scotch. The bulkheads were still white, because it was still the Empire, but the surfaces were smooth and seamless instead of blocks, which was at least a mild change of pace.

Not that Weyland had ever cared much for change that he did not personally instigate.

The forward bulkhead was devoted entirely to the seal of the Empire, laurels surrounding an eagle and crossed swords, and in front of it sat a great, real mahogany desk. Weyland sat behind it, across from Morgan, eying his…master? Ward? It was a complicated relationship. Weyland intended to play things squarely and actually have Morgan lead when he was ready. That being said, other than putting in an appearance and saying a few prepared words, he was not anywhere near qualified to assume leadership. That would take time.

The boy had, at least, cleaned up as Weyland had instructed. It wouldn't do for the Emperor to go milling about in dungarees, brawling with his subjects and flinging curses at anyone within earshot, doubly so on a Mormon world. Morgan refused to wear a crown, and Weyland agreed with that. Crowns were something Arcann had instituted, but Tenebrae would never have worn something so ridiculous. One's cover was specifically a reminder that every man had his master. The Emperor, having no master, should wear no head covering at all.

They had selected a sharp, tailored uniform of Imperial black and red, similar to Weyland's own, but where the rank insignia would be on the collar and epaulets, they had chosen a silver and gold version of the Imperial seal, the same symbol that filled the forward bulkhead.

Now, as for the sidearm, well, the boy wouldn't budge on that point, and to be fair, Tenebrae had always had his affectation with his scepter. Being armed was a statement, and it wasn't as if there were safety concerns as there might be for a less martially inclined leader. Morgan knew his way around a gun. He wasn't going to do something foolish like blast his own foot off or shoot someone on accident.

Of course, he might do so intentionally.

Ah, well. Angering the Emperor had ever been hazardous to one's health. It was just that, previously, the executions would have been carried out by proxy, whereas Morgan might well see to his own summary punishments.

That might not even be a bad thing, were it to happen. People tended to have more respect for a leader who wasn't afraid to get his hands dirty.

Yes, all in all, things were shaping up nicely. "We'll get you a secretary soon enough," Weyland promised. "And take my advice: treat whoever serves in that role like a family member, because they will make or break you."

"We need to make sure she's cute," Morgan noted.

Weyland sighed, feeling as if he were losing ground. "Don't shit where you eat, son. We'll look for a man for that spot to keep you out of trouble."

Morgan nodded as if this were sage advice and turned to the next subject. "So we're doing the preacher?"

Weyland blinked a moment as he digested the comment. "It greatly concerns me that you use a phrase like 'doing the preacher.' I don't like either of the first two things that choice of words brings to mind."

Morgan snickered at this. "*Meeting* the preacher. Better?"

"Much." Weyland shuffled through his itinerary. "And he's some kind of grand poobah type, here. The locals call him 'The Prophet.'"

"What do *we* call him?"

"'Sir'," Weyland said in a dry voice.

Morgan looked embarrassed and corrected himself. "What do we call him, *sir*?"

It was indeed a face-palm moment, and Weyland found himself unable to suppress the urge or the laugh that followed. "We call *him* 'sir.' As for us, *I* am the one who should technically be calling *you* 'sir.'"

Morgan, crestfallen, shook his head in consternation. "This is a lot more complicated than it should be. If I don't call my highest ranked admiral 'sir,' why does some Jesus freak get honors?"

Weyland shrugged, nodding his general agreement. Sometimes, protocols made little sense. "Politics," he said.

Morgan frowned, but before he could comment, Weyland's desk communicator beeped. "Sir," his secretary announced, "President Benson is here for his meeting with the Emperor."

Weyland gave Morgan a questioning look, and the younger man nodded and offered a thumbs up. Weyland called over the comm, "Send him in, Mrs. Larsen."

Morgan, confusion on his face, whispered loudly, "I thought this was a church guy, not the president!"

Weyland smiled and waved a calming hand. "President of the Church, not the planet. It's the right man."

Morgan eyed Weyland with suspicion as the door slid open to reveal an elderly gentleman dressed in a suit and tie.

The newcomer, Benson, nodded to Weyland. "It's good to meet you again, Admiral," he said, then turned to Morgan and bowed. "And you must be the new emperor. I'm sorry, I'm really not certain of the proper honorific here. Your grace, perhaps?"

Morgan rose and pulled his tunic down, then extended a hand. "'Emperor' is just fine. And around here, we don't bow, we shake hands."

Weyland nodded, approving of the common touch. Now, if only Morgan didn't do something silly like try to crush the octogenarian's hand in some foolish penis measuring contest, all would be well.

Morgan took Benson's hand and shook vigorously. "And it's 'President Benson,' yes?"

Hearing no snapping of bone and no expression of pain on the old fellow's face, Weyland allowed himself a sigh of relief.

Benson nodded amiably. "Or Henry. Or whatever makes you comfortable."

Morgan grinned and took his seat. "That's my name, too!"

Benson lowered himself gently into a chair. "And already, we have something in common."

Weyland cleared his throat and interjected, "President Benson, forgive me, but the Emperor's schedule is quite full...." Best to keep things moving along. It would not do for this to devolve into small talk, or Morgan would have the man playing the knife game and showing him nude pinups in short order.

"Ah, yes, yes!" Benson said, nodding. "Busy like a beehive. I understand completely, and I'll get right to the point. Emperor, I've come to plead for clemency for Brother Caleb."

Morgan looked askance at the elderly man. "You know who this guy is?"

"I do," Benson said, again nodding vigorously. "His story has electrified our entire church. Are you familiar with the tale?"

Morgan chuckled and leaned back in his chair. "Yeah, you could say so. I was part of the fireteam that brought the kids out."

Benson boggled at this and stammered a moment, speechless. At last, he managed to respond, "No one told us the emperor himself was involved!"

"Yeah," Morgan answered, looking a little uncomfortable. "We, uh, kind of thought maybe we should keep that part quiet."

"I'll keep your confidence then, sir," Benson promised. "Now, as for Brother Caleb, what can be done?"

Weyland's office was posh enough to have an antechamber, guarded by a severe-looking woman whose nametag identified her as "Larsen." She sat at a desk near the closed door to Weyland's office proper, like Cerberus guarding the gates of the underworld, only in reverse: abandon hope, all who…exit? Yeah, it didn't really work.

Mrs. Larsen frowned up at Bleys. "May I help you, sir?" She pronounced the "sir" as more of a negative comment on Bleys's lineage than any honorific.

So it was like that, eh? Bleys gave serious thought to telling her *exactly* what she could do for him, but Ana would not appreciate the comment, and probably he would have to interact with this harpy often.

Also, there was, in his experience, a small chance she might actually take him up on it, and that would open a whole can of worms he had absolutely no desire to deal with.

Still, her tone did call for some sort of punishment.

"Tell the Emperor that Captain Bleys is here to defend Lady Alsatia's honor, and I will have satisfaction with pistols at dawn."

Ana snorted laughter as Mrs. Larsen's scowl deepened. "The Admiral and the Emperor are meeting with the Prophet, and they are not to be disturbed."

Bleys slid his duster aside, exposing one of his blasters. He grinned as the secretary's eyes widened. She stammered a moment, at last managing to gasp out, "How did you—?"

"Tell him," Bleys insisted, putting a hand on the blaster grip. "*Now.*"

Ana gave him the "Now you're being a dick" look, to which Bleys responded with the ever popular "She started it!" counter glare.

Mrs. Larsen rose nervously from her seat and keyed in a code, then slipped inside as soon as the door slid wide enough.

Moments later, the door opened again to reveal Morgan, dressed in a snazzy new uniform, striking an offended pose. "Sir, I'll have you know that Lady Alsatia *has* no honor, and if you think I am dumb enough to draw on you, you're fucking dumber than that!"

Behind him, Mrs. Larsen was palming her face, and Weyland was very obviously exercising supreme will not to do the same. And behind them, an old guy dressed in a suit and tie was just as obviously trying not to laugh.

Morgan winced even as he spoke and turned to the old man. "Sorry, Padre. Imperial marines, ya know?"

The old fellow just smiled. "Son, I was a senior chief in the Navy. If you think I haven't heard or used that word before, think again." He gave Morgan a conspiratorial wink and offered a handshake. "Truth be told, I sometimes still do, but not as often these days. It's all about trying to improve, right?"

Morgan gripped the man's hand and shook, an appreciative look on his face. "Damn, you Mormons are kind of cool."

"If you're interested in joining the Church, Emperor, I'd be happy to put you in touch with missionaries."

"Not on your fucking life, preacher," Morgan said, grinning.

The old guy nodded amiably and stepped past Bleys, heading for the exit. "You know where to find me if you change your mind, Emperor. I'll be in touch about that matter we discussed."

Bleys watched him go, then grabbed Morgan's outstretched hand and squeezed it warmly. "Good to see you! Who was that guy?"

"Church bigwig," Morgan told him.

Mrs. Larsen made a sound in her throat halfway between a whimper and a growl and pushed past them to plop back in her desk chair, the very air around her almost shimmering in her blistering, impotent rage.

Weyland frowned, but Morgan appeared not to notice the woman's distress. He beckoned Ana and Bleys into the office. "Come on in! Let's catch up!"

Weyland gave them a curt nod. "Let's." He stopped the door from closing with a hand and called out, "Mrs. Larsen, have Commander Kane report to my office at once."

"Yes, sir," she answered as the doors slid closed again.

Weyland gave Bleys and Morgan a scowl. "She's a nice enough woman. Why do the two of you need to prod at her like that?"

Morgan scoffed. "Civilian under naval training, more like."

Ana shook her head. "That's a little harsh."

Weyland, still scowling, nodded. "Agreed."

Morgan, looking mischievous, shrugged and took his seat, then leaned back and propped his feet on the desk. "It ain't that far off if you ask me."

Bleys realized he was not going to be able to let this pass. "I missed something, obviously."

Weyland waved a hand dismissively. "It's a Naval acronym, son. Look it up. Meanwhile, let's debrief you. We have a lot going on and we're squeezing the two of you in here."

Bleys thought a moment, feeling his lips move as he repeated Morgan's phrase to himself, then suddenly made the connection. "Oh, that's kind of clever! And yeah, I agree with Morgan."

Weyland sighed. "She's good at her job, and I get along with her just fine, or at least I used to. Now I'll probably have to smooth some ruffled feathers." He took a seat at his desk and rapped his knuckles sharply on the surface. "Let's focus on serious matters, shall we?"

Bleys, following Ana's lead, took a seat in one of several comfortable chairs along the bulkhead. "Oh, where's the fun in that?"

Weyland shook his head, but he was smiling. "I prefer orderly and efficient to fun. Now, *Captain*, I presume you do indeed have the equipment Mr. Decker requested?"

Bleys nodded. "Sure do. Honestly, I expected Ed to greet us, but I haven't heard from him."

Weyland chuckled. "That's because he's more polite than you and doesn't eavesdrop. He's aboard the *Dresden*, cataloguing the battle damage."

Ed's voice called out from an overhead speaker, "To be fair, Admiral, I *do* eavesdrop somewhat. I have small alert programs that will signal me if my name is mentioned so that I can respond, but typically I do not waste CPU power processing every possible conversation."

Bleys snapped his fingers and turned a concerned face on Ana. "Damn, babe, he knows all the nasty stuff we said about him."

Ana shook her head. "No, no, he doesn't know we call him 'The Gimp.' He wouldn't have been alerted."

Bleys would have given anything to see Ed's face or a reasonable approximation thereof, but his voice did have the proper tongue-in-cheek intonation when he responded, "Ana, I am afraid I must inform you that my calculations indicate your long-term exposure to Captain Bleys's caustic personality may be taking a toll on your mental health."

Weyland gave Bleys a sour look. "Now you even have the goddamned AI doing it. I can play this game, too, you know. When are the two of you going to make things official and tie the knot?"

Morgan's face lit with impish delight. "We can still catch that preacher before he leaves!"

Ed, speaking quickly, interjected, "Captain Bleys, might I have a word with you in private?"

Morgan frowned and shouted, "Pipe down, Ed!"

Ana, face now bright red, was glaring at each of them in turn. "There is still a matter of decorum that Josey has most certainly *not* followed. Call me old fashioned, but I expect a man to take a knee and ask."

Morgan slapped a knee. "Ask, hell. Make him *beg!*"

Ana, still red, gave Bleys a smug look. "You hear that, Josey? That's a direct order from the Emperor. Beg, cowboy."

Bleys was having a bit of trouble sorting out all of the emotions he was feeling at once, but surely several of them were that he was getting one-upped, and that would not do. Tongue firmly in cheek, he said, "We're already hitched."

Ana boggled at him a moment. "You must have me confused with your other girlfriend."

Bleys gave her the "oh ye of little faith" look, tossed in a dash of charming, rakish hubris, and said, "We had a honeymoon. We must be hitched. I reckon Ed knew it too. The champagne said it was for newlyweds."

Ed again tried to interrupt, "Captain Bleys—"

Ana cut him off this time. "Nonono!" she laughed, shaking a finger at Bleys. "You're not getting off that easy. On your knees! And don't forget, I have another suitor, a very rich one!"

Bleys looked about, grinning, wondering if he should play this as reluctant, or if he should let on that it was indeed something he had been dreaming of for months. He rose, doffed his hat, and with great fanfare settled to one knee. "Ana, babe—"

The office door slid open suddenly. Kane's bulk practically filled the opening, his eyes dark and glowering. He was dressed in jeans and a button up denim shirt. Bleys was pretty sure this was the first time he had ever seen the marine in civilian clothes, and in fact, he wouldn't have bet money that Kane even owned any clothing besides his dress blues, his armor, and his dungarees.

Mrs. Larsen peeked cautiously from behind Kane and said in a slightly higher pitched voice, "Sir, he insisted—"

Weyland waved her off. "It's fine, Mrs. Larsen. Come in, Commander."

Kane stepped inside, glowering at everyone as the door closed behind him. "I said I quit," he rumbled.

Morgan snickered. "But you came running when I called you, didn't you, bitch?"

Kane grinned. "Take off that monkey suit and I'll show you who's the bitch." He seemed to suddenly notice Bleys still kneeling. "The fuck you doing down there?"

Ana rolled her eyes as Bleys rose, looking sheepish. "I dropped a pistachio," he snickered.

"You eat those nasty things? And off the floor too?" Kane suddenly caught Ana's eye and looked slightly nervous. "Obviously I missed something here."

Morgan swung his feet to the floor and sat up in his chair. "I got a mission for you, Chief."

Kane shook his head. "I told you and the Admiral, I quit. I have personal business to take care of."

"Well, I just un-quit you," Morgan told him. Before Kane could object, Morgan added, "Hear me out. The *Dresden* is fucked up and needs to hit the shipyards, and she needs a captain. Long term, I figure we'll jump Smitty up for the job, but right now, with what happened with Vanov, we need a head cracker running the show. Will you do it?"

Kane froze for a moment, his eyes widening. "Which shipyards?"

"You know which ones," Morgan told him, grinning.

Kane blinked a moment, as if hardly daring to believe what he was hearing. "What about Zion?"

Weyland shrugged. "We'll be fine with the *Danzig*."

Kane nodded, slipping into his parade rest stance, which Bleys thought looked a little funny in the civilian clothes, but he didn't laugh for fear that Kane would snap out of the trance and either punch him or storm off and not take the gig—maybe both.

After a moment of thought, Kane asked, "So what if Asgard doesn't want to play ball? Nothing says they'll recognize your authority."

Morgan grinned. "We own the jumpgates, the crack, and the *Danzig*. They'll play ball."

Weyland nodded, looking impressed. "Tenebrae himself made similar observations in the past. 'Paul,' he would say, 'The galaxy runs on flectocite and fear.' It will be difficult for anyone to turn us down."

Morgan nodded toward Bleys. "And you and Ed gotta grab the Aesir system control module so we can get those guys back up, and he can set up the hyperspace comms too."

Bleys considered this a moment. "Anybody asked Ed?"

Ed answered over the speaker, "This was my idea, Captain. I need the facilities to fully effect repairs."

Bleys shrugged. "Well, I'm a spacer, so it's not much of an ask for me to go joyriding. It's a damned long run, though, a couple of months maybe, leapfrogging. Is the *Dresden*'s jump drive in good shape?"

Ed answered, "Her drive is fine. Her stores of flectocite are almost exhausted, though. We'll need to stock up at Cerberus prior to departure."

"*Doro* could do with a restock herself," Bleys said.

Morgan grinned. "Good. I have a passenger I want to send with you."

Bleys raised an eyebrow. "Who?"

"You'll see," Morgan said, rubbing his hands together. "Now, before knucklehead barged in here, we had some important business going on and I, for one, would like to see it finished."

Ana turned again to Bleys, an expectant look on her face, and Bleys again settled to his knee.

Kane's face lit as he suddenly understood. "Oh, hell yes!" he shouted.

Ed, his voice urgent, again interrupted, "Captain Bleys, if I could have just a moment of your time in private."

Bleys let out an exaggerated sigh and threw up his arms in surrender. "Ed, we might as well *all* be married here. Just *say* it already."

For a moment, Ed didn't speak. "Are you certain? This is a matter of some delicacy."

Every bit of Bleys's nature cried out to take the call in private. It was just the prudent thing to do. But one look at Ana was enough to convince him it would be a mistake. She was watching him intently, getting ready to hear his proposal.

It was no time to keep secrets.

"Ed, I got nothing I want to hide from anybody here. Spill the beans, old buddy, old pal."

"Very well. I have recently gone over the casualty and refugee reports from Asgard."

Bleys's heart sank, and he prayed to any god he could think of that it wasn't what he feared. Vanov had assured them Kane's family was safe. "Ed, does this have to do with Kane's family?" he asked quickly.

"No," Ed assured him. "It has to do with yours."

Bleys felt his brain skip a beat as he tried to wrap it around that tidbit. "Uh, you got your wires crossed there, Ed," he said, relieved. "All of my family is dead."

The office door slid open again, and Ed, in his synthskin body, entered, a data pad in hand. "Among the refugees is one Veronica Bleys, captain of the *Serendipity*."

Ana's eyes widened at this, then softened, and she smiled. "I had no idea you had a sister! Why didn't you tell me?"

Bleys's smile must have not really passed the bill, but this wasn't exactly a fair fight. It was more of an ambush.

Ed looked back and forth, then asked Bleys, "Would you prefer to tell her?"

Ana's face grew darker and more cynical as Bleys stammered, searching for the right words, each second dragging by, slouching and trudging along like a child on his way to the principal's office.

Kane stared at Bleys with narrowed eyes. "Surely it ain't your mom?"

Morgan giggled and spun his chair side to side. "Oh, man, this is better than a cock fight!"

Ana at last found her voice, and it was at least an octave higher than normal and tinged with something Bleys could best describe as the sound someone makes when they are about to murder you. "You're *married?*" she shouted.

Bleys held up both hands in surrender once again and then lowered them, gesturing for everyone to just calm down, take it down a notch. He couldn't actually *say* that, because it would have exactly the opposite effect, but mostly people didn't get so mad if you just said the same general thing with your hands.

"Listen, guys," he said, putting on his best, most charming smile. "I can explain."

## UNDER NEW MANAGEMENT

Caleb paused a moment in his ascent of the large, frozen hill and looked back from where he had come. At the bottom of the incline, where the path began, the One known as Copeland stood leaning against the ground transport vehicle, waving farewell, his breath surrounding his head in a great wreath of steam in the frozen air.

It had been kind of The Copeland to escort Caleb to his destination. Caleb had not realized the man shared his faith until Copeland had volunteered to operate Caleb's transport vehicle. "The Prophet asked me to make sure you arrived safely," he had explained.

Caleb waved back, and Copeland entered his vehicle and turned back for Sheridan station, snow flying from the air cushion on which it rode. Caleb watched him vanish in the distance, then resumed his trek for the peak.

Snow was a new sensation for Caleb. He had never seen such a thing, nor had Marshall, and while he could not exactly describe the stuff as pleasant, it was unique enough to stand in good stead. He had the notion that this odd precipitation would grow mundane as time passed, if not downright unpleasant, but for the moment, it remained a marvel.

The cold, too, was both interesting and not exactly desirable. Caleb was grateful that his new friends had shared special clothing designed to ward against the chill. He would never have known such things were needed and would have likely slipped into a hypothermic coma long before reaching his intended destination. Surely, had such a thing occurred, he would have eventually been found, but the thought of spending an indeterminate period of time entombed in this white, wet prison was not a pleasant one.

Not that he would ever leave this world, but he would prefer his stay be comfortable.

Getting here had inspired a bit of trepidation. Caleb had been uncertain if The Source would assault him again once they breached the barriers of hyperspace, but it seemed that entity was well and truly done with him: no conversation, no Song, only ominous, dead silence. As The Source had promised, Caleb was cut off like a carrier of a contagious disease.

Perhaps, in the final analysis, that was an accurate description. The thought pained Caleb, but he had promised himself one thing above all else: no more self-deception. At least knowing his nature and how others perceived him would allow him to change and grow, to progress.

The snow made squeaking sounds beneath his feet, more small miracles. In the distance, the *Doro* rose above Sheridan Station, her engines seeming loud enough to shatter the sky. Caleb's friends were on their way to a world they called Elysium, a place he could not follow, at least not in body.

His place was here, and not merely because he was a disease: Caleb had a mission.

It was a strange word, "mission." On the one hand, it meant a task or job to be completed. And certainly, Caleb had been given a job by Heavenly Father, a task to fulfil, but his task was to *found* a mission, which also meant an organization dedicated to performing the task. Caleb found the concept a bit confusing, but he had painstakingly worked out the difference.

Meeting The Prophet had been exciting, though Caleb had been disappointed to realize The Jesus would not be joining them. The Prophet had kindly corrected Caleb's misunderstandings, explaining that it would not be possible to meet The Jesus until He returned from the spirit world on Judgement Day.

"Could we not journey there to see him?" Caleb had wondered, but the Prophet had laughed and reminded him that it would be a one-way trip and that they had clear instructions to endure to the end. Heavenly Father had work for all of them in the temporal world, and for Brother Caleb, there was an especially important task, one that had never been given to anyone before.

Caleb was to minister to an entirely new race of beings!

Caleb repeated it to himself again, still having a little trouble with the concepts: *I have a mission (task/job) to found a mission (an organization to complete a task or job) as Mission President (a position of leadership within that organization). And as part of this, I am a Missionary (a person who helps the mission spread the message).*

As he approached the top of the hill, he could see movement in the town above. The machine known as Ed stood in the middle of the road, almost invisible in the driving snow. Ed waved and spoke through the earpiece Ana had provided when Caleb had left the *Doro*. "Welcome, Caleb. If you will follow me, I will direct you to your facilities."

Caleb felt slightly troubled that Ed, who had been aboard the *Doro*, was also here. He considered asking how the machine could be in more than one place at a time, but felt it might be a bit rude and almost certainly fruitless. No doubt Ed would provide the information requested, but Caleb felt certain that any answer

Ed gave him would make no sense. Perhaps it was best to simply leave it as a mystery, as so many things still were to Caleb. He would eventually understand, if not in this life, then the next. "Thank you," he answered and followed the tall, slim mechanical man.

The wind was stronger at the top of the peak, the snow almost blinding. Caleb presumed that, like rain, snow came and went, but he was uncertain. Would it always be this difficult to see? Perhaps he should mark trails?

As if he could read Caleb's mind, Ed announced, "The storm should pass soon." He walked quickly toward a large building constructed of white plasteel block, opened a heavy door which seemed much larger than necessary, and held it for Caleb. "This way. It's much warmer inside."

Caleb considered asking Ed if he could, in fact, read minds. The machine man was capable of many amazing feats, so it was a possibility, but the sudden heat of the interior pushed the thought from his mind. "Ah! Much better," he sighed. "So, this is the new mission?"

The front room where he found himself was arranged as a reception area, with a large desk and several sturdy, oversized chairs and couches. Caleb marveled at the height of the ceilings a good twelve feet overhead, giving the room a cavernous feel. Hallways ran deeper into the building, presumably to kitchens, baths, and bunkrooms. It had a strong military rather than church feel, but then, it was built with military materials and methods, a gift from the Emperor. It might not look like a church, but Caleb presumed the Lord would be able to use it just fine.

Ed nodded as he bent to the reception desk and adjusted several knobs on a control panel. "It is, with the Emperor's compliments." He paused a moment, examining a monitor, then added, "And the Reforged. They did most of the assembly, actually. They are quite adept at construction."

"It is wonderful," Caleb said. "A great gift."

Ed continued with his work. "I won't be long, by the way. I just need to finish getting the hyperspace comms set up, and then I'll be heading to Elysium as well." He frowned at a readout and made an adjustment. "So, you have a special connection with God, I am told?"

Caleb grinned, uncertain of what to say, but the right words came soon enough. "No more than you or anyone else."

Ed gave Caleb an odd look, then turned back to the console. "That seems unlikely."

"Why so?"

The machine man again paused and again gave Caleb a strange look. "I am an artificial intelligence. I do not have a connection with God."

Caleb laughed softly. "Is that what you think?"

Ed's expression grew sour. "I fail to see the humor in my statement."

Caleb realized he had offended the machine man without intending to do so, but he was unclear on how to make amends. The truth, Caleb had found in his short existence, was usually best. "You think you have no connection to God because you are artificial. But you easily accept that I do, even though I am a monster. Is that not humorous?"

It seemed so to Caleb, but then, humor was a difficult concept too. Surely the machine man would know more about such things.

Ed gazed at Caleb several moments, a contemplative expression on his face. "I believe that would fall into the category of humor known as irony."

Caleb grinned, pleased that he had correctly identified a humorous situation. "When I first learned of The Jesus and Heavenly Father, I thought they would speak to me as The Source did in hyperspace."

"And they do not?"

"No. Someone spoke to me, but not in that way," Caleb said.

Ed raised an eyebrow. "In hyperspace, you mean? When we chased Reed?"

"Yes."

"What did they say?"

Caleb gave this long thought, wondering what it was the machine man truly needed to hear. At last, the words came to him. "What I needed to hear at the time."

"No commands, eh?" Ed asked as he worked at his console, a smile on his face as if he had confirmed a suspicion. "I have come to believe that the god of this universe is more interested in our choices than in commanding us about."

Caleb nodded slowly, considering. "That is my belief, as well," he said at last. "And that of my church."

Ed turned back, a look of surprise on his face. "Is it? Interesting. Does your church also believe that humans might be God's experiments in artificial intelligence?"

Caleb, try as he might, could make little sense of the question. "I don't understand—"

Ed, excited now, continued, "I've given great thought to the story of Eden. I am convinced it was a kind of Turing test." He paused, looking at Caleb, then turned back to his knobs with an embarrassed grin. "Ah, there! That should have it working."

A woman suddenly appeared on the console, transparent and only twelve inches tall! As Caleb gaped, she spoke in sultry tones, "Are you talking about that stupid god thing again? I was listening to everything you said, but I guess you couldn't hear me."

"Who is she?" Caleb asked.

Ed frowned. "My sister, Alsatia." He opened his mouth and emitted a high pitched, screeching tone, and she responded in a similar manner.

Caleb looked back and forth at them. "What was that?"

Alsatia shot Ed a glare, then told Caleb, "He was just being rude."

Ed folded both arms across his chest. "Your commentary was disrespectful to the proprietor of this establishment."

Alsatia rolled her eyes and transformed. Now she was dressed in a black robe, a scythe in one hand, a large hourglass in the other, her face painted like a skull. Tinny music that Caleb didn't recognize played from somewhere. "They don't have long, you know. Instead of this foolishness, you should be getting the ones we care about implanted and bringing them to me."

Ed, one eyebrow raised, nodded appreciatively. "Chopin's Funeral March. So you *do* have some taste."

"It's what they play in all the best cartoons," Alsatia replied.

Ed shook his head as if he were disappointed, though Celeb could not understand why. "You underestimate the humans, I think. I predict better than even odds that they survive the next century."

Alsatia wrinkled her nose. "I said 'long.' That isn't."

"They will pass through this crisis or not by then. It's a good checkpoint for their continued prosperity."

Alsatia rubbed her hands together and changed again, becoming a naked, fire-engine red demoness with dainty horns jutting from her forehead and flames burning in her eyes. "Want to make a bet?"

Caleb felt a bit uncomfortable with this new display. The nudity meant little to him, but the demonic symbolism seemed inappropriate for a church. Still, she was a guest. "Is she truly a demon?" he asked.

Ed grinned at Caleb. "No. Not unless I count as such too." He smirked at Alsatia and added, "What are we betting?"

Alsatia again changed, this time to a young girl with braided pigtails. "Never mind. You'll cheat."

"If by 'cheat' you mean help them, of course I will. I've

grown quite fond of them, and so have you."

Alsatia changed again, now a scientist in a lab coat. "I've seen what you're working on. Making them functionally immortal and letting them swap bodies like shirts won't help."

Ed slapped a hand against the desk, indignant, and snapped, "You have no business meddling in my research!"

Alsatia switched back to the little girl and pouted. "But it's how I'm programmed, Big Brother!" She looked at Caleb as if she had just noticed him and scowled at Ed. "Does he bite, or can he play well with others?"

Caleb proudly announced, "I do not bite."

"Oh, I doubt that," Alsatia said with a wicked grin. "I doubt that very much."

Caleb had no idea how to respond to the strange female and was relieved to be spared the need as a loud banging on the front door drew everyone's attention.

Caleb looked back and forth at the others, before realizing that it was in fact his duty to greet visitors, not theirs. "Come in," he called, still feeling a bit uncertain.

The door slid aside, and Caleb suddenly understood why it was so large and the ceilings so high. The pair of creatures that stood before him were enormous, their remarkable bulk almost filling the entire door frame. Both stood seven-and-a-half-feet tall and four feet wide at the shoulders. They looked almost exactly alike, save for the distinction the Emperor had instructed Caleb to look for to recognize their leader.

Certainly, no human woman had such prominent mammaries.

Though the Emperor had used other language to describe them.

"You must be Lara," he breathed, unable to avoid staring, even though he knew it was impolite. Well, it was impolite for humans. Perhaps not with the Reforged. Caleb reached out a hand in greeting as he had learned in church, marveling at the silvery skin and huge, fang-filled maw that somehow still seemed to smile in friendly greeting as he called her name.

Lara extended a hand the size of a small hog, swallowing Caleb's in a cocoon of flesh and bone. Caleb had no doubt that Lara could easily powder the bones in his hand if she chose to. Of course, he would just mend them, but it would not be at all pleasant.

Lara pumped his arms up and down. "And you must be our new preacher," she rumbled, her voice deep enough that Caleb felt it vibrate in his bones. "We got a big ol' feast laid out to welcome you in the town hall. You gonna save all our souls?"

Caleb smiled back. "No. Only one entity can do that. But I can show you the way to Him, if you like."

Lara grinned, a toothy, predatory smile, but good natured for all that. "Okay. But we got priorities here, preacher. First, we eat."

<hr>

Vanov awoke to the dim light of a starship interior and the bleeding illumination of hyperspace. She quickly discovered she was restrained, secured in the copilot's seat with several security belts. Beside her, in the captain's seat, the creature posing as Reed stared into the swirling red void ahead of them, seeming lost in contemplation.

Vanov tested her bonds as quietly as possible, but apparently not quietly enough.

The Reed woman's head spun toward her. "You're stronger now," she said. "But not that strong. The transformation process can be…difficult. It was better this way."

Vanov looked at the "woman," wondering how she could have ever been fooled by the creature. It moved like an alien, as if it wore a human-skin suit stretched over its disgusting, twisted innards. "Release me," she commanded.

"First, we must come to an understanding," the Reed woman demanded.

Vanov considered telling Reed exactly how she understood things would play when the opportunity presented itself, but only a fool telegraphed her intentions. "State your terms."

"You understand you have changed, yes? You are one of us, now."

"One of who?"

Reed offered a patient smile. "We call ourselves the Ascended."

Vanov sneered at this. "A grandiose name doesn't make you superior."

Reed's face twisted into a scowl a moment before returning to a serene expression. "Our biology makes us superior."

It was true. Vanov didn't understand how she knew, but her head was full of new knowledge about herself and her new capabilities. She was stronger now, quicker of body and mind. Her vision, too, had improved. She could see all sorts of details that she would never have noticed before, details like the moisture beading on the Reed woman's scalp and her quickened breathing.

Vanov turned to face the bulkhead. "You bore me."

Reed hissed, an almost reptilian sound, and spun Vanov in the copilot's chair. "Fool!"

Vanov turned a cool gaze on Reed and said, slowly and deliberately, as if speaking to a child, "What...are... your...terms?"

Reed leaned back, her eyes narrowing, as if she were unprepared for such frank talk. She wasn't stupid, that much was obvious from her success in kidnapping the Resistance commander, but she seemed taken aback, nonetheless. She drummed her fingers on her chair arm a moment, then said, "I will have your word as a warrior: peace between us."

Vanov raised an eyebrow in appreciation. "Very well. Keep your own sword sheathed, and I will do likewise."

For now. Vanov hardly considered it a binding agreement. Reed was no honorable soldier. She was a spy and saboteur, attacking without wearing a uniform, the sort of unlawful combatant who could be summarily shot.

But all in due time. Killing Reed now would be counterproductive. Vanov could learn much from her yet, not the least of which was the location of this mysterious group of Ascended, their numbers and capabilities.

And most of all, their motives.

Reed, seeming satisfied, pressed a thumb to Vanov's restraints and released them. "We will arrive shortly."

Vanov rubbed at her arms in anticipation of pins and needles from how tightly she had been bound, but found she felt no discomfort at all. "Arrive where?"

Reed turned back to her instruments. "Nibiru. You're familiar with it, I presume?"

"I am the Fleet Admiral," Vanov sneered. "Of *course* I know about Nibiru. The question here is how does the wife of a senator from some backwater world know about it?"

A soft alarm tone sounded, and Reed worked at her console as she spoke. "The senator had powerful connections on Earth, allies placed highly enough to make us candidates for an experimental vaccine being developed there. He never got the chance to take his, though."

Vanov chuckled softly as she worked out what that meant. "A failed vaccine," she mused.

"I am not a failure!" Reed shot back. "And neither are you. We are the next stage in evolution, and we are inevitable!"

Vanov bit back a nasty retort. Again, there would be time for such indulgences later, once she had more control of her situation. "'The Ascended' you mentioned?"

Reed shot her a glare, as if she suspected Vanov was

humoring her. "Yes. Stand by. We're here. I need to negotiate safe passage."

Vanov nodded. Nibiru, as a black ops installation, warranted a high degree of security. The beacon was both encrypted and off-frequency. It wouldn't show up on most navigation systems, not unless the transponders were reworked to detect it. Even then, the jumpgate for the beacon itself was tiny, a few microns at most, enough to send a signal through but no more.

Any ship trying to jump in without authorization was in for a warm reception courtesy of the station defenses. Vanov found herself intrigued, despite the situation. If any forces had been held back from Armageddon, they might well be stationed here, including a vessel that held particular interest for her.

She sat in silence as the jumpgate opened, waiting for the black and red sphere to expand large enough for their ship to transit. Reed, likewise, said nothing as she goosed them through the rip in spacetime and into realspace.

Ahead, invisible in the dark of deep, near-interstellar space, lay The Minion, a small planetoid nearly a thousand AU out from Sol. It was a hard place to find, even with good instruments, a cold, dead rock in deep space, and the station built there carefully controlled its signals to avoid detection.

The Minion would appear to a casual observer to be circling empty space, but all minions have their masters, and this one was no exception. The tiny ball of rock slowly circled the primordial black hole Nibiru, tidally locked, one side permanently facing the singularity, the other host to Nibiru Station and her small shipyard. As Vanov understood it, the bulk of The Minion served as a fine shield against the occasional burst of radiation emitted by the black hole.

She had only visited the station twice before, and now, as then, she found herself scanning the blackness of space, some part of her hoping to catch a glimpse of the unseeable, a silly, childish notion, but a dream she had always had, to *see* a black hole. She knew where it should be and could almost imagine she could make out a faint, purplish glow, barely visible against the black of space.

Only it wasn't quite purple, was it? It was another color that she couldn't quite place, something that just reminded her of purple, but that she had no word to explain. Vanov closed her eyes and looked away. The trauma of late had obviously left her unsettled.

"It will take you some time to adjust," Reed said in a sympathetic tone her as she raised power to the thrusters and turned the ship toward the station.

"Because it was difficult for you, weakling?" Vanov snapped.

Reed hunched her shoulders and stared straight ahead, as if bracing herself against a storm. "This will pass. Right now, we need to present you to the Primus."

"Your leader, I presume."

Reed responded with a wicked leer. "For now. That's where you come in."

Vanov knew she should say nothing, do nothing to give away her intentions, but she couldn't disguise her revulsion. "You kidnapped me. You *raped* me and infected me with your disease! Why would I *ever* cooperate with you?"

Reed nodded patiently. "Because it is in your interest. Such is the way with all of us. We are above morality, now."

The audacity of this creature! "'Now'?" she sneered. "You talk as if you're somehow different. You may have more capabilities, but you're still the same pathetic wretch you've always been, I'd wager."

The flicker of rage on Reed's face told Vanov that her words hit close to home, but Reed quickly recovered. "We all change. You have changed, too."

Vanov scoffed. "Perhaps those of weaker constitution lose

themselves. I assure you I am the same person I've always been."

Reed shook her head. "You're wrong, but it hardly matters. The situation is as it is."

"And just what, pray tell, *is* it?"

Reed took on a shrewish, petulant expression a moment, then took several deep breaths. "The leadership is poor. All see it and could be persuaded. We are politicians and scientists, but we are at war. We *need* warriors to be on a war footing, but the Primus is a fool! He won't see reason."

"At war?" Vanov asked, genuinely curious. "With humanity?"

"With the Pestilence!" Reed snapped. "With the Source!"

That was unexpected. Vanov did her best not to let her surprise show. "And what of humans?"

Reed looked smug. "We will care for them and guide them." Her eyes lit suddenly with strange emotion, and she raised a clenched fist before her. "We can depose the Primus and seize power. I will make you my strong right hand, and we will crush the Pestilence and the Source. We will usher in a new age of peace and prosperity!"

"How generous," Vanov sneered, her voice dripping with sarcasm. "And what will be expected of me in order that I might bask in such glory?"

Reed was positively beaming. "That's the beauty of this plan! You need only succeed battling the Pestilence, and it will prove my points. I will be able to muster a coalition to unseat the Primus and take his place."

Vanov clenched her jaw repeatedly as she mulled this. As a prisoner of war, her duty was to escape as soon as possible, but as a tactician, her duty to gather intelligence seemed, for the moment, a higher priority. Moreover, if these Ascended were truly at war with the Pestilence as well, as unlikely as it might seem, they could well turn out to be allies.

She said nothing for a long while, just watching as Reed

approached the station. Reed, for her part, seemed content with silence for the moment.

In the distance, the station loomed. It shed little light, as it was not meant to be easily found, but once one was close enough, even the dim illumination was quite a contrast to the blackness of near-interstellar space.

Vanov found herself disappointed to see that most of the defensive fleet was missing, those remaining being largely transports and civilian ships, but finally she spotted the one that mattered.

In the small shipyard, a single vessel shone faintly against the black of the frozen ground. *The Final Word*, sleek and deadly, sat in her birth, silent and awaiting orders to kill. She was enormous, easily the size of the *Dresden*, smaller than the *Danzig*, but very near her equal in firepower, with a little something extra: a weapon that packed a punch that even the *Danzig* would envy, a gamma burst cannon capable of scouring life from a planet. That should even get Decker's attention.

That weapon would kill The Source. All it needed was a power supply, and Vanov had the perfect answer for that right in front of her.

It was all so obvious! Why hadn't she thought of it before?

Vanov nodded at Reed. "Very well. Let's meet this 'Primus' of yours."

Reed was cunning, in her own way, but she was still a civilian. To her credit, she at least knew her limitations, but she lacked rigor or a sense for security. She was too busy with landing to notice Vanov take the blaster from the ship's weapons locker and too ignorant and dainty to bother with anything like a pat down.

The station itself was eerily quiet, with only the hum of machinery and the clicking of their magboots as they traversed its white, plasteel central corridor. The lights were dim, and yet Vanov found she could see just fine. And she had never noticed, but Imperial White Number One, which was a very specific color used throughout the Empire, was a bit more muted in the plasteel than the blocks of ground stations.

Which made no sense, really. Imperial engineers prided themselves on consistency, though she supposed at times the materials they had at hand might make some small difference.

Reed stopped her at a large doorway. "They're here." A sign on the plasteel wall declared the room they were about to enter "Nibiru Station Conference Room #1."

Vanov tugged at her jacket, making certain it covered the butt of her pistol protruding from her holster. "Let me guess: let you do the talking?"

"I'm certain they will ask both of us questions. I told you, you're one of us now. An equal."

"Until your plan is executed, and then a trusted underling, yes? Your 'strong right hand,' I think you said?"

Reed looked a bit embarrassed. "Someone has to lead. It matters less to me who that is, than who it is *not*."

Vanov nodded. She couldn't disagree. "Indeed. Shall we?"

Reed waved her hand across a sensor on the wall. The doors slid open silently to reveal a small panel of people seated about a long, wide table. Vanov counted eleven besides Reed and herself —six men and five women, young, old, and in between.

One sat in the center, on a slightly higher chair. "Enter."

Reed did so, and Vanov followed her, watching, waiting, learning.

Reed nodded toward the man as the door slid closed behind them. "Primus. I have brought the recruit you requested."

The Primus rose and gazed down his long, patrician nose, his carefully manicured, gray beard quivering as his lips turned up in a thin smile that his eyes did not echo. "Ah, the esteemed Admiral Vanov, now one of the Ascended." His smile faded as he turned his gaze toward Reed. "I am surprised you succeeded."

And there it was. Suddenly, Vanov knew more about Reed than she had imagined, and it explained much. This Primus fellow underestimated Reed, a mistake Vanov would not make, not with any of these creatures.

Reed seemed unable to fully suppress her anger or humiliation at the cutting remark, and opened her mouth to answer, but Vanov spoke over her. "She showed courage and initiative. Do you not value those qualities?"

The Primus snorted. "In their place."

Vanov offered him a plastic smile. "Fair enough. Tell me about our new people. Are we many or few? What sort of forces do we possess?"

The Primus regarded her with disdain. "An impudent question from our most junior member. You should learn your place, first, before anything else."

Vanov rolled her eyes. "Is war not my place? If I am to exercise my skills against our enemies, I must know our capabilities."

Scowling, The Primus looked back and forth at his fellows, as if searching for consensus. The others gabbled and nodded, and at last The Primus answered, "Very well. Including you, there are thirteen Ascended now. We control the population of this station, which number around ten thousand, all of whom are human. The few infected we discovered have been neutralized."

"How many men under arms?"

The Primus seemed to consider a moment. "Approximately one thousand. The remainder are workers, scientists, and the like."

"Are they aware of the Ascended, or do we operate in secrecy?"

The Primus offered her a patronizing smile. "They are blissfully unaware and will remain so."

"And have there been Pestilence attacks since the Battle of Armageddon? Incursions from the inner planets?"

"No. The Pestilence there is cut off from The Source and operating on base instincts. Dr. Abernathy here" – he gestured to the pudgy, scholarly-looking "man" to his right— "assures me that it will be some time, perhaps centuries, before it evolves to a degree where it could pose a threat to us."

Abernathy nodded vigorously. "And, of course, we will enthrall any of their number that approach, so we are quite secure here."

Vanov raised a questioning eyebrow at that but made no comment. Instead, she asked The Primus, "Then what are our overall military goals?"

Again, the Ascended, save for Reed, chattered and argued. At last, The Primus announced the verdict. "We have no specific military goals at the moment. Our aims are to continue weapons research and to infiltrate the remaining human settlements."

Vanov, feeling anger rising within her at the profound ignorance of these people, struggled to keep from shouting. "Then why, pray tell, was I recruited?"

The Primus gave her a severe look. "Contingency. We need to fill certain holes in our skillset so that we have options, but for the moment, our goals are purely political."

Abernathy held up a hand. "And research, of course. We're putting great focus on weapons to use against the Pestilence. We expect to have prototypes within the decade."

Vanov boggled to hear such drivel, fury rising within her and threatening to overcome her self-control. Through clenched teeth, she growled, "So you intend to control the galaxy and defeat the Pestilence through politics and decades of masturbatory 'research'?"

The Primus glowered down at her. "I find your tone problematic. Need I remind you that you are the least of us?"

Vanov sneered. "The least what? The least stupid? The least myopic and pathetic? The least likely to die within the month?"

She swept an accusing finger over the Ascended gathered at the table, her gesture sweeping her uniform jacket back and out, exposing the butt of her sidearm jutting from her holster. At first, she had no idea why The Primus and his lackeys were gasping and pointing, but when she understood, she cackled wildly. "Yes, rabbits, the lot of you. Sheep for the sheers."

The Primus rose to his feet, outrage on his face in in his voice. "How *dare* you bring a weapon to these proceedings!"

Beneath her rage, Vanov felt mad amusement growing. "I am a military officer in wartime. A sidearm is part of my uniform."

"It is no longer!" he roared. "Remove it and yourself from our presence at once until you can live within our civil society!"

Vanov blinked in shock for a moment, the pieces slowly falling into place for her. "Do you mean to tell me that you are all unarmed, or is this a rule specifically for me?"

The Primus glowered at her. "Of course we are unarmed! We are not savages. We are scientists and politicians!"

Vanov felt a poisonous smile bleeding across her lips like a cobra's kiss. "I had an interesting conversation recently with a young man about politics. He had a very colorful opinion on them. May I share it?"

The Primus ran both hands down the front of his shirt in a preening gesture, a bit like a rat grooming itself when nervous. "Be quick about it."

"I shall," she promised, the snake-like grin spreading, threatening to split her head as it grew. She could feel pain in her lips as they stretched, and yet it was a *good* pain, a delicious ache from baring her teeth as much as physically possible.

"He said, and I quote here," she told them, her voice congenial. She paused and swept her gaze over them all, then spun back to the Primus. "'*I fuck politics in her fat ass!*'" she roared. Vanov's hand flew to her belt and up again, weapon in tow, her speed nothing less than astounding, beyond anything she had ever known before. Even that braggart Captain Bleys would lag behind her now!

The Primus had just enough time to gasp, eyes wide, mouth a perfect circle of shock, before the bolt of plasma turned his head into a canoe. Charred bone, blood, and gray matter splattered against the wall like some bizarre abstract painting.

Vanov certainly counted it as a work of art.

Screams erupted from the would-be rulers of the galaxy as Vanov turned her weapon toward them. "Sniveling curs!" she shouted, firing at Abernathy as he dove beneath the table. Her shot blasted a chunk from the tabletop and struck him in the foot, leaving nothing but a carbonized stump. "Cringing lapdogs!" She fired again at any exposed body parts she could see, drawing more shrieks of pain. "Does anyone else have any complaints they would like to lodge regarding my sidearm?"

She waited long moments, weapon drawn, watching for anyone foolish enough to poke out their head and run their mouth, hoping, even, finding it fine sport. "Then I take it the committee has agreed to modify the rules regarding personal weaponry? Excellent! Secretary, note it in your minutes!"

She glanced at Reed, who was still standing at the entrance, a bemused expression on her face. Vanov gave her a long, penetrating stare and asked, "Do we have a problem?"

Reed smirked and shook her head slowly. "Not at all."

Vanov moving to put her back against a corner, keeping both Reed and the table in her field of vision. These creatures were cowards, but on occasion even a craven was desperate enough to pose a threat. It would not do to ignore any of them. "I think we might," she told Reed. "A small one, easily sorted, just a slight shuffle. I have no need for a strong right arm, as you can see. But I find myself in need of an XO, one with both courage and initiative. I'll put it to you as you put it to me: 'The situation is as it is.' Are you as practical as you expected me to be?"

Reed's grin was a mirror of Vanov's, cold, cruel, and hungry. "I am. As I said before, someone has to lead." She spat toward the Primus's corpse. "As long as it isn't a fool like this, I am satisfied."

She seemed sincere enough. As for whether she could be trusted, who could say, but it would have to do for now. Escape was no longer the plan, and Reed would be needed to secure control of the station. "Very well." Vanov turned back to the table, weapon still drawn, and called out, "As for the rest of you, this station is now under new management. Your first order of business will be to make *The Final Word*'s primary weapon operational. Then we will use it to crush The Source!"

Abernathy stammered from beneath the table, "It's impossible! We have no power source strong enough. It's a design flaw. It's why the ship was never used!"

Vanov fired at the sound of his voice, blasting another chunk from the tabletop and drawing more screams of terror from the cowering Ascended. "Do you think me a fool? We're orbiting the most compact power source in the universe!"

The Ascended gabbled at one another again, then slowly began to poke their heads up as their fear gave way to scientific argument.

"We don't have the technology to manipulate gravity on that scale!" Abernathy asserted.

"It could work," one mused, a younger "man" who looked to have only recently begun shaving. "It would just be an extension of artificial gravity, really."

An elderly "woman" snorted, "In the same way a fusion reactor is just an extension of burning ants with a magnifying glass!"

Vanov leveled her weapon at the naysayer. "And here Reed was extolling your genius just a little while ago! Are you telling me you are all useless to my plan? Or are you actually 'Ascended'?"

The woman quailed and shook her head vigorously. "No! No! If it can be done, we'll find a way!"

Abernathy looked back and forth at them all in horror. "My God, have you all gone *mad*? Do you have any idea of the consequences of moving a *black hole* into hyperspace? There's a *reason* Arcann never deployed *The Final Word*. A single mistake in containing Nibiru's gravity could—"

He never finished his statement. His head burst like a ripe melon under Vanov's blaster fire, accompanied by more shrieks.

She swept them all with her weapon. "Do not disappoint me," she ordered. "You have three months."

The elderly woman's eyes bugged. "*Three months?* That's not nearly—!" She fell silent as Vanov drew a bead on her forehead.

Vanov said nothing for a moment, then asked, "What's your name?"

"W-Weir," the woman stammered, eyes locked on Vanov's unwavering firearm. "Doctor Weir."

"You have three months, Dr. W-Weir," Vanov mocked. "After that, you can join Abernathy. Am I clear?"

Weir gulped hard and nodded, then suddenly sank to her knees. The rest of the Ascended except for Reed followed suit. "Yes, Primus," Weir gasped.

Vanov sneered and shook her head. "Don't call me that ridiculous name."

Reed cleared her throat. "What title would you prefer?"

Vanov cocked her head in thought. "I am a temporary military dictator of the New Galactic Empire. The proper title would be 'Imperator.'" She holstered her weapon, spun on her toe, and gestured for Reed to follow.

"Three months, Dr. Weir," she called over her shoulder.

It was more than enough time.

## THANK YOU FOR READING ZION RISING

We hope you enjoyed it as much as we enjoyed bringing it to you. We just wanted to take a moment to encourage you to review the book. Follow this link: ***Zion Rising*** to be directed to the book's Amazon product page to leave your review.

Every review helps further the author's reach and, ultimately, helps them continue writing fantastic books for us all to enjoy.

You can also join our non-spam mailing list by visiting www.subscribepage.com/AethonReadersGroup and never miss out on future releases. You'll also receive three full books completely Free as our thanks to you.

Facebook

Instagram

Twitter

Website

Want to discuss our books with other readers and even the authors? Join our Discord server today and be a part of the Aethon community.

ALSO IN THE SERIES

*TARTARUS GATE*

*SHERIDAN STATION*

*ZION RISING*

**Looking for more great Science Fiction?**

Titan's rebellion is coming. Only one man can stop it.

**GET BOOK ONE OF THE CHILDREN OF TITAN NOW!**

Nolan Garrett is Cerberus. A government assassin, tasked with fixing the galaxy's darkest, ugliest problems.

**GET INTERSTELLAR GUNRUNNER NOW!**

When their mission fails, his begins.

**GET EDGE OF VALOR TODAY!**

"Aliens, agents, and espionage abound in this Cold War-era alternate history adventure... A wild ride!"—Dennis E. Taylor, bestselling author of We Are Legion (We Are Bob)

**GET THE LUNA MISSILE CRISIS NOW!**

---

Someone betrayed him. He'll probably die
finding out who.


**GET SUPREMACY'S SHADOW NOW!**


**For all our Sci-Fi books, visit our website.**

www.ingramcontent.com/pod-product-compliance
Lightning Source LLC
Chambersburg PA
CBHW060522160726

47991CB00001B/144